MW00777267

Men Working

Men Working

a novel

JOHN FAULKNER

Foreword by Trent Watts

Brown Thrasher Books

The University of Georgia Press

Athens & London

Published in 1996 as a Brown Thrasher Book
by the University of Georgia Press, Athens, Georgia 30602
© 1941, 1969 by Murry C. Falkner and James M. Faulkner
Foreword © 1996 by the University of Georgia Press

Printed in the United States of America

00 99 98 97 96 P 5 4 3 2 1

Library of Congress Cataloging in Publication Data

Faulkner, John, 1901–1963.
    Men working: a novel / John Faulkner ; foreword by Trent Watts.
        p.   cm.
    "Brown Thrasher Books".
    ISBN 0-8203-1827-2 (pbk. : alk. paper)
        1. United States. Works Progress Administration—Fiction.
    2. Working class—Mississippi—Fiction.   3. Sharecroppers—
    Mississippi—Fiction.   4. Depressions—Mississippi—Fiction.
    5. Family—Mississippi—Fiction.   I. Title.
    PS3511.A8554M46   1996
    813'.52—dc20   95-46728

British Library Cataloging in Publication Data available

Men Working was originally published in hardcover by Harcourt,
Brace & Co.

TO DOLLY AND BUB AND CHOOKY, WHOSE

STEADFAST FAITH NOT ONLY MADE THIS WORK

POSSIBLE BUT MAKES ANY TASK SEEM SMALL

Foreword

TRENT WATTS

In 1950 William Faulkner was awarded the Nobel Prize for literature. That same year Arthur Zeiger, a New York University English professor, wrote to his brother John Faulkner about the article entitled "My Favorite Forgotten Book" that he was writing for *Tomorrow* magazine: "I've by no means forgotten it—I doubt if many who read it have—but I've selected *Men Working* to write about, because I don't think it achieved nearly the audience to which its merits entitled it."[1] In 1950 John Faulkner was known, to this New Yorker at least, as the author of two novels of Mississippi life, *Men Working* (1941) and *Dollar Cotton* (1942), both of which had enjoyed encouraging reviews and sales. Zeiger was puzzled, then, by Faulkner's nearly decade-long silence, as well as the general critical inattention to his work.

A self-taught painter of real ability, Faulkner was, in his later years, sometimes noted more for his depictions of Mississippi scenes in water colors and oils than in words. When a friend organized a showing of his works in 1960 she found it necessary to ask Faulkner: "we would like to know what books you have written and send us any publicity that you have on hand."[2] Although Faulkner published seven novels and a number of short stories, his literary reputation has not, like that of his famous brother, waxed fat over time. By the end of his life in March 1963, and to a greater extent today, the one inescapable fact overshadowing John Faulkner's reputation is that in the red hills of north Mississippi he was "the younger brother who also wrote."[3] "Everywhere I looked," recalled John Faulkner shortly after his brother's death, "there was Bill and his stories: Oxford, Jefferson, and Lafayette County, Yoknapatawpha."[4]

An avid aviator, John Faulkner enjoyed writing stories of wartime flying exploits, but like his brother he displayed a surer touch when he stayed close to home, working with the hill people of north Mississippi and their wary confrontations with modernity. Along with the two early novels, Faulkner wrote a collection of stories for his son, *Chooky* (1950), and *My Brother Bill: An Affectionate Reminiscence* (1963), as well as a string of Fawcett paperbacks [*Cabin Road* (1951), *Uncle Good's Girls* (1952), *The Sin Shouter of Cabin Road* (1955), *Ain't Gonna Rain No More* (1959), and *Uncle Good's Week-End Party* (1960)], all featuring the rural Mississippians of Lafayette County's Beat Two.[5] The *Cabin Road* series sold hundreds of thousands of copies each, and *Cabin Road* itself was issued in an edition of one million copies. However, the novels were considered bus-station ephemera by most critics and went largely unreviewed.[6] Upon his death Faulkner left a wealth of unpublished fiction, including a novel, none of which has attracted much attention.

Men Working is a solid first novel, perhaps John Faulkner's best writing. A satire of the New Deal's Works Progress Administration in Mississippi, *Men Working* traces the fortunes of the Taylor family who, forced by the Great Depression and the collapse in cotton prices to abandon their marginal tenure as sharecroppers, move to town hoping to obtain government relief—to "work on the WP and A" (9). The novel introduces themes and displays the tensions and ambiguities that run throughout Faulkner's work. Like William Faulkner's *As I Lay Dying* and Erskine Caldwell's *Tobacco Road*, *Men Working* examines the cultural dissonances, and consequent humor and horrors, that befall uprooted agrarian people.

From the first pages of the novel, the reader senses a tonal ambivalence that prevents an easy interpretation of the text. Like other novels of depression-era America, *Men Working* begins with the land. "The women and the children," Faulkner writes, "followed the flashing plows and dropped seed one by one into the wide deep furrows and covered the seed and the black land slept with the seed under the growing sun" (3). But this opening image of the fecund earth and its cultivation by the "country people" and their mules is quickly complicated. In the beginning of the novel there is the land, yet Faulkner quickly juxtaposes the hard realities of market forces and their pressures on southern landless farmers. In the springtime the people long to sow the land, but it seems indifferent to them and cannot support them, even though the crop promises to be the "best stand ... since Nineteen Twenty" (3). The country people are caught between the two fixed powers of nature and the market. Unable to wring a living from the soil, they are equally incapable of reconciling themselves to city people and their ways. Even after the novel's setting changes from farm to town, agrarian rhythms remain a palpable presence, an elemental force: "And the fields lay idle beneath the sun. For the people were moving to town" (64).

But for all of these serious overtones, the novel strikes the reader most forcefully with its broad comic vision and with the impression it gives that John Faulkner enjoyed recounting this tale. For indeed, John Faulkner wished to be known as a good storyteller, even insisting that his brother Bill's writings had been overanalyzed by people who did not understand that like his brother Bill, he too sought principally to entertain. With *Men Working*, John Faulkner succeeded in his aim; for, whatever else may be said of the novel, it is entertaining. Drawing on the traditions of the Old Southwest humorists and southern gothicism, Faulkner plays skillfully upon benighted South hillbilly and redneck stereotypes. The death and delayed burial of the Taylors' retarded son, the "monst'ous cur'osity" Reno, may strike the modern reader as crude; the shopkeepers' swindling of these naive country folk may appear cruel. But more important, these events show the novel's affinities with a persistent regional literary tradition: echoes of Addie Bundren's odyssey in *As I Lay*

Dying and the sharp dealings of "Spotted Horses" are unmistakable.

The novel's ambivalent tone is perhaps a product of the events of the story, which operate as a critique of New Deal policy by a southerner who is deeply and publicly suspicious of "progress" yet well aware of its attractions. Specifically, Faulkner takes aim at the Works Progress Administration (later the Works Projects Administration). Created during the second phase of the New Deal in 1935 with the passage of the Emergency Relief Appropriation Act, the WPA (and the New Deal in general) played a remarkable and sometimes under-appreciated role in the economic, social, and cultural life of the twentieth-century South.[7] The WPA took millions of southerners off local relief (such as there was) and put them to work building streets, roads, and highways; constructing bridges and airports; painting post offices; and improving land for parks. WPA workers restored historic areas of such cities as New Orleans and Charleston. Southern historians have special reason to be grateful for the WPA's archival work, as WPA employees cataloged one of their richest sources, the Southern Historical Collection at the University of North Carolina at Chapel Hill. The WPA also provided federal support for the arts, including the Dance Theatre, the Federal Art Project, the Federal Music Project, the Federal Theatre Project, and the Federal Writers' Project. The FWP produced the remarkable American Guide Series and helped some of the South's finest writers ride out the Depression, among them Richard Wright,

Ralph Ellison, and Eudora Welty, whose photographic record of depression-era Mississippi, while not a WPA project, provides a fascinating documentary record in its own right and serves as a complement to the writings of her contemporaries.[8]

With such projects it was hoped that the WPA would avoid the stigma attached to earlier forms of poverty relief. Federal WPA Administrator Harry Hopkins stressed: "Give a man a dole and you save his body and destroy his spirit; give him a job and pay him an assured wage, and you save both the body and the spirit."[9] But both John and William Faulkner objected to the WPA and the larger New Deal, insisting that they did in fact "destroy the spirit." Being on the dole, as John Faulkner characterized the WPA, robbed people of initiative and created a demoralized populace dependent upon the government. "This God damned WPA is ruining the whole country," lamented Mr. Young, the Taylors' landlord. "You can't get a man to stay with you long enough to make a crop and when you do get one he's been leaning on one of those WPA shovels so long about all he's good for is to stand in a watermelon patch for a scarecrow" (29).

In practice, the WPA fell short of its promises. Not all the work offered was as meaningful as Hopkins might have wished. Black Americans and women did not share equitably in the federal bounty, regardless of the protests of Mississippian Ellen Sullivan Woodward, who administered the Division of Women's and Professional Projects.[10] And despite the wishes of the Roosevelt administration, especially WPA Administrator Hopkins, the WPA compromised with Jim Crow. While Frank, one of Faulkner's fictional characters in *Men Working*, insists that "the government don't make no difference between black and white" (6), southern state governments certainly did. Conservative critics in Washington and the states, never comfortable with the WPA, were alarmed both at the precedent of large-scale federal relief programs and at specific challenges to local power and customs. Like other programs, the WPA suffered when "Dr. Win the War" replaced "Dr. New Deal," as Roosevelt put it, and finally succumbed in 1943.

In *Men Working*, the WPA and the New Deal are hardly the unalloyed boons their admirers claimed. Faulkner casts a sardonic eye on both the naive Taylors and the WPA administrators (though, ironically, he was one himself) who tell the country folk any lie to convince them to loiter somewhere other than in their offices. Faulkner is clearly scornful of an agency that brings the rural poor to town only to neglect them. He criticizes the empty lure of consumerism and shows how it further blights the lives of the Taylors; Paw will have his radio over medicine for the children, and all seem to prefer an automobile to food. Early on in the novel, the mass WPA-driven exodus to town is prefigured by the "steady stream of country people" who come to town each Saturday, milling around the Square uneasily, admiring the shop goods that they cannot afford. "The powder soon wore off their faces but the glaring spots of rouge remained. Their fresh starched dresses were soon crushed from much passing and pushing in the throngs and they walked with unaccustomed stride in their stilted high-heeled shoes" (6). Faulkner, however, does not presume that there are simple solutions to the plight of the southern poor, such as telling these women that their consumerist reveries are misguided. He mistrusts the presence of the modern administrative state in Mississippi, as represented by the WPA; but *Men Working* is no Agrarian tract. Faulkner does not romanticize the lives of tenant farmers and sharecroppers and does not suggest that anyone can be restored to either innocence or wisdom by walking away from town to follow a mule. The Taylors are caught, then, between two icons of Western culture, the Garden and the City. John Faulkner offers neither as salvation; furthermore, he was too sympathetic an observer to ridicule the Taylors and their limitations mercilessly. He finds an unaccountable persistence in these people that draws his amazement, if not always his admiration.

John Faulkner, too, was a southerner who owed a debt to the WPA. For in the New Deal he saw the coming of the modern state to rural Mississippi. He saw the transformation of farming, of government, and of society, and felt that the southern way of life was being permanently altered. The historian C. Vann Woodward has partly accounted for the resurgence of southern letters called the Southern Renascence by pointing out the acute historical consciousness of southern writers. These writers saw themselves poised between two worlds, however they delineated them and their value and used this particular vantage point to speculate on community, history, and time. Without claiming that John Faulkner thought as systematically on these matters as Robert Penn Warren, for instance, we can at least maintain that the transition Faulkner witnessed in his own corner of north Mississippi provided him with inspiration and material for his fiction. We do not, of course, have to share or applaud his diagnosis. To many Mississippians, especially African Americans, twentieth-century changes have been a boon. The legacy of the Roosevelt administration's attempts to reach southern blacks and the southern poor still shapes their attitudes toward the national government. John Faulkner, obviously, did not hold these views. He was no negrophobe, but he was a paternalist, with attitudes toward black southerners typical of his time, place, and class.

Highly readable, genuinely funny, and with a serious attempt to engage uneven modernization and its discontents—one of the central issues of twentieth-century southern history—*Men Working* and John Faulkner deserve the attention of students of southern history and literature. Despite its reprinting in 1975 by Yoknapatawpha Press (run by Faulkner's niece, Dean Faulkner Wells) in Oxford, Mississippi, *Men Working*, like John Faulkner's work in general, has attracted remarkably little attention. This is surprising, considering the explosion of interest in William Faulkner's writing and its cultural context, coupled with the wealth of historical research on the twentieth-century South, and the greater willingness of contemporary historians to consider fiction to illuminate their interests in southern culture. However, *Men Working*, by the standards of decades of literary criticism, displays shortcomings in its "literariness" that even ardent readers cannot ignore. These faults in the novel as literature suggest at least a partial explanation for the general critical inattention to John Faulkner's work.

Modernist literary critics, who dominated English departments through Faulkner's productive years and whose tenets continue to exert an influence on literary judgment, especially outside the academy, give the writing of John Faulkner low marks. Among the desiderata of modernist criticism, Jane Tompkins notes, are the "notion that fullness and depth of representation are preferable to variety . . . and the premium that formalism placed on making judgments about the aesthetic as opposed to the historical significance of works of art."[11] *Men Working* is not a unified social protest novel; there is no unified critical vision apparent here and certainly not a powerful unified aesthetic. In the same letter in which he announced his enthusiasm for *Men Working*, Arthur Zeiger asked Faulkner: "What were your social motivations and purposes, if you had any?" This fundamental question from a real admirer of the novel points to a problem that detracts from the overall effect of *Men Working*, and *Dollar Cotton* as well for that matter.

Contributing to the novel's unevenness is Faulkner's at times uncertain handling of several literary traditions. Some of the novel seems pure naturalism, most striking, for instance, in the Taylors' lack of agency. When they strike out, as when Hub robs a drugstore to pay for an operation for his brother Buddy, their attempts are as futile as those of Norris's or Dreiser's pawns: Hub is shot stealing two hundred and fifty pennies; Buddy dies during surgery after calling pitifully for Hub in one of the novel's moving scenes. Faulkner's fondness for the Old Southwestern humor tradition also leads at times to trouble. On the one hand, *Men Working* echoes its contemporary, *Grapes of Wrath*, in its attempts to make readers aware of the plight of the agricultural South's dispossessed. But social realism and Old Southwestern humor, with its dependence on tall tales, broad humor, and grotesqueness, meld uneasily. The novel is precariously poised— not merely between comedy and tragedy but on a deeper level. A struggle exists between John Faulkner's fundamental uncertainties over what we are to make of not only the Taylors and their misadventures but also the larger impact of the Depression and the New Deal—the effect of the market and its solvent force on the organic community that Faulkner clearly prizes. Almost like the Taylors, Faulkner is caught between a visceral attachment to the land, a sense of its goodness, and the siren song of modernity.

But if we follow the lead of cultural criticism, denying the supreme importance of the modernist criteria of "literariness," and treat *Men Working* as a cultural artifact, it is apparent that the text is exceedingly valuable for the student of twentieth-century southern culture. In fact, it is precisely John Faulkner's inability to balance the cultural and philosophical tensions of modernization in a traditional society that make him well worth reading. *Men Working*'s ambivalences—its tensions and paradoxes—are an expression of the fundamental apprehension of the dominant culture of the Deep South toward modernism during the mid-twentieth century. John Faulkner was a man with strong and perhaps irreconcilable contradictions in his thinking about the direction he wished his region to take. Like more than a few twentieth-century southerners, he was torn between romanticizing the past, valorizing the wholeness of southern communities, and embracing the not entirely illusory promise that by welcoming broad changes in their institutions and mores life could be better for his people in his part of the world.

For John Faulkner, his family and his home of Mississippi were early and lasting influences. Born in Ripley, Mississippi, in 1901 (William was born in New Albany in 1897), John Wesley Thompson Falkner III and his parents moved when he was one year old to Oxford where he grew up with his three brothers, William, Murry, and Dean. Earning an engineering degree from the University of Mississippi in 1929, John Faulkner served eventually as Oxford's city engineer. He worked on highway and bridge construction for the Mississippi Highway Department on projects between Greenwood and Clarksdale and from Clarksdale to Memphis, helping to survey and plan the famous Highway 61 that carried so many impoverished

Mississippians out of the Delta and into the urban centers of the South and Midwest.

Early in 1938 John Faulkner returned to Oxford to take up farming in Beat Two of Lafayette County on land owned by William. The latter was temporarily flush, having recently sold the movie rights to his novel *The Unvanquished*. Determined to be a land owner, William offered John a job managing his new farm. The time hardly seemed auspicious for farming, especially when undertaken by two men who were not well versed in its frustrating variabilities. After all, that same year the National Emergency Council issued its "Report on Economic Conditions of the South," prompting President Roosevelt's labelling of the region as the "nation's no. 1 economic problem." The brothers never expected to make a fortune off the land, though, and wanted only "to raise mules and enough grain to feed them."[12]

The venture was enriching for John Faulkner in other ways, however. For in northeastern Lafayette County, some seventeen miles from Oxford, he began to write and paint and to discover an artistic voice of his own. "I began writing on the farm," Faulkner remembered, "making up stories to tell my youngest son, Chooky."[13] In managing the farm owned by his brother, in taking up the craft that William had mastered, John Faulkner perhaps felt the pinch of envy. Their mother did not help sibling relations when, as John later wrote, she asked William to read John's stories and give advice on getting them published.

In "Feud," an unpublished short story that takes a great deal of effort not to read autobiographically, John Faulkner tells of two brothers, both writers:

> William, newly famous, newly rich, an undoubted genius and a trifle mad, became obsessed with the lust for power which confined itself to a desire for subservient obedience from the members of his own family. . . . Having subjugated his immediate family, he induced his brother, John, to return from a distant City to act as manager of his farm on an agreement quite suitable to both. . . . During the long winter evenings of John's enforced sedentary existence he had turned his hand to writing, more to pass the time than anything else, and had discovered a latent talent for it. . . . John's first thoughts were, of course, freedom, at last.[14]

Though we should resist the temptation to read too much into the conclusion of "Feud," in which the brothers die, still feuding, John admitted that "I did not get along too well with him [William] through his last years."[15] Readers of *Men Working* and John Faulkner's other fiction cannot help but be aware that the creator of Yoknapatawpha cast a shadow over the former's work that he found difficult to escape. John Faulkner rarely spoke publicly of William Faulkner's towering literary achievements and growing reputation and probably did not discuss these matters very often with his brother Bill. But in conventional terms,

John Faulkner was successful and happy, probably more so than his brother.

Curiously enough, when writing on Beat Two in 1963, albeit in his recollections of William, John stressed its meaning to Bill, although the place and its people became as much his own fictional domain:

> Bill found more than just a farm out there. He found the kind of people he wrote about, hill people. They made their own whiskey from their own corn and didn't see why that could be anybody else's business. They fought over elections and settled their own disputes. We had a killing just across the creek from us, over redistricting a school zone.[16]

This characterization of Beat Two people brings us again to the tension at the heart of John Faulkner's Mississippi writings and paintings. In considering his series of paintings, "Scenes From the Vanishing South," and the descriptions he wrote of each, among them "Possum Hunt," "Old Linker's Mill," and "Chit'lins," it is easy to label John Faulkner as a southern writer who set his teeth against modernity and pined for the alleged good old days of sturdy, independent men and women, who coaxed a living from the soil and asked quarter from no one. Late in his life Faulkner no doubt encouraged this characterization by criticizing the federal government and labor unions for undermining independence and initiative and by displaying (especially in the 1950s) an alarming tendency to shoot from the hip when speaking to the press on southern mores, particularly segregation. John Faulkner's self-description as a "staunch segregationist," coupled with the criticisms of the New Deal that run through his fiction, may lead one to dismiss him too quickly as a reactionary or even that protean creature, a southern conservative.

However, a writer's public pronouncements, even on writing, are never gospel, especially in the case of John (or William) Faulkner. *Men Working* is more than a slap at Big Government and must not be sold short by taking Faulkner's criticisms of the New Deal as the novel's only feature, or even its principal purpose. While we certainly do not have to accept his as the last word on the subject, it is worth considering John Faulkner's own ambivalent connection to the WPA. "After about two years on the farm," Faulkner wrote, sounding remarkably like the people of his fictionalized Beat Two, "Bill's money ran out and I moved back to town and got a job on the W.P.A." But unlike the Taylors, he was a superintendent, a Project Engineer, from 1939 to 1940. In his obituary, the *Jackson Daily News* observed that "while working as a superintendent for the WPA, he rigged two trucks into buses to transport his workers and 'really got to know folks and their tragedies.'"[17] Turning these encounters into his first novel, he wrote *Men Working* in the summer of 1940, seeing it published the next year; he later claimed that the novel's criticisms of the WPA got him fired.

In an unpublished story, "Homefolks," Faulkner provides an abstract of his attitudes on southern life and a meditation on the world he valued and feared was disappearing. Two Mississippians, one black and one white, find themselves in a Washington, D.C., zoo admiring a caged pig and discover in their common homeland a tie that overcomes race and other distances. I would suggest that something of real value can be carried away from a story as seemingly slight as "Homefolks," from the lightly regarded *Cabin Road* series, and certainly from the more fully developed *Men Working* and *Dollar Cotton*. In "Homefolks," pig and men are united under John Faulkner's vision of an organic southernness. Similar to the Agrarians, he sees the forces of science and "progress" undermining these ties. One might regard this attitude as retrograde, paternalistic, or at least an inadequate basis for society in a twentieth-century industrial, urban nation. But we should by now know that it is a mistake to dismiss too quickly Faulkner's argument that change has its costs, which proponents of the new order rarely publicize. Certainly, if we wish to more fully understand the Deep South in the twentieth century, John Faulkner's writings merit a place in our discussions. His work provides insights into southern thought between the era of populism and the era of massive resistance, and has lessons to teach us about social class in the region as well.

Despite the many books that have appeared recently on southern economic development and the effects of New Deal programs on the South, John Faulkner's novels (like other "minor" fiction of the 1930s) have long been nearly unavailable. *Men Working* is more than a neglected southern novel. It is a key document in the fields of Mississippi history and the history of the New Deal–era South. It is an important regional novel—one of the best satirical works of the period on southern government, politics, and manners. And as John Faulkner would have wished, *Men Working* and his other novels can still be read with amusement by anyone who has ever found the South a singular place.

NOTES

1. Arthur Zeiger to John Faulkner, October 30, 1950, John Faulkner Papers, Private Collection, Oxford, Miss. See also Arthur Zeiger, "My Favorite Forgotten Book," *Tomorrow* 10, January 1951, 39.

2. Hosford Latimer Fontaine to John Faulkner, January 17, 1960, John Faulkner Papers, Mississippi Department of Archives and History, Jackson, Miss.

3. Redding S. Sugg Jr., "John's Yoknapatawpha," *South Atlantic Quarterly* 67 (summer 1969): 343. Sugg explains that John Faulkner's publishers insisted that he add the "u" to his surname, as William had done.

4. John Faulkner, *My Brother Bill: An Affectionate Reminiscence* (New York, 1963), 276.

5. For a fuller listing, see Helen White and Redding S. Sugg Jr., "John Faulkner: An Annotated Check List of His Published Works and of His Papers," in *Studies in Bibliography: Papers of the Bibliographical Society of the University of Virginia* 23, ed. Fredson Bowers (Charlottesville, 1970), 217–29. Thomas and Judith Bonner of Xavier University are currently writing the first full biographical/critical study of John Faulkner and his work.

6. Michel Bandry, "*Cabin Road*: John Faulkner's Lafayette County," in *Interface: Essays on History, Myth and Art in American Literature*, ed. Daniel Royot (Montpelier, 1985), 72.

7. A good discussion of this is found in Roger Biles, *The South and the New Deal* (Lexington, 1994); see also James C. Cobb and Michael V. Namorato, eds., *The New Deal and the South* (Jackson, 1984); Frank Freidel, *F.D.R. and the South* (Baton Rouge, 1965); and George B. Tindall, *The Emergence of the New South, 1913–1945* (Baton Rouge, 1967).

8. Biles, *New Deal*, 76, 78.

9. Anthony Badger, *The New Deal: The Depression Years, 1933–1940* (New York, 1989), 203.

10. Larry Whatley, "The Works Progress Administration in Mississippi," *Journal of Mississippi History* 30 (February 1968): 35–50; Martha H. Swain, *Ellen S. Woodward: New Deal Advocate for Women* (Jackson, 1995).

11. *Sensational Designs: The Cultural Work of American Fiction, 1790–1860* (New York, 1985), 194, xii.

12. Faulkner, *My Brother Bill*, 176.

13. Ibid., 204–5.

14. John Faulkner Papers, Private Collection, Oxford, Miss.

15. Faulkner, *My Brother Bill*, 204.

16. Ibid., 177.

17. Faulkner, *My Brother Bill*, 200; *Jackson Daily News*, 29 March 1963.

Men Working

One

The good land lay beneath the sun. And the mules with their sleek sides dark splotched with sweat slid the flashing plows through the good land and laid it wide for planting. The women and the children followed the flashing plows and dropped seed one by one into the wide deep furrows and covered the seed and the black land slept with the seed under the growing sun. When the rain came, the seeds burst with growing and pushed their tendrils experimentally through the earth and disrupted the light crust with their swelling and their growing and the black fields became striped with pale green and the owners of the pale green striped fields pushed their feet deep into the pulverized ground and nodded their heads in satisfaction.

We've got a good stand, they said. Best stand we've had since Nineteen Twenty. We'll make a whopper of a crop this year.

It was Saturday afternoon in the early summer and the orange colored school bus with its black lettered "London High" sign stood parked in its usual place against the curb in front of the Corner Grocery. The driver sat nodding behind the wheel waiting to begin his homeward trip with the load of farmers, both black and white, and their wives and families that he had brought to town for the day.

A young fellow about the same age as the driver, tanned to a nut brown and dressed in cheap new yellow brogues, new cotton pants with the tag still showing from beneath the belt and a new straw hat, stepped down from the sidewalk and strolled up to the side of the truck. A wrapped package with the twisted end of paper stuck out of one hip pocket and his handkerchief flapped limply out the other. He stopped even with the truck cab and pulling his pants leg carefully up to preserve the crease rested one foot on the running board. The driver raised his head.

"Hello, Hub," said the driver to the young man standing at the cab.

"Any of the rest of 'em here yit?" said Hub.

"Naw," said the driver.

"Mind if I git in the cab with you?" said Hub.

"Crawl in," said the driver. "Old man Dewey thinks he owns the cab though and you'll probably have to get out when he comes."

"Damnf that's so," said Hub. "My money's just as good as his."

"Well, crawl in," said the driver. "You can settle that with him when he comes. I don't give a damn, myself."

Hub walked around the truck and crawled into the cab.

4

"I wisht Tommy would come on," said Hub. "Then I'd like to see old man Dewey put us out."

They sat without talk, in the untiring patience learned from years of regulating the compulsions of their existence to the growth of a crop, watching the Saturday crowd on the walk in front of the truck.

"Here comes some of them," said Hub a few minutes later as two Negroes loaded down with bundles pushed their way through the mild consternation of the crowd on the sidewalk and sidled in between the fenders of the bus and the car parked next to it.

" 'Bout ready to pull out, Mist' Frank?" said one of the Negroes.

"Soon's they all get here," said the driver.

"Kin we leave dese things in de truck?"

"Yeah. And don't you all get too far away. We'll be leaving here pretty soon."

"Yassuh. We jes' git in now den."

The Negroes pushed on between the bus and the car next to it and Hub and the driver heard them fumble at the rear door and then felt the bus sag as they climbed in.

The crowd on the sidewalk before them, mostly Negroes, milled and seethed and their soft ejaculations and mellow laughter hung above them in the sunlight like an audible halo and a benediction.

"Wisht I was happy as a nigger," said Hub.

"If you didn't have any more to worry about than they have, I guess you would be," said Frank.

"I don't begrudge anybody, white or black, a day's

work," said Hub, "but it does look to me like the WP and A could pay a white man more for a day's work than they do a nigger. It just naturally costs a white man more to live."

"That's right," said Frank. "But the government don't make no difference between white and black."

A steady stream of country people worked their way through the crowd on the walk; mostly girls, black and white, arm in arm, in twos and threes with an occasional woman dragging a small wailing child at arm's length behind her. They came to town at nine in the morning and spent the day walking round and round the Square. The powder soon wore off their faces but the glaring spots of rouge remained. Their fresh starched dresses were soon crushed from much passing and pushing in the throngs and they walked with unaccustomed stride in their stilted high-heeled shoes.

The bus sagged again as some new arrival climbed in at the back.

"There's somebody else," said Hub. "They ought to be coming in pretty fast now. It's done past four."

"Yeah," said the driver.

"Look," said Hub. "There goes that girl that old man Dorsey is crazy about."

"Old man Dorsey? Why, hell. He's old enough to be her great-grandfather."

"That don't make no matter. Maybe she wants him that way. She shore drags him around all over the country. Some of 'em saw them over on Twenty-one

6

the other night at the Log Cabin. He was passed out but she wasn't."

"Having a time, was she?"

"Man, you tell 'em. She just wants him to foot the bills. She passes him out and then she has herself a time."

"Looks like his folks would stop it. Ain't he got a brother here?"

"What the hell can a brother do or for that matter anybody else with an old fool like him? I'm glad somebody can jar him loose from some of his money though. He shore is tight as hell with it."

"I guess she's getting her share."

"Fifteen or twenty dollars every week-end I heard some of 'em say. Some say he's fixing to marry her."

"That beats the WPA," said the driver. "Did your old man make it today?"

"Yeah," said Hub. "His Four Oh Two come this morning. He's going to start work Monday."

"What's he going to do about his crop?"

"Let Mr. Young worry about that."

"Will Mr. Young let him keep on staying on the place, you reckon?"

"We ain't asked him. We're moving to town tomorrow. Paw wants to see you about moving us in."

"Well, I guess I can. I've got to take a load to the London Church singing in the morning but I can move you in tomorrow evening."

"That ought to suit all right," said Hub.

"You coming to town too?" said Frank.

"Hell, yes," said Hub. "You think Mr. Young would let me stay on after paw left?"

"Couldn't you stay on and work the crop out? There ain't a whole lot more to do to it."

"Ain't got nothing to work it with," said Hub. "Paw had to sell the mules and all the plow tools before they'd certify him."

"Well, I be damned," said Frank. "Who'd he sell the mules to?"

"We sold 'em to Bill Good."

"That crook? What'd you get for 'em?"

"Well, paw still owed him some on 'em. We just give 'em back for the balance due on the note."

"What'd you do with your plow tools?"

"We give 'em to maw's brother."

"God-o-Mighty," said Frank. "Does Mr. Young know about your leaving yet?"

"That old bastard?"

A stoop-shouldered man in faded and patched overalls and jumper and a wide-brimmed felt hat pulled low over his eyes against the sun glare pushed his way through the crowd and came up to the bus.

"Hello, Frank," he said. "Can we make arrangements fer your truck tomorrow to haul a load into town fer us?"

"I guess so, Mr. Taylor," said Frank. "Hub has already said something about it. I've got to haul a load to London Church tomorrow morning but I can haul you in tomorrow evening."

8

"That'll be all right, I guess," said Mr. Taylor. "It oughtn't to take us long to git in and git settled."

"I hear you're going to work on the WPA," said Frank.

"Yes. I've took a job with 'em. Start work next Monday morning."

"Found you a place to stay here in town yet?"

"Well, no," said Mr. Taylor. "Not just exactly. I been pretty busy today with gitting my Four Oh Two and all and I ain't hardly had no time to look around none. But I reckon as many houses as they is here we won't have no trouble finding us a place to stay."

"I hope you won't," said Frank.

"Is ever' body here yit?"

"Naw. There's still several to come but we'll be ready to leave as soon as they all do get here."

"Well, I'll just run down the street a minute and I'll be right back. I got a little more trading I got to do."

"Don't be gone long," said Frank. "We're about ready to go."

"I don't aim to stay over a minute," said Mr. Taylor.

"Paw's always got some last minute trading to do," said Hub.

"Yes, by God, he's worse than old man Dewey," said Frank. "Old man Dewey goes in every store in town every evening. We have to wait on him every time."

"He's on the WP and A, is he?"

"Yes. And he waits in his house in the mornings until I blow for him and then comes poking out and then we have to set here every evening for thirty minutes for

9

him to get through trading so we can leave. And having to drive twenty-two miles throws us past dark every evening getting home."

"Where does he git all the money to do so much trading?"

"Hell, he don't buy but about a nickel's worth in every third store. Comes out every evening with his pockets stuffed full of little old packages about the size of a spool of thread."

"Well, I'm glad we are moving to town so we won't have to ride the bus every day. Save us twenty-five cents a day apiece."

"Are you going to work on the WPA too?"

"Me? Naw. They won't certify me on account of they done already certified paw. They won't certify but one to a fambly."

"You ought to get you a family, Hub. Then you could get certified, too."

"I been thinking 'bout that," said Hub.

"I wish they would come on now," said Frank. "I'm ready to go home."

"Me, too," said Hub. "I wonder how many we are short now."

"Several of 'em got in in the last few minutes," said Frank. "I'll ask Will."

He leaned his head out of the cab window and called over his shoulder into the small ventilator in the tin frame body in which the passengers rode.

"Will? . . . Will. How many we like now?"

"Lemme see, Mist' Frank," came from the inside of

the truck. "Here's me an' Thomas an' Abe an' Sis Mc-
Carty an' . . . Whah's Miz Thompson and Mist' Ed?
. . . Dey awl heah cep'n Mist' Dewey an' Mist' Taylor
an' Mist' Hub up dar wid you . . . Bout fo' five, Mist'
Frank, I reckons."

"Crank up and maybe they'll come on," said Hub.

"I believe I'll try it," said Frank. "Tommy ain't here
yet."

"He dropped off down to the café as we come by
while ago. He'll be here."

Frank turned the switch and engaged the starter and
the motor caught with a roar. He put the truck in re-
verse and backed carefully away from the curb.

"Here comes paw and Tommy, now," said Hub.
"And there's the rest of 'em coming out of that crowd
there on the corner. That's all of 'em 'cept old man
Dewey."

"I'll just drive around the Square as soon as they all
get loaded and maybe we can see him," said Frank.

"Come on up here, Tommy," called Hub.

Tommy ran around to the front and opened the cab
door and Hub hitched over to make room for him. The
rest got into the back. The bus moved slowly forward,
threading its way between the cars parked two-deep
against the curb and the double row of cars in the
narrow parking strip along the center of the pavement
on two sides of the Square.

"What's old man Dewey going to say about not getting to ride in the cab?" said Tommy who was a regular

rider on the bus and knew that Mr. Dewey looked on the cab as his private seat.

"What do you care?" said Hub. "First come, first served. Frank done already said it don't make no never mind to him who rides up here."

"Let him holler then," said Tommy. "See if I care."

They drove slowly on around the Square looking for old man Dewey, slowly because of the pedestrians that moved in a two-way stream between the sidewalk and the courthouse, dodging around the talking groups that stood out in the pavement, stopping for the line of cars and trucks that wound around the flat toadstools in the traffic lanes.

"There he is," said Tommy, suddenly spying Mr. Dewey on the sidewalk. "Just come out of that store there."

"Holler at him," said Hub.

"Mister Dewey," called Tommy. "Oh, Mister Dewey."

"Hey?" said Mr. Dewey.

"Ready to go?"

"Just a minute. I've got to go in this next place here. Just a minute."

"See?" said Frank. "What did I tell you?"

"Hurry up then," called Tommy. "We haven't got a place to park."

Mr. Dewey disappeared into the store door and they cruised on around the Square.

"Where do all these cars come from?" said Hub. "They're parked double against the curbs and that

12

center strip along each side the Square is full and the curb around the courthouse is packed and jammed. Ain't hardly enough room left in these two little old narrow tracks for a car to git through."

"I don't know where they come from," said Frank. "It beats anything I ever saw. You can't hardly get on the Square and once you do get on it you can't hardly get off again."

"A bunch of them belong to the folks working on the WP and A," said Tommy.

"WPA?" said Frank. "How can a man working for the WPA buy a car?"

"Oh, lots of 'em got 'em," said Tommy. "Some of 'em gits ratings and gits 'em and some just pitches in together and gits up the down payment."

"I guess we'll git us one soon's paw gits him a rating," said Hub.

"There's old man Dewey again," said Tommy. "Going in to another store."

"Call him quick," said Frank. "We can't fool around here all day."

"Mister Dewey. Oh, Mister Dewey," called Tommy. "You better come on here. We're leaving."

Mr. Dewey paused, holding the store door open, and looked at them undecided.

"I'll be out there as soon's I go in here," he finally said.

"We're gone then," said Tommy, straightening in his seat.

"Hey," said Mr. Dewey. "Hey. I'm coming."

"That got him," said Tommy. "Look at him run."

Mr. Dewey ran up to the cab but Tommy made no move to open the door or relinquish his seat. Mr. Dewey put his hand on the door handle and opened the door. The bus had been inching along with the cars behind it blowing impatiently and now Hub stomped Frank's foot which was held poised lightly on the accelerator and the truck bucked and jumped forward. The projecting edge of the home-made body caught Mr. Dewey on the shoulder and spun him half around, throwing him off balance and up against the rear of a parked car they were abreast of. Tommy and Hub laughed uproariously.

"Go on and leave him," said Hub.

"Hell, I can't," said Frank. "You oughtn't to have done that."

He declutched the motor and brought the truck to a full stop and Mr. Dewey caught up with it and stuck his wrath-filled face into the cab window.

"I'm sorry, Mr. Dewey," said Frank. "My foot slipped."

Maybe I can smooth it over before the whole thing gets us in trouble for blocking traffic, he thought.

"I know about how it slipped," said Mr. Dewey. "Hubbard just about did that. I know him and all his folks. That's just about the kind of tricks they play on folks."

"My folks are a damn sight better than yourn," said Hub.

The cars behind them were becoming more impa-

14

tient. Their horns were a continuous raucous squawking.

"Come on. Come on. Let's go," said Frank. "We've
got to get away from here."

"I'm waiting for Hubbard and Thomas to git out,"
said Mr. Dewey.

"What for?" said Tommy.

"That's my seat in the cab," said Mr. Dewey. "I allus
ride the cab."

"Well, this is one time you ain't," said Tommy. "And
if you want to go home with us you better git in the
back of the truck."

"That's the stuff, Tommy," said Hub. "Tell 'im 'bout
it."

"Frank, are you going to make them git out and let
me have my place? Remember, I ride every day with
you and they just ride Saddy."

"Well now, Mr. Dewey," said Frank, genuinely worried, "we always go by the rule, first come, first served.
You get the place every day during the week because
you live furthest out and get on first. These men pay
for their rides just the same as you do and I can't hardly
make them get out if they don't want to."

"Don't forget that I pay you a quarter every day to
ride. That's a quarter every day against a quarter onct
a week."

"Hell," said Tommy. "Let's go. He's got to ride with
you if he keeps on working on the WP and A. They
ain't no other trucks comes in from out our way. If the

old bastard don't want to git in the back this evening, why, just let him spend the night in town."

"Thomas, I intend to tell your paw on you. I'll git in the back but I shore intend to tell your paw on you."

"Well, tell him," said Tommy, "and see if I give a damn."

Mr. Dewey gave up the losing argument and went around to the rear of the bus and crawled in the door and the truck, now fully loaded, got under way and with the sun at its back began the twenty-two mile run out into the county.

The passengers began dropping off about ten miles out. As each one neared his particular turnoff he would bang his hand against the tin body of the truck and Frank would pull to a stop. The rider would scramble over the legs between him and the door and drop to the ground. Then those nearest the door would assist in the collecting of his bundles and packages and hand them down to him and call cheery farewells, and the one who had descended would stand in the midst of his heaped bundles until some self-appointed conductor in the lessening crowd inside the bus would sing out, "All aboard." The truck gears would clash and the truck with its laughing, carefree Negroes and its poor whites who resented the Negroes' happiness would jolt off down the road under the interested regard of the one who had just gotten off, and their last sight of him before they rounded the first curve would be of him busily moving between the lessening pile of bundles in the road and the growing pile on the bank. Once the bundles were collected on the roadside bank he would sit there by them and await the coming of the wagon or the children who would help transport the bundles the intervening half mile or mile or five miles to the cabin that he called home.

Sixteen miles out the truck stopped and Tommy and Hub got out of the cab and Hub's father let himself down from the rear door and came around to the cab.

"You say you can move us tomorrow evening?" he said to Frank.

"Yes sir," said Frank. "It may be a little late but I'll be there as soon as I get back from the singing at London Church."

"I've a mind to go to the singing with you," said Mr. Taylor. "They ain't no man enjoys a good singing more than I do. But I reckon I dasn't. Maw might need me to help pack. Well, we'll look fer you tomorrow evening. I want to be in town in time to go to work Monday morning, shore."

"I'll be there," said Frank. "See if Mr. Dewey wants to get up here in the cab."

Mr. Taylor went back around to the rear door and returned almost at once.

"He said, 'Naw,' kind of madlike."

"Well, all right," said Frank and put the gear in first.

Tommy and Hub and Hub's father stood watching the truck roll off down the gravel road and saw it stop just before it got to the first curve. Mr. Dewey descended from the door at the rear and went around to the cab and got in; then the motor roared and the truck moved on off.

"Wanted somebody to beg him," commented Tommy.

They gathered what few bundles they had and trudged off down the side road that passed close to Mr. Taylor's cabin.

"Well," said Mr. Taylor, "I don't rightly know how maw's going to take this about me gitting on the WP and A."

"Why, she's been talking about it all week and we done already sold ever' thing but what we are going to take to town with us," said Hub.

"I know," said Mr. Taylor, "but we ain't never just set the day yit."

"I'd druther move than git throwed off," said Hub.

"I guess Mr. Young will be right put out," said Mr. Taylor.

"Serve him right too," said Hub.

They walked along, patient, unhurried in the dusk, and the early night sounds began to fill the air. Frogs piped shrilly beneath the flickering fireflies. A whip-poor-will yodeled his mellow, "Chips flew out of the white oak."

"I kind of hate to leave, myself," said Mr. Taylor.

"Why, hell, paw. What is there left for us out here? Mr. Young, the old bastard, taking the whole par'ty check and paying us day wages. What are we going to do after the crop's laid by? There will be a dozen farmers then trying to git on the WP and A for every job there is. Let him have the crop. We can make twelve

18

bales of cotton, near 'bout, every year in town instead of about four like we do now and we won't have to pay no one a share outen them neither."

"Well, I reckon you are right about that," said Mr. Taylor. "I just hope maw sees it that way."

"There ain't no way else fer her to see it," said Hub.

"I wisht I could make my old man move to town," said Tommy. "It was hell gitting up at three-thirty last winter to catch that damn bus."

"How long you been on the WP and A, Thomas?" said Mr. Taylor.

"I been on ever since it started," said Tommy. " 'Bout four year come this fall."

"How do you manage to stay on through crop time?"

"Tommy quits about two weeks before they lay off all the farmers ever' spring and plays sick. Then when he gits ready to go back to work they done already laid off all the farmers and his card was over in the sick pile and they couldn't find it. Then when he gits reported as ready to begin work again they git his card out of the sick pile and put him back on and they done already forgot the farmers till next spring. He does it ever' time and they ain't caught him at it yit."

"That's a pretty good trick," said Mr. Taylor. "We'll have to remember that next spring."

"Hell," said Hub. "We don't need to remember it. We ain't farmers no more."

"That's so," said Mr. Taylor. "I kind of hate to think about it."

A path led off down a scrub-oak covered hill and

19

Hub said, "Here's our turnoff. Come on and spend the night with us, Tommy."

"Don't care if I do," said Tommy, "this being your last night out here. We might stir around a little after supper."

They could make out the light in the kitchen window at the back of the house now and as they followed on down the path through the woods it flickered through the small oak leaves and as they left the small oak and came into the stand of larger timber in the little valley they walked in alternate light and darkness as the light seemed to jump in behind the tall tree trunks then out on the other side as if impelled by the tension of a rubber band. The house itself sat on a small rise of ground and in the dip between them and the house was the spring, fenced off with pine slabs, one of which was rotted and fallen to the ground.

"I declare," said Mr. Taylor. "I aimed the last two year to fix that slab back up and somehow it looks like I just never got around to it. There's the bucket on that limb, Hubbard. Maw likely wants you to fetch some water to the house. I declare, I hate about forgetting that slab. Seems like a man just can't git around to ever'thing that needs to be done around a place. Watch out fer that little shoat when you git the water, Hubbard. He stays in the spring a whole lot since it's done got so warm."

Hub unhooked the tin bucket from the limb over the path and slapped it against the moss-covered bank above the spring.

"Sooey out of here," he said.

The shoat gave a grunt of startled surprise and scrambled out of the spring and ran squealing into the bushes.

"You best wait a few minutes fer the water to settle," said Mr. Taylor. "I'll go on up to the house."

They watched his stoop-shouldered gait toward the house along the path of light thrown by the lamp through the kitchen window, his head tilted down so that his hat brim shaded his eyes against the glare of the lamp.

"Now, I wonder why he don't move out of the light so's he can see where he's going," said Hub.

Tommy squatted down on the bank and now Hub dropped down beside him.

"I wisht we had some likker fer tonight," said Tommy.

"I got most a half gallon in a jug out to the barn," said Hub.

"I got a couple of dollars here," said Tommy. "I wonder if Frank's going to town tonight."

"I guess he is. He takes a crowd in ever' Saddy night. But it's too far to walk over to his house and we might miss him if we try to catch him up at The Rock. Let's go over to Stan's. He might can git his car tonight."

"All right."

"Git your water and let's git on to the house. We'll leave soon's we eat supper."

Hub rose and, moving over to the spring, squatted down beside it, tilting one edge of the bucket into the water and letting it settle under his hand as it filled. He lifted the bucket, letting it drip back into the spring as he straightened up.

"I don't guess it's very muddy now," he said. "Let's go."

Tommy followed Hub across the swept yard, keeping carefully to one side of the path of light, and up to the broken steps and across the worn floor of the porch. The front door stood open and they walked in and across the dark room and into the strip of light thrown from the kitchen lamp onto the front room floor. They entered the kitchen door and Hub's mother stood over the stove, slowly stirring the contents of a blackened pot.

Her figure, even through its shapeless faded mother hubbard, was heavy and cumbersome with unattended child-bearing and her feet were flat and encased in low tennis shoes—"tennises" she called them—with the laces carelessly flapping around her bare dirt-stained ankles. Her stringy, once-abundant hair was coiled on top of her head in an indifferent knot and her face, once pretty but now resigned and flaccid, drooped to the corners of her snuff-stained mouth. A year-old baby, big and strapping for its age, straddled her outthrust hip and her arm encircled it casually, easily, as it sat quietly sucking its thumb.

She hitched the baby to a more comfortable position on her hip and, twisting slightly, spat into the meager pile of wood beside the stove.

Gwendolin and Eugenia, five and seven, sat on the edge of the empty wood-box, staring at the open door through which Tommy and Hub were entering. Their ferret-like eyes were fixed on Tommy's face and their lips were fixed in a self-conscious grin.

Harold and McKinley, ten and twelve, paused an instant in their wrestling to study Tommy with their over-sharp eyes, and Jutland, fifteen, sat leaning back against the wall in one of the few cane-bottom chairs with a half-smoked cigarette dangling from his lips. Mr. Taylor stood with his hat still on, leaning against the table, his whole attitude one of vague indecision and innate bewilderment.

Buddy, aged nine, sat on the edge of the wood-box opposite Gwendolin and Eugenia, with his crutch leaning against the wall beside him and his shriveled leg drawn partially from sight beneath the shadow of the stove. His pale pinched face was turned unswervingly toward Hub and his pale lips and over-large eyes lit with an ethereal expression as he caught Hub's glance. He attempted to rise and knocked the home-made crutch clattering to the floor and Hub moved quickly to his side and taking the wrapped parcels from his pocket extended them. Buddy took them without removing his gaze from Hub's face and his long, sensitive fingers explored the wrappings and retrieved the box of crayons and the clean sheets of white paper and he knew even before he dropped his eyes to them what they were.

"Colors . . . and paper," he breathed.

Hub grinned down at him and tousled his hair.

"O.K.?" he asked.

Buddy nodded and his expression changed to one of

shyness as he unbuttoned the middle button of his shirt and his hand found its way in against his naked flesh and withdrew with a torn-edged piece of paper sack which he extended to Hub.

"Well, I declare," said Hub. "Now ain't that a purty pitchur."

"He's been a-setting there all evening drawing that," said Mrs. Taylor. "I declare, he's the beatin'est child I ever saw. Give 'im a piece of paper and a pencil and he'll set quiet all day. I do believe the whole house could fall in on 'im and he'd never look up . . . Rinno's about to fall outen his cheer to git to you, Hub. Ifen you don't say something to him soon, he'll have a pure fit."

Hub moved around the stove to Reno, named for Doctor Rheneau who chanced to be passing at the time that Mrs. Taylor gave birth to the baby that she had tried unsuccessfully for seven months to get rid of by every means known to the midwives and Negro women of that section. Then in the desperation of imminent unwed motherhood she had jumped off a ten-foot bank, landing stiff-legged in the bottom of the sand ditch, and her involuntary groans of labor had halted the horse-back journey of the doctor long enough for him to perform what part of the delivery the jump had not, and to threaten and coerce and bribe a passing Negro to turn his team and wagon around and haul the spent girl and the premature baby to her maiden home. After which he figuratively and literally washed his hands of the whole affair, never knowing that he had bequeathed his name in abortion to the baby.

24

Now Reno, twenty years old and six-feet-two inches tall and weighing less than fifty pounds, drooled saliva from between the scattered yellow snags that were his teeth and it dripped from his lax, trembling lips and ran down into the fuzzy black of his sparse beard. His hoarse, impatient croaks changed to rasped mewlings of pleasure as Hub approached and patted him on his knob of a shoulder.

"Hello, big boy," said Hub. "Look what Buddy drew."

At the word Buddy, Reno's head rolled across the dirty pillow which was tied to the chair-back and his eyes came to a belated focus on Buddy, and Buddy grinned shyly back at him. Then Reno's head rolled jerkily back to Hub and his knees trembled and his hands clutched with an almost audible dry clatter as he strove mightily to raise himself in his chair. Hub laid a soothing hand on his head and he relaxed once more against the pillow. Hub stooped and rearranged Reno's feet which had been disturbed in his twistings. One had fallen over the edge of the foot-rest of the half-reclining chair that Hub had built and the other had crumpled at the ankle, leaving the foot twisted under and the weight of the leg on the side of the ankle. Hub slipped a hand underneath the bony knees and lifted Reno's legs and fitted the long thin feet back to the foot-rest. He straightened Reno in his pillows and Reno gurgled his delight.

"I declare," said Mrs. Taylor. "I don't know which is better fer Rinno. To not see Hub and fuss about it

25

or to git to see him and twist around so he hurts hisself against that chair. Hit looks like when he even gits scratched now hit just won't never heal."

Reno quieted at last, Mrs. Taylor turned and took notice of Tommy.

"Hello, Tommy," she said. "How's your maw and paw?"

"Paw's doing right well, thanky, ma'am, but maw's kind of ailing."

"Hot weather, I 'spec'," said Mrs. Taylor. "Hit makes us all feel ailish and complainy sort of."

"Yessum."

"Hub, you didn't see nothing of Virginia in town today, did you?"

"No'm. She ain't home yit?"

"I haven't saw her since Tuesday," said Mrs. Taylor. "I'm gitting right disturbed about her."

"I'll have to give her a talking to the next time I see her," said Hub.

"I guess you'll have to," said maw. "Looks like what me and your paw says don't do no good a tall. Y'all pull up your cheers. Supper's 'bout ready."

They pulled up boxes and chairs to the table and Hub made room for Buddy beside him. Maw worked between stove and table, serving the plates with warmed-over turnip greens and pone bread. They ate in silence, a meal in the country being no place for conversation. They rose one by one as they finished, and left the room.

26

"I'll be late gitting in," called Hub to maw as he left. "Me and Tommy are going out fer a while."

"Keep a watch out fer Virginia," called maw.

Hub and Tommy left through the kitchen door that opened into the back yard and Buddy's eyes followed Hub as he and Tommy merged with the shadows of the path that led down to the barn.

They stopped at the barn door and Hub said, "Wait here a minute. I'll git it."

He left Tommy standing in the lighter square of the door and he felt his way along the wall to the ladder that led up into the loft. Tommy heard his feet scrape on the rungs of the ladder and heard the thud as his feet found the boards of the loft, heard him moving across to the corner above the door and felt the scraps of dislodged hay sift down into his upturned face. He heard Hub scratch around in the hay then move back across to the ladder and descend to the ground floor.

"Got it?" he called into the darkness.

"Year," said the barely discernible moving shadow.

Then Hub was at his elbow with the jug in his hand and he pulled the stopper and extended the jug.

"This is mighty soon after a meal to take a drink," said Tommy.

"Take a big one," said Hub. "You'll feel it."

Tommy tilted the jug over his forearm, lipped its mouth and slowly raised his arm. He swallowed, gagged, and lowered the jug quickly.

"Hell, I can't drink this soon after supper."

"We'll wait then," said Hub. "By the time we git to Stan's we'll be ready for one."

Tommy handed the jug back to Hub and Hub put the stopper in and tapped it firm with the heel of his hand.

"Who is that coming up to the door?" said Tommy, pointing toward the front of the house.

"I don't know but I better put this jug somewhere," said Hub.

He stepped back into the shadow of the barn and set the jug against the wall, then he and Tommy walked quietly back up to the house. They heard voices before they reached the porch and they stopped in the shadows to listen.

"—and you mean to tell me that you are going to just go off and leave this crop?"

"Well, that's what we were sort of figgering on doing," said paw.

"Why, God damn it, you can't just go off and leave a man's crop like that. I let you have this piece of land with the understanding that you would make a crop on it. You haven't made a crop yet. You are not good started. And so far you've got the best stand you've had in twenty years."

"Well, it's a good stand, all right," said paw. "I don't aim to just leave no man. I seen lots of men in town today what was looking for work. Seems like you ought to be able to git enough hands to finish just this one crop."

"One crop, hell," said Mr. Young. "This makes seven

families I've lost this week. This God damned WPA is ruining the whole country. You can't get a man to stay with you long enough to make a crop and when you do get one he's been leaning on one of those WPA shovels so long about all he's good for is to stand in a watermelon patch for a scarecrow."

"Well, Mr. Young. Hit don't seem just right fer you to stand in the way of a man's bettering hisself."

"Bettering himself? How much will you get in town?"

"They say they will pay me about twenty-six dollars a month."

"And you expect to feed and clothe you and your wife and—how many children? . . . Seven?—Seven-eight-nine children on twenty-six dollars a month?"

"Well, that's a right smart more than I'm gitting now. I don't hardly ever see no money a tall."

"Money?" said Mr. Young. "Money?"

He glared down in furious abnegation at paw standing mildly puzzled and ineffectual before him.

"Get off my place," he shouted at last. "Get off."

"You mean tonight?" said paw.

"No," said Mr. Young. "No. I take that back. Just take your time about moving. Don't hurry at all. But just as a favor, a personal favor, don't come by my house to tell me you are gone. Then I won't have to look at you again."

And Mr. Young stalked out the door.

"Well," said maw. "I thought he was mad at fust, but that was right narce of him telling us to just take our time about moving. I guess he knows a body cain't just pick up and move all at onct. Hit takes time. I do sort of feel bad about leaving him without nobody to make that crop fer him. He's a real narce man. I wonder why he don't never want to see our faces no more? Hit might make him sad to think about us leaving. I allus git sad when I hear about folks leaving and all."

"I cain't just rightly understand him, myself," said paw. "I thought maybe he would put us off soon's he heared about us fixing to leave."

"Are ye got your mind set to go, paw?"

"Yes. I reckon we'll leave tomorrow. Frank says he can haul us in late tomorrow evening. Air you content to leave?"

"Well, I feel some better since Mr. Young acted so narce about it. I was kind of unmindful about it at fust. Kind of hated to leave. But since I got my mind made up like, I'm eager to git on in. I ain't seen town in seventeen year neither. I doubt ifen I will know it. Hub was telling me just the other day that they done cemented all the streets now. I bet hit's right purty. Seventeen year . . ."

"The bastard," said Hub from the shadows. "The bastard. Thinks he can hire us for day hands and take all the par'ty checks and the crop too and then in the winter when we go to him for supplies he'll say, Why don't you git on the WP and A? By God, we'll just git on the WP and A now and let him have the crop.

30

I wish we had two crops to let him have . . . and both of 'em was full of grass. Come on. Let's go."

Maw handed the baby to Gwendolin, who with the rest of the children had been hanging onto her dress and peering around her wide sleazy hips at paw and Mr. Young. She returned to the kitchen where Buddy sat hunched over the table amid the pushed-back dishes in the glare of the lamp, his crayons and his clean white sheets of paper before him. Maw swished past on her rubber-soled feet and stooping over Reno picked him up as one would a baby and carried him to the table where she seated herself with Reno's dangling length spilling over her lap onto the floor. She chewed some food reflectively, then took the sodden mass from her mouth and placed it in Reno's and he gulped it greedily and croaked impatiently for more. And across the table Buddy's long tapering fingers created artificial light and shadows with photographic clarity on the clean white paper and he sat walled from them in the obliviousness of his creation.

Two

Stan's father had been allotted the piece of ground adjoining Mr. Taylor's and his cabin was half a mile farther down the path through the woods. Hub and Tommy walked single file down the path, Hub leading with familiar feet and the jug of whiskey gripped tight in his swinging hand.

"I'm glad you know this path," said Tommy. "I can't see a thing."

"I've walked it enough times. I ought to know it," said Hub.

"How much farther is it?"

"Ain't far. We're almost there."

"Looks like we ought to be seeing the light from Stan's."

"We're coming up from the back side. Most likely they done et and moved up to the front of the house."

The path merged suddenly into a clearing and they felt the hard-packed dirt of a yard beneath their feet. Out from under the trees it was a little lighter and they could now make out the house and see a crack of light beneath the closed front room window shutter. As they came even with the light crack, Hub stopped abruptly and set the jug under the edge of the house.

"Stan's old man is on the front porch, I guess," he said.

"Hell. He won't care," said Tommy. "He drinks, hisself."

"I know it," said Hub. "That's the reason I hid the stuff."

"Oh," said Tommy.

They rounded the corner of the house and walked into the carpet of light thrown by the lamp through the open front door.

"Hello," called Hub into the house as he came to a stop at the foot of the steps.

"That you, Hubbard?" said a dim figure tilted back against the wall.

"Yessir, Mr. Browning. Didn't see you setting there. Is Stan to home?"

"Ain't got in yit. He'll be here toreckly. Hear you folks are moving to town."

"Yessir," said Hub. "Paw's got on the WP and A. Got his Four Oh Two this morning."

"I ain't got no hankering to git on the WP and A," said Mr. Browning. "How-some-ever, I've saw them that does want to git on try and try but it seemed like they just couldn't git certified. I reckon they just didn't know exactly who to tech on the shoulder at the office."

"I wonder if they ever saw Mr. Will about it? He might could help 'em."

"Yes. They said they've saw him. He tells 'em ever' time he'll have 'em certified by next pay period but somehow they ain't got on yit."

"I'm glad paw got on," said Hub. "A man can't do much good farming anymore. Specially for a bastard like Mr. Young. Work the insides outen a feller then tell him to go to hell."

"That's right," agreed Mr. Browning. "Lots of the folks is moving to town. I seen Steve Joe today and he told me the Social Worker had done notified him to come to town next Tuesday to have a intercourse with her so I guess he will be on the WP and A soon."

"I hope ever' body leaves Mr. Young," said Hub.

"Is Stan off in the car?" asked Tommy.

"Well, Tommy," said Mr. Browning, recognizing him for the first time, "I didn't know who you was. Yes. He went over to Ormand's fer some tobacco fer me."

"That must be him coming in now, then," said Tommy.

The three of them watched the lights from the approaching car as the glow above the rise changed from luminousness to pattern, then narrowed and burst into two overlapping glares.

"Them's the brightest lights I ever seen," said Tommy.

The whole yard stood in sharp-cut relief from the lights a quarter of a mile away. They dropped their eyes against the glare but still stood facing the approaching car, silent and waiting as it bored through the intervening distance, growing brighter and brighter as it approached, then wheeling into the yard and stopping even with them as their shadows sped in the opposite direction to the movement of the car and jumped into the protection of the enveloping darkness behind the lights.

"Don't cut the motor," Hub called to Stan.

"Where you boys going?" said Mr. Browning.

"Thought we might run over to The Lake tonight," said Hub. "If Stan ain't too tard. How about it, Stan?"

"I ain't never too tard to go somewhere Saddy night," said Stan. "Here's your tobacco, papa. Tell maw I won't be home till late."

He handed the tobacco to Tommy who in turn handed it to Mr. Browning. Mr. Browning took the cloth sack of tobacco and leaning over into the light pulled the papers from beneath the paper band that held them to the sack. He opened the folder containing the papers and patiently blew on the end of them and picked at them with a gnarled forefinger until he loosened one and stripped it off the small pad. He creased it and picked the tobacco sack open and filled the paper without paying any more attention to the three young men.

"Tell Stan to back down to the side of the house to turn," said Hub to Tommy.

Tommy opened the door and crawled into the front seat by Stan. He spoke to Stan and Stan backed the car around the side of the house. Hub was standing in the shadow at the edge of the porch with the jug in his hand. Tommy pushed the door open for him and he stepped to the running board and placing one knee on

35

the seat he reached over and down and set the jug on the floor behind the seat.

"Let's go," he said as he turned around and scrouged down beside Tommy and slammed the door. "We'll stop over the first rise and take one."

Stan put the car in low, let the clutch in and pressed the accelerator against the floor. The car rushed out of the yard, spewing dust, and Stan slapped it into second and high, then braked suddenly to ease over a small wash in the road. He speeded up again, as soon as they felt the back wheels take the dip, and flipped over the first rise. He threw the car out of gear and cut the switch with a flourish to let the car coast down the rise on its own momentum, braking it to a stop at the bottom of the slant. He cut the lights off and turned half in his seat as he watched Hub kneel over the back of the seat and retrieve the jug from the floor. Hub twisted back around with the jug on a hooked forefinger and pulled the stopper and extended the jug to Stan. Stan sniffed the open mouth of the jug and tilted it to his mouth. They followed his swallowing in the darkness and swallowed with him. He lowered the jug and Tommy took it. They drank in turn and sat silent, Hub holding the jug in his lap. Stan rolled a cigarette and passed the half-full sack of tobacco around and they all sat smoking and feeling the whiskey warm their insides.

"Let's take another one and git going," said Hub at last.

They drank again and Stan started the car and they

36

drove on down the dirt side road and whirled into the gravel highway, The Rock.

"What'll she do?" said Tommy.

For answer Stan pressed the accelerator against the floorboards and the speedometer hand moved forward until it hung quivering just above sixty.

"Pretty good for a car this old," shouted Stan above the roar and clamor of the motor.

They sat feeling the exhilaration of wind in their faces and Stan kept the accelerator pressed down. They rocketed across the levee road and up the hill on the far side and the car slowed to fifty.

"Stop before we git to Ormand's and we'll take another one," Hub shouted.

Stan braked the car to a stop at the top of the hill and they drank again.

"Put it over in the back so's they won't see it at Ormand's," said Stan, and Hub replaced the jug on the back floor.

Stan started the car again and drove along at forty miles an hour until they rounded the turn and saw the single yellow light of Ormand's at one side of the road. He pulled in to the gas pump and stopped and shut the motor off. They climbed out of the car and walked into the store.

"How 'bout some gas, Ormand?" said Tommy.

"You got the money?" said Ormand.

"You don't think I'd ask for the gas if I didn't have, do you?"

"I just wanted to be sure," said Ormand. "I ain't forgot that sixteen dollars you been owing me over a year now."

"I ain't trying to beat you out of it, am I?" said Tommy.

"Naw," said Ormand, "but it's been running quite a spell. How much gas do you want?"

"About two gallons," said Tommy.

Ormand went out to the pump and hosed the gas into the car tank.

"Trying to get tough, wasn't he, Tommy?" said a young fellow lounging against the counter.

"He knows who to fool with," said the whiskey in Tommy.

"Was two gas all?" said Ormand as he came back in the door.

"You better give me a sack of North State," said Tommy.

"Gimme one too," said Hub.

"Take it all out of that dollar," said Tommy.

Ormand reached two sacks of tobacco from a carton and slid them across the counter and took Tommy's dollar and gave him the change.

"Well, men. Let's go," Tommy said.

"Where you fellers going?" said Ormand.

"Up 'bout The Lake, I guess," said Hub.

They got back in the car and drove along the gravel highway toward the lake eight miles away, stopping frequently to drink from the jug.

"Boy, I hope that little black-headed girl that was

38

there about a month ago is back tonight," said Tommy.

"Hot, was she?" said Hub.

"Boy, you tell 'em."

"I wouldn't mind tying into something tonight," said Stan.

The glow from the lights of the jook house at the lake appeared above the trees and they stopped and drank again.

"Let's go, men," said Tommy. "Up and at 'em."

"Don't start another fight tonight, Tommy," said Stan.

"Hell, I ain't going to fight anybody," said Tommy.

"You always do," said Stan.

"If you don't want to go in with me, you stay outside," said Tommy.

"Aw, I didn't mean it that way, Tommy. Just be careful."

"I don't never mess with nobody that don't mess with me," said Tommy.

"Here's a good place to park," said Hub. "Pull in here."

They drove past the lighted front of the hastily erected frame building and the stamp of feet and the beat of the nickelodeon smote their ears.

"Boy, howdy," said Tommy. "Let's go."

Stan parked the car at the edge of the cindered parking space and they got out.

"Reckon this whiskey will be all right in the car?" said Hub.

"Sure," said Stan. "Everybody inside has got their

own. Won't nobody bother ours. Let's go catch Tommy."

Tommy was already in the door. He staggered slightly as he moved out among the dancers. The building was new, of unpainted lumber, and the floor, from waxings and the scraping of many feet, was worn slick already. Two electric lights glared down on the dancing couples on the floor as they swayed and staggered in the open space between the curtained booths that lined each wall.

"Hello, Red," said Hub to the tough-looking individual who stood by the beer box and regarded the dancers and the newcomers with the expressionless stare of a combination night-club owner and professional bouncer.

"Hello," returned the tough guy shortly.

Tommy was at the edge of the dancing couples now and he caught the arm of the nearest girl and tried to pull her away from her partner. The partner shoved Tommy roughly and Tommy staggered back and almost fell. With a drunken man's perversity he laughed instead of getting mad and caught at the next girl that passed him. Her partner swung her away from Tommy and said, "Better get back over there with your friends, Shorty. You'll need 'em if you keep that up."

"Who the hell do you think you are, telling me my business?" said Tommy.

Hub and Stan caught Tommy by the arms and led him protestingly to a booth. They parted the curtains and a man inside pulled quickly away from a girl who looked up at them with too bright eyes and strands of disarranged hair across her forehead.

"Get the hell out of here," said the man.

The hard-looking individual by the beer box moved quickly across the floor on surprisingly light feet and spoke quietly at their shoulder.

"Get your buddy out of here if he can't behave."

"Who thinks they can put me out of here?" said Tommy.

For answer the tough guy caught him by the back of his collar and the seat of his pants and marched him kicking and cursing across the floor and threw him out the door. Tommy landed on his feet but out of balance and he took several lengthy, running, plunging strides before he finally piled up in the cinders on his face. He stumbled erect and shook his head and wiped the cinders off his face.

"You can come back in here when you decide you can act sober," said the hard guy and he turned his back and resumed his post by the beer box.

"You big son-of-a-bitch," muttered Tommy.

Tommy brushed the cinders from his clothes and walked over to the car. He climbed in and retrieved the jug from the back floor and pried the stopper out and drank. He lowered the jug to his lap and sat feeling the whiskey inside him and nursing his wrath. He drank again and yet again and tried to roll a cigarette. He poured the tobacco into his lap and on the floor and tried to twist the few flakes he managed to keep on the paper into a cigarette and his head sank lower and lower and finally he slept. The jug rolled out of his lap onto the floor but there was not enough whiskey left in it to spill and it lay on its fat side on the floor between his feet.

Hub and Stan stood undecided as Red threw Tommy out the door. Finally Stan said, "Hell, let him go. I told him before we came in he was going to git in trouble. Serves him right."

"Reckon he'll git into the whiskey?" said Hub.

"Tommy can't drink much. He'll either git sick or go to sleep. Let him go."

"O.K.," said Hub. "This is my last night out here and I kind of hate to spoil it."

"Let's git one of these girls," said Stan.

"Which one?" said Hub.

"There's one over there we can git in a minute. Look at that bastard with her."

They looked at the couple in the far corner. The girl was half drunk and giggling at the obscene efforts of the fifty-year-old man who was dancing with her. The dancers on the floor had stopped to watch and they egged the old man on with suggestions and laughter while the hard-looking owner at the beer box watched with unblinking indifference.

"Go on, dad," called one onlooker.

"Dad cain't," said another. "He's done about reached his limit."

The old fellow turned a silly drunken grin on them and his out-of-focus eyes wavered over the entire group and came to rest on one of the bright lights overhead.

"He's calling on heaven for a little help now."

"You can't get the kind of help he wants in heaven."

"What's your wife going to say in the morning, dad, when she finds you done left your check with Red?"

Dad mouthed unintelligible sounds and saliva drooled from the corners of his uncontrolled mouth. His movements had stopped now. He was too drunk. He merely clung to the giggling girl for support and swayed, his eyes still fastened on the light overhead and a fatuous grin on his lips. His eyes gradually closed and he started slumping to the floor. Two of the onlookers caught him beneath the armpits and eased him to the floor against the wall. The hard-looking owner pushed through the crowd and picked the old fellow easily from the floor and strode out the door with him over his shoulder. He returned in a few minutes with empty hands. The crowd had already started dancing again.

"You take this dance, Stan," said Hub, "and I'll take the next one."

The old man's girl walked readily into Stan's arms and plastered herself against him and they moved out onto the floor. Hub stood leaning against the wall by the last booth waiting for the nickelodeon to play out the record. It finished with a lingering minor note and Stan walked the girl up to Hub.

"Your time next," he said.

"Let's drink a beer," said Hub. "You got any money?"

"Sure," said Stan. "I won two dollars off Book and a couple more niggers this evening."

Hub turned and pulled the curtains of the closest

booth aside. He took a half step into the booth and stopped with one foot lifted from the floor and stared at the occupants of the booth. There, with her head leaned back beneath the lips of a city-dressed stranger, was Virginia. Empty beer bottles littered the table and there was a half-full bottle of whiskey there. The man had Virginia's dress pulled up high over her knees and his hand was fumbling with the inside of her thighs.

Hub grasped the man by the collar and yanked him around and out of the booth and the man overbalanced and fell sprawling out into the floor. Virginia opened her eyes and saw Hub above her and cringed back into the far corner of the booth, stark terror in her look.

"Come out of there," said Hub hoarsely as he held the curtain back.

The owner had left his post at the first sign of the disturbance but the stranger had scrambled to his feet before even he got there. He grasped Hub by the shoulder and attempted to swing him around.

"What the God damned hell do you think you are doing?" he grated out.

Stan took him by the elbow and shook him to gain his attention.

"Feller, you better git going. That's the girl's brother."

"The hell it is," said the stranger.

He released Hub's shoulder and almost ran to the door and disappeared into the night.

The owner, hearing Stan, stopped and stood watching Hub and Virginia.

44

"Come out of there," said Hub again.

Virginia cringed farther back into the corner and as Hub leaned into the booth raised her hand to her mouth. He slapped her savagely and caught her arm above the wrist and yanked her out of the booth and to her feet. He turned and stalked across the floor and the owner moved aside and made room for them to pass. Virginia stumbled behind Hub, almost running, bent forward and twisting her shoulder to the pain of his grip on her wrist.

"Don't, Hub," she whimpered. "You hurt."

Hub stalked on across the dance floor and slammed the door wide and yanked her through behind him. He whirled her up to the car and opening the door flung her into the back seat and crawled in beside her.

"You bitch," he said furiously. "You bitch."

Stan followed them and now he took his place silently beneath the wheel and pushed Tommy over against the door. He tried to shove Tommy's feet over and found the jug. He set it upright on the seat between them and striking a match found the stopper and stuck it in the mouth of the jug. He started the car, backed out from the parking space and headed down the road they had come.

Three

The baby woke first the next morning as usual and woke maw in nuzzling at her for milk. Maw hunched over on her side and pried her bulging breast out of the top of her knit underwear and placed the nipple of it in the baby's opened, seeking mouth. Paw waked at the disturbance, grunted, and turned his back to them and closed his eyes again. The baby filled itself and slept and maw slid quietly out from under the cover and stood barefoot on the worn plank floor in her knee-length union suit. She reached her dress from the foot of the bed and slipped it over her head. She moved, still barefoot, to the window and stood staring out of it as she knotted her hair on the back of her head. Her hair done she walked past the pallet on which Reno lay and on between the children in their sagged iron beds. The door to Virginia's room was closed.

A fire was already going in the stove and a fresh bucket of water stood on the shelf by the door. Hub entered with an armful of wood and placed it quietly on the floor beside the stove.

"You're a good boy, Hub," said maw. "I don't know hardly how I'd git along without you. The chillun is most too little to help and your paw . . . I dunno. Seems like he just cain't try much any more."

Maw picked up her snuff stick from the edge of the table and placed it between her lips. She took the slices of fat back from the water in which they had been soaking overnight to get rid of the excess salt that the fat back had absorbed in curing and dipped the slices one by one into the sack of meal and dropped them into the hot skillet. She walked to the back door with the coffee pot in her hand and holding the top back flung the watery mass of yesterday's grounds into the back yard. Two bedraggled hens ran squawking to the grounds and scratched tentatively in them, cocking an inquiring eye first at the grounds, then up at the now empty door before moving slowly away in their search of food.

Maw threw a handful of fresh grounds into the pot without ever rinsing it and added water and set it on the stove. She turned the sizzling meat with a two-pronged, bone-handled fork and slid a pan of biscuits into the oven.

She heard the sounds of the family stirring about as the noise and the smell of cooking food from the kitchen filled the house.

"Y'all come on and git your breakfast," she called.

The two younger girls threw the sheet made of wheat-short sacks back and scrambled giggling into the kitchen in their rumpled clothes that served as dresses in the daytime and nighties at night.

Buddy was standing on the front porch leaning on his crutch and gazing into the full flush of dawn and his paper and crayons were clamped tight beneath his arm. Harold and McKinley were standing at the edge of the porch wetting into the yard. The damp marks showed plainly in the dust.

"I did it furthest. I did it furthest," sang Harold.

"You ought to," said McKinley. "You're the biggest. But you didn't beat me fur."

"I did too."

"You didn't."

"You kids stop fussing and go git your breakfast," said Jutland, who was standing in the front door, shoeless and with tousled hair, smoking a cigarette.

Harold and McKinley ran whooping into the house, racing for the breakfast table.

"Be careful," maw warned. "Don't knock the baby over."

The baby had waked again and crawled down from the bed and was walking into the kitchen on tottery, bowed legs. Harold and McKinley divided around it and knocked it over. The baby squalled shrilly and maw said, "Now look what you've did."

She picked the baby up from the floor and crooned to it and taking a piece of the fried meat from the platter on the table, sucked the hot meal from it and gave the piece of fat to the baby. The baby took it in two hands and, raising his fists to his face, tried and worked at the strip of greasy fat until he got one end of it into his mouth, after which he sucked contentedly and noisily as he sat astride his mother's hip.

"Where's paw?" maw asked.

"Went to the barn," said Jutland.

Maw looked toward the barn to call and saw paw coming around from behind it snapping the straps of his overalls over his shoulders and settling the seam in place at his crotch.

"Come on, paw," she called. "Breakfast's ready."

"I'll git Hub and Tommy," said paw and he called into the barn, "Hub? . . . Hub . . . You and Tommy come on to breakfast."

Hub was sitting in the door of the opened and empty feed room and he turned and leaned into its dimness and caught Tommy by the shoulder and shook him.

"Tommy . . . Tommy . . . You want some breakfast?"

"Ugh," said Tommy from the pile of hay on which he was sleeping.

"You want some breakfast?"

Tommy woke up and lay looking at Hub with bloodshot eyes.

"You want some breakfast?" repeated Hub.

Tommy pushed to a sitting position and held himself there by gripping his ankles with his hands. His hair was stuck with pieces of broken hay and his back was covered with it and he stank of stale whiskey and vomit.

"No. Hell, no," he finally managed. Then he said, "Is there any of that whiskey left? Maybe if I had a drink to settle my stomach I could eat some breakfast."

"I don't know whether there is or not," said Hub. "I left the jug in Stan's car last night."

"You go on and eat your breakfast," said Tommy. "Soon's I git able I believe I'll go down to Stan's and see if I can find that jug."

"If Mr. Browning's awake the jug is about all you'll find," said Hub.

"You all coming to breakfast?" said paw.

"You go on," said Hub. "I'll be in soon's I find what Tommy is going to do."

Paw walked on to the house and Hub sat quietly in the door.

Tommy, with a vast effort, got to his feet and out the door into the barn hall where he stood blinking his aching eyes at the light.

"Jesus," he said, holding his hand to his head. "I smell like a son-of-a-bitch, don't I?"

"You smell right strong," said Hub. "I got a extra pair of overalls you can put on if you want to go to the creek and wash. Maw can rinse out them clothes you got on and they'll dry pretty fast soon's the sun gits good up."

"Hell, I believe I'll go get that drink first and then wash up," said Tommy. "Tell your maw I won't be to breakfast."

Tommy stumbled across the yard to the path that led to Stan's and Hub stood in front of the barn until Tommy passed from sight in the trees. Then he turned and walked over to the back door and entered.

50

"Didn't you bring Virginia home last night?" said paw as Hub entered the door.

"Yes," said Hub.

Maw caught his eye and shook her head slightly and her eyes said, Don't tell him where you found her. He'll shut the door on her. Don't tell him. And his eyes answered and she was content and turned back to her stove and her cooking.

"Where was she?" said paw.

"Over to Spences' with Margaret Ann."

"I'm glad she was there," said paw. "I git kind of feared fer her at times. She don't take lightly to correcting. Virginia ain't what you'd call a godly girl. Her mind runs too much to pleasure. And I don't aim to have a daughter of mine laying out at night with no man."

"I don't guess Virginia's any worse than the rest of them," said Hub. "Most all of them like a little fun now and then."

"A little fun don't hurt no one, I don't guess," said paw. "But you mustn't take it too fur."

They finished breakfast in silence and Hub took the baby while maw ate her breakfast and fed Reno and washed the dishes.

"Well," she said when she had finished, "I wisht we could go ahead and pack and git it over with. I hate to just set."

"We could, I reckon," said Hub. "Git ever'thing ready on the porch. Ever' thing but the stove. We'll need that to cook dinner."

"Well, let's do it then," said maw. "We kin leave the stove and pots out. We kin eat offen the back shelf."

Paw was sitting in a cane-bottom chair on the front porch tilted back against the wall with his hat pulled low over his eyes when Hub walked to the front door and called to Gwendolin and Eugenia, "Come git this baby. We are fixing to pack. Watch him now and don't let him git hurt."

Gwendolin came up to the front steps and took the baby and set it astride her hip in the style of her mother and walked with out-thrust hip back to where Eugenia was playing beneath a tree. Hub moved Reno's chair to the porch and returning to the kitchen took Reno's dangling length in his arms and carried him to the porch and placed him in his pillows where he rolled his head in anger at Hub's departing back and drooled into his whiskers. Then Hub called Jutland and the other two boys and turned back into the house and brought out the first of the meager furniture. Broken and patched chairs, lumpy, knotty cotton mattresses, scarred and bent iron beds, deal tables. And paw sat tilted back against the porch wall with his feet hooked in the rung of his chair and his stained felt hat pulled low over his eyes. Buddy was nowhere in sight.

They had finished packing their torn quilts and their cotton blankets and their few clothes and had them stacked with the rest of their possessions against the front porch wall by ten o'clock with the exception of Virginia's bed and dresser and the cookstove.

Jutland started into her room and Hub said, "Let her sleep. We didn't git in until late last night."

Virginia came out of her room when the noon meal was served. Her eyes were heavy with sleeping and she refused to meet Hub's gaze. She was pretty, with petulant mouth and over-developed bust, and she emanated discontentment. She glanced defensively at her mother and defiantly at her father as she took her place in the line at the shelf on the back porch at the far end from Hub and Buddy.

They ate turnip greens and cabbage and new potatoes and plain cornbread and washed it down with buttermilk.

"That's the last of the milk," said maw. "I hate to think about how we've parted with our cow."

"I don't," said Jutland, who did the milking. "I'm glad she's gone. I hope I don't never see another cow or another cotton-chopping hoe."

Virginia had not been apprised of the fact that they were moving to town nor had she noticed the absence of the furniture from the front part of the house, her room opening into the kitchen from one end. She wondered at them eating on the shelf on the back porch and now her curiosity was whetted further, but rather than draw attention any more than was necessary to herself and her last few days' absence from home until she was sure how much her father knew of last night she thought it better to forego asking questions.

They finished eating and Hub said, "We can git Virginia's things packed now. Come on, Jut."

Jutland followed him into Virginia's room and they took the bed down and moved it to the porch and came back for the dresser. Virginia was standing at the window when they entered.

"You better put on your things," said Hub. "We are moving to town this evening."

"Town?" said Virginia, and her eyes lighted at the prospect.

"Yes," said Hub. "Paw's on the WP and A now."

Virginia stooped and pulled a pasteboard suit-box from under the dresser and laid it open on the floor. She opened the dresser drawers and took out a pair of panties and a brassière and two checked gingham dresses and a pair of stockings and placed them in the box, then she slipped out of the wrinkled and stained wrap-around she had donned for dinner and, as Hub and Jut watched, took her last night's dress from the back of a chair and pulled it on over her head. They waited while she painted and powdered her face and combed her hair, watching her reflection in the small cracked mirror nailed to the wall above the dresser.

"I'm through with it now," she said.

They lifted the dresser and carried it out while she stood with her hands full of dime-store rouge and powder and lipstick and two wrinkled and powder-stained hair ribbons. She placed these things in the suit-box and tied a string around the box to keep it from coming open. She was still barefoot but her white shoes stood beneath the window and she wouldn't wear stockings.

They had moved the last piece of household goods

out onto the porch now and they sat waiting for the truck.

"Frank ought to be showing up most anytime now," said paw. "They ought to be back from the singing by now. I wisht now I hadda gone. If I had knowed how easy it would be to git packed I would of."

"Yonder comes somebody," said Jutland.

"That ain't Frank," said paw. "Who is it?"

"Looks like Steve Joe and his woman," said maw.

"Well. So it is," said paw. "Come to see us off, I bound ye."

"That's who it is," said maw. "Well. That's right neighborly of 'em. Makes me kind of hate to leave."

"Come in. Come in," called paw as soon as Steve Joe and his wife were in talking distance.

Steve Joe waddled along ten feet ahead of his wife. His jowls hung so heavy they pulled his lower eyelids open past normal and the red granulated lids watered copiously. His droopy lips were stained with tobacco juice and his size fifty overalls cut into his waist and bulged out over his behind and hips which quaked and trembled with each waddling step. His nondescript wife shuffled along behind him, her face almost hidden underneath an old-fashioned sunbonnet, and a few wispy strands of mouse-colored hair hung limply across her scrawny neck.

"Come in, Steve," said paw. "Come right in and set. You too, Miz Wright. Come in. We're proud to see you."

The steps creaked beneath Steve Joe's weight as he

hoisted himself up on the porch by pulling with one hand on a support post and pushing with his other against his keg-size knee.

"Good evening, Hubbard," he said to the senior Taylor. "Evening, Miz Taylor. Hot, ain't it?"

"Just right to make cotton grow," said paw.

"I reckon you ain't got to worry about that any more, have you? I heared you had done got your Four Oh Two."

"Yep," said paw. "Go to work in the morning. We are moving into town this evening. Soon's Frank gits here."

"He went to London Church this morning," said Steve Joe. "Took a load from up 'bout Ormand's."

"I knowed he was going," said paw. "I wanted to go right bad myself but I figgered I better stay to home and help git packed and all. I don't want to be late to my first day's work."

"No. That's right. That's right. Give a man a honest day's work fer what he pays you. That's a mighty good rule."

"That's what I figger," said paw. "Give a man a honest day's work fer ever' day's pay and then they won't be no complaints on neither side."

"Yep. That's right. I'm expecting to git on real soon," said Steve Joe.

"We'll be proud to see you all come into town," said paw. "Yes sir. Hit will seem like home to see all the folks moved into town. Maybe maw won't hate it so bad then."

56

"Miz Taylor don't want to move, does she?"

"Well, it ain't just that," said paw. "She's just sort of skittish about it. A old dog learning new tricks, like."

"Yep. Yep. Well, hit'll be mighty convenient in there. Ever' house has got a hydrant to it. All you got to do fer water is turn a tap. Don't have to walk no half mile to no spring. It makes washing pretty easy fer the womenfolks."

"Maw ain't seen town in seventeen year. She'll git used to it after a while, I guess."

"Well, I envy you folks. Wisht I was going on in now, myself."

The sun crossed the meridian and began its slow journey down the western half of the brassy sky. At three o'clock Frank still had not come.

"I wonder what's keeping Frank?" paw said for the fiftieth time.

"He'll be here pretty soon," said Steve Joe.

"Yonder he comes. Yonder he comes," suddenly screamed one of the children.

They heard the roar of the motor and at last could make out the bus through the trees. Halfway from the side road to the house they heard the motor idle, then die.

"I wonder what's wrong now," said paw.

"I'll walk up there and see," said Hub.

He left the porch and was gone about twenty minutes and then returned.

"Get the ax," he called from the edge of the yard. "Frank cain't get over that stump in the road and we are going to have to cut some brush and sprouts and stuff so he can drive around it."

Jutland picked up the ax from against the porch wall and slung it over his shoulder and stepped down into the yard. Hub stood waiting for him at the edge of the clearing and he and Jutland, followed by the children, disappeared up the woods road toward the truck.

"I guess we might's well walk up there with them," said paw. "I don't guess maw will need me fer a while."

"Yep," said Steve Joe. "We might can help push."

They got up from their seats and paw descended the steps first and waited for Steve Joe to let himself down into the yard. The two men walked across the swept yard and followed the road up to the truck. When they got there Hub was swinging the ax, clearing a path wide enough for the truck to pass around the stump. Frank was stepping off distances and measuring clearances between trees and Jutland stood to one side with the children behind him and the baby riding Gwendolin's hip.

"You take it awhile, Jut," said Hub, straightening up and wiping the sweat from his face with his hand and flipping the drops into the bushes.

Jutland took the ax and went on with the clearing and Frank said, "I'll crank her up and try it this far."

Paw stood to one side with his hands behind his back, watching, and Steve Joe shifted his weight from one foot to the other, looking first at Jutland swinging the ax, then at Frank through his bushy brows.

58

"You couldn't git over this stump, could you?" he said to Hub.

"Naw. That's the reason we're cutting this path around through the woods."

"You don't think the truck would just push them bushes down?"

"Naw. They're too thick."

"I seen Mr. Young one day in that pick-up of hisn just sail out through the woods over stumps and bushes and ever' thing."

"His pick-up clears the ground more than Frank's truck and besides this is going to be loaded coming back up this hill. We couldn't make it loaded even if we could make it going down empty. These bushes would slow it down too much."

"You don't think we could have brung the stuff up this fur and loaded hit up here?"

"I don't reckon Frank could of backed all the way out to the road."

"That's right," said Steve Joe who had now exhausted every suggestion for doing something any way except the way it was being done. "I guess he couldn't of, shore 'nough."

Frank backed the truck up about ten feet and eased it into the path they had cut. About halfway through he stopped.

"We are going to have to cut that tree there," he said, pointing to a six-inch oak on the right. "These duals ain't going to clear it."

Hub took the ax from Jutland and soon had the tree

down. He passed the ax back and bent once more to the sprouts.

"Is Jut about through?" said Frank.

"Just about," said Hub. "Ease her on down some more."

Frank drove on a little further and stopped again behind Jutland as he cut the last of the bushes out of the way, leaving the path clear into the road. The truck passed through and jolted back into the badly washed ruts and Frank stopped.

"You all want to ride on down?" he said.

The children, who had been watching wide-eyed, now scrambled into the rear door and Hub got into the cab. Jutland swung on the running board with the ax in his hand and stood poised on bent knees, giving to the roughness of the road and ready to duck the low branches that overlapped above.

"Go ahead," paw had called. "Me and Steve Joe will just walk on down."

Frank swung the truck expertly into the bare, hard dirt of the front yard and backed it against the porch.

It took only a few minutes to load. The chairs and beds and dressers and stove were loaded into the front of the truck bed and the mattresses were placed in last for maw and the children to sit on. The children scrambled in and maw climbed in last and Hub picked Reno from his chair and carried him over to the truck and placed him in maw's lap, then returned for the chair and pillows and came and loaded them in.

Steve Joe and Mrs. Wright stood watching and Mrs.

Wright said, "Cain't you just let him lay on the mattress? Looks like you might git right tard a-holding him all the way to town."

"Well, you see," said maw, "Rinno's done got so 'he bruises so easy and hit looks like when he does git bruised hit just won't never heal, till I reckon I better just hold him. He ain't so very heavy nohow and Gwendolin has done got so's she can tend to the baby most as good as I can."

"Hit's a great blessing when the chillun gits so's they can take the baby offen a body's hands," said Mrs. Wright.

"Yes, ma'am, hit is," agreed maw.

She hunched herself into a little more comfortable position with her back braced against the side of the truck and her legs stretched out flat on the mattress before her. The children were squealing and tumbling about over the mattress and over maw's feet but Virginia sat far back in one corner of the bed in silence. Paw had already crawled into the cab when Hub appeared at the rear door and said, "We ready to go?"

"Well, I guess so," said maw.

"Where's Buddy?" said Hub, peering into the truck.

Maw craned around and looked past the tumbling children.

"Well, I do know," she said. "He ain't here."

"I'll get him," said Hub. "You all set still."

He disappeared around the corner of the house and once in the side yard, called, "Buddy? Oh, Buddy."

He called again, then spied Buddy down by the spring.

He walked up to where Buddy sat sketching, and there, coming to still life beneath his long sensitive fingers, was the fern-surrounded spring with its blue shadows and the huge old pine towering above it and the down rail that paw never found time to nail up.

"You better come on here," said Hub. "We'll go off and leave you."

"Look," said Buddy, holding up the sketch with shy pride.

"I declare, Buddy. I don't see how you do it. Looks just like it, fer the world. And even purtier. But come on, feller. We got to go."

Hub squatted with his back to Buddy and said, "Git on."

Buddy placed his paper and crayons carefully under his arm and mounted Hub's back and Hub took the crutch in his hands and swung it behind him for a seat for Buddy and straightened and trudged back to the house and up to the truck.

"Drawing, I bound ye," said maw as Hub helped Buddy in.

"Ready to go now, I guess," said Hub and he disappeared around the side of the truck and they felt the sway as he climbed into the cab and then heard the door slam shut.

Frank started the motor and the gears ground as he meshed them and Steve Joe and his wife stood in the eastward tip of the lengthening shadows and watched them drive out of the yard.

"You take them chickens, Miz Wright," maw called

above the clattering of the moving truck. "We ain't taking them to town with us."

Mrs. Wright bobbed her head in acknowledgment and Steve Joe stood bent slightly forward watching them through drawn brows.

The truck bumped and jerked up the rutted lane and around through the detour they had cut and on up the hill and maw sat braced against the lurching and Reno mouthed his delight at the swaying and bouncing. When they reached the side road at the top of the scrub-oak hill Frank slipped into second gear and then high. Half a mile down the dirt road they came to the gravel high-way—The Rock—and Frank wheeled to the left and they drove on toward town and into the setting sun.

Four

The good land lay idle beneath the sun. The pale green stripes of growing corn and cotton and sorghum against the rich black land had become solid green mats of weeds and grass. The mules stood idle in their pastures for there were no longer people to work the good land. The plows stood unused at the ends of the rows and the weeds grew taller and taller and hid all but the sweat-stained handles from sight and the plow-gear grew moldy from disuse. The willow sprouts multiplied along the creek bank and sent their roots out into the rich black fields and the roots sent up new sprouts and the fields became smaller and smaller. Grass grew over the turnrows, covering the wheel tracks, and the ditches choked with weeds and filled and overflowed. And the fields lay idle beneath the sun. For the people were moving to town.

And the town talked.

Another load of the bastards came in last night. Sunday night of all times. Fellow with a wife and about forty children. Got in about dark . . . On Sunday.

Said he thought with all the houses there were here in town he ought to be able to find some place to stay without any trouble.

Another one on the WPA, I guess?

Hell, yes. Got one of their damned Oh Two's or whatever it is they get that makes them leave their crops and come to town. Left a good crop on the Young place and come to town for twenty-six dollars a month.

Jesus Christ. And with a wife and a truck full of children. What did they do last night?

They parked on the Square until nine o'clock with the man and one of the oldest boys running around all over town trying to find a place to stay. Went to the hotel and when they told them at the hotel that a room was worth a dollar and a half a night they said that looked awful high but they guessed they would have to pay it. Wanted to know if the room had a flue in it and Mark, at the hotel, thought they meant heat of some kind and told them yes but as hot as it was they wouldn't need no heat and you know what the bastard said? Said they didn't need no heat but they'd have to have some place to set up their cooking stove.

Jesus Christ.

They would have spent the night in the truck but the fellow that drives the truck had to get back to the country to haul a load of WPA workers in in the morning. He took 'em out to Three Way and dumped their stuff out on the side of the road and they spent the night out there. Got a damn good-looking girl with 'em and a little crippled boy and looks like a sick old man. Needed a haircut and a shave. Looks like he must be sick as hell, lying under a pile of old quilts. I drove by there this morning.

Town was dotted with the architectural monstrosities of the Nineties painted in flaking drab colors and covered with gingerbread scroll work. The buildings were huge, the rooms large and high ceilinged and few in number, and the water works, installed after the completion of the houses, was now obsolete. Most of the houses were built close to the Square which in the day of their construction was the edge of town, and the desirable residential section, but now was overlapped and surrounded by Automobile Row and Rotten Row and was noisy and dirty and undesirable. The influential citizens who built the huge houses had built new houses in the new edge of town and the new desirable residential sections and placed these old, drab, flaking houses in the hands of the rental agencies.

The day of the automobile came when young couples no longer bought homes, they bought cars and the cars became homes and the houses became places in which to change clothes and from which to go to supper at the café or to the picture show. Then the rental agencies coined the word "Apartment"—and each two rooms in the big houses became an apartment and they placed two and three young couples in each of the big houses in the apartments. Then someone built a regular apartment house in the new desirable residential section, each one with private bath and kitchenette, and the young couples who lived in automobiles moved into these new apartments and the huge old houses were empty again.

When the WPA started the share-croppers on their migration to town they searched out places to live and they found these huge old vacant houses and the rental agencies were glad and they cut the rent from fifty dollars to forty dollars and the WPA workers said, Out of twenty-six dollars I can't afford to pay more than five dollars rent, so if I can get seven other families to move in with me we can take this big house to live in. And so they moved into the big old houses. Eight and nine and ten families in six and eight rooms and they put mattresses side by side on the floor in the big old halls and the children slept on the mattresses in the halls and the parents and older daughters and babies slept in the rooms and each family was apportioned one room or at least one side of one room.

"Well, maw. How do you like this?" said paw that first Monday evening.

"Hit's right crowded," said maw, "but hit ain't as bad as if we had all the chillun in just one room with us. It helps some fer ever' body's chillun to sleep in the hall. Hit's right narce having neighbors so handy like. Hub got us settled right well. Me and you and the baby kin sleep in this bed here and Virginia and Gwendolin and Eugenia kin sleep in the one in that corner and the boys are going to sleep in the hall on the mattress."

"What are you going to do with Rinno?" said paw.

"I'm skeered to leave him out in the hall with the

boys. I guess I better make him a pallet here by the bed like out to home. The boys might not remember to turn him on a different side ever' night and git them sores started again."

"You going to leave Buddy out there with 'em?"

"Hub will look after him. I don't have to worry about Buddy as long's Hub's around. Hit's a cur'ous thing the way Buddy's face gits all shiny like ever' time he looks at Hub."

"Yes, hit is," said paw. "And Rinno seems to take to Hub a pow'ful lot too."

"Hub's right kind to the pore feller," said maw.

"Rinno," said paw. "He's a monst'ous cur'osity."

"Yes, he is," said maw.

"What did Hub do about the cookstove?" said paw after a few moments' reflection.

"They weren't no place fer another one in the kitchen so ever' body just takes time about cooking on the two they done already got set up down there. Did you come by the grocer store?"

"Yes," said paw. "They's some bread and stuff in them two sacks."

Maw took the two sacks and pulled their contents out and laid them on the bed. There was a loaf of bread, a can of mackerel, and a small sack of meal.

"Hit's right narce being able to git fresh stuff ever' day," she said. "I'd most fergot how handy things was in town."

The children, with their natural shyness accentuated by the unfamiliar surroundings, had been in the room all day and at paw's entrance they had crowded excitedly around him for a peep into the paper sacks, but when maw poured the contents out on the bed and it was revealed to be only the familiar mackerel and the not quite so familiar store bread, they lost interest and moved back to their places on the other bed and sat listlessly.

Maw gathered the meager supplies in her arms and started for the door.

"I'll go down and see kin I git the use of one of the stoves," she said. "Gwendolin, you mind the baby until I git back and kind of see after Rinno ever' now and then. Don't let him fret none."

She thumped out the door in her dirty, untied tennises with their rubber soles swish-swishing across the bare floor and paw seated himself in his cane-bottom chair and tilted it back against the wall. They sat unmoving, staring at each other and at nothing and the only movement was the occasional shifting of the baby in Gwendolin's lap to a more comfortable position and Reno's head rolling from side to side on the dirty pillow tied to the chair back.

Hub came in a few minutes later with Buddy astride his back and soon after Jutland followed.

Reno rolled his head toward the door at the disturbance and focused his eyes on Hub and his hands twitched and hoarse excited croaks burst from his drooling mouth and he began to tremble violently.

"God-o-Mighty," shouted paw. "Ketch him, quick. He's 'bout to shake hisself outen the cheer."

69

Buddy slid from Hub's back and Hub stepped quickly across the floor and caught Reno just as he pitched forward. He settled Reno back into the pillows and Reno mouthed happiness under Hub's hands. Buddy's face had paled as Reno pitched forward and now it flushed alarmingly and paled again in resurgent waves and his crutch slid to the floor out of his nerveless grip.

"Great God," paw shouted this time. "Ketch Buddy. He's 'bout to faint."

Buddy held onto the door until Hub could reach him and lead him to the bed where he slumped in uncontrollable trembling with Hub's arm supporting him.

"What's the matter with you, boy?" said paw.

"He's all right," said Hub. "I'll have to fix something across Rinno's chest so's he cain't fall out again."

"Hits a-going to be a job carrying him up and down them stairs at mealtimes," said paw. "Ifen you could rig up something so's we could just leave him up here whilst we eat, it'd help."

"I'll see what I can do," said Hub. "I might could fix him up a swing of some kind we could tie him in."

"Now that's a good idea," said paw. "The pore feller might enjoy hit."

They heard maw's voice from the foot of the stairs calling them to supper.

"You all go on and eat," said Hub. "I'll stay up here with Rinno."

"I'm going to stay with Hub," said Buddy.

"Well," said paw, "I reckon if you are going to you

are just a-going to. We'll tell maw so's she won't worry."

They trooped down the stairs, passing a family on the way up who had finished eating and were on their way to their own room.

"Who's with Rinno?" said maw as they entered the kitchen.

"Hub 'lowed as how he'd stay with him," said paw. "Says he's going to make Rinno a swing tomorrow so's we can leave 'im in it while we eat."

"Well now," said maw. "Won't that be narce. I bound ye Rinno'll like hit too. Where's Buddy? He ain't been in all evening."

"He come in with Hub," said paw. "I never ast 'em where they been."

"Buddy's been drawing some more them pitchurs, I reckon," said maw. "I never seen nothing like the way he'll just set all day with them colors and draw. He draws things right narce, too. Well, I'm glad Hub's up with Rinno. Seems like the pore feller's right contented long's Hub's around."

"Yes, hit does," said paw. "When Hub come in while ago Rinno got to jumping around in his cheer so I made shore he was a-fixing to pitch right out into the floor."

"Would've ifen Hub hadn't caught 'im," said Jutland.

"Seems like he notices Hub and Buddy more'n the rest of us," said paw.

Maw had taken the baby from Gwendolin and was familiar once more over the stove with the baby straddling her out-thrust hip and the snuff stick dangling

71

from the corner of her mouth. Two women, almost counterparts of maw, stood at the sink washing dirty dishes into the accumulation of the leavings of other meals that covered the drain, and the crumbs of the previous suppers littered the blackened boards of the bare deal table.

The family took their seats on the chairs and boxes and paw said, "Where's Virginia?"

"She went up to town this evening and ain't got back yit, I guess," said maw.

They ate in silence and got up one by one as they finished and left the room.

Hub and Buddy came in and sat side by side at the table and maw ate her supper as she moved back and forth between the table and stove. As Hub and Buddy finished eating she collected the mismatched dishes at one end of the table and scraped food into a bowl, which she pushed to one side, and stacked the rest of the dishes in the sink and with the bowl of food in her hand followed Hub and Buddy up the stairs to their room. She sat on the bed by Reno and masticated his food for him and placed it in his mouth and he gulped it down and mouthed unintelligible sounds of impatience between swallows.

When he finished maw laid him on his pallet on the floor by her bed and changed the short sack diaper and turned him carefully on his right side and soon he slept.

Paw rose and crossed the room to the bed and slipped his cracked brogans off his sockless feet and stripped off his jumper and overalls and sat back on the bed and heaved himself across to the side next the wall and turned his back to the room. Gwendolin and Eugenia pushed the wheat-short sack sheet back and got into bed as they were and maw laid the baby in the middle of her bed. She cut the light out and pulled her mother hubbard off over her head and kicked her tennises off. She walked to the window and placed her snuff stick carefully on the ledge, then returned to the bed and sat heavily down on its edge. The springs groaned beneath her weight as she swung her legs over and lay back with a sigh. Harold and McKinley were already asleep on their mattress in the hall. Buddy, alone on his pallet with his home-made crutch beside him and his shrunken leg and twisted foot awkward beneath the quilt, lay in the dusk that was peopled with the fine shadings and pale, soft colors of his imaginings. Hub and Jutland had gone to town.

The house settled into the first part of its night sleep and was quiet until nine-thirty when the older boys started coming in from the picture shows and beer parlors. Each one created a mild disturbance as he stripped off his outer clothing and found his particular section of mattress. The house quieted again until eleven and twelve when the older daughters began coming in from the jook houses in the clattering old jalopies that their escorts owned. The children on their pallets were disturbed and the parents were awakened. Muffled sounds came from the rooms and an occasional angry voice or the sound of a slap, then the house settled once more until daybreak when the country people who had spent a lifetime rising with the day got up and began stirring around.

Hub and Jutland were in and asleep by ten but Virginia did not get home until after twelve. She tiptoed through the dark hall and between the mattresses on bare feet, opened the door quietly and slipped into the room.

"Virginia?" said maw from her bed.

"Yes," said Virginia.

Paw groaned and turned over and she stood poised by the door. Paw settled back into regular snoring and she moved noiselessly to her bed and stripped her dress off over her head as maw lay watching. She stood for a moment in the light from the street-light that filtered through the window, white and soft looking in her indistinguishable panties and brassière, then slipped into bed by Gwendolin and Eugenia and maw closed her eyes and slept.

By sunup the next morning they were up and through breakfast and sitting about the room waiting until it would be time for paw to go to work and for Hub and Jut to go hang around the Square.

"We'll need something for supper tonight," said maw as paw opened the door to leave.

They all sat looking at paw as he stood with his hand on the knob of the opened door. He shuffled his feet uncertainly, looked at the ring of eyes staring at him and fumbled at the paper-wrapped parcel of lunch in his pocket.

"Hub can see about some arrangements at one of

74

the stores uptown," he said. "I'll be right busy working today. I lost yestiddy with gitting us moved and all and I'll be right busy today."

He closed the door and they heard his steps as he walked across the hall and clumped down the stairs.

"I was talking to one of the men here," said Hub, "and he told me most any of the stores up to town was glad to credit us WP and A folks. I might talk to some of 'em today and git a credit fixed up fer us."

"You better tend to it right away, then," said maw. "Your paw ain't apt to since he's done gone to working."

"I'll see about it," said Hub.

Hell, yes. Charge the stuff to 'em, said the merchants. They get one of them blue government checks every two weeks. All they got to do to get it is to get in a bunch and stand around leaning on a shovel for sixty-five hours and then go to the post-office and get one of them blue government checks. Charge it to 'em. Add about half again onto everything they buy and it's cheap at that. They been used to running one of them furnish accounts and them rich furnish merchants add three hundred per cent to every one of their accounts and then charge them eight per cent interest to make it legal. Charge it to 'em.

"They were pretty nice about it," said Hub to maw. "First place I went to fixed us up a credit. Asked where we was living and I told 'em and they said, Well, that settled it. They knowed we was on the WP and A. Said not to bother about paw coming around to stand fer it. Said just tell him to come around when he got his check. Right nice folks."

"Well, hit makes me feel a heap better about coming to town," said maw. "With ever' thing kind of strange like, it makes a body feel good for folks to be friendly."

"You better git me up a list of what we need and I'll go git it," said Hub.

"I'll do that right now," said maw. "You git a paper and pencil and I'll call hit off to you. Me and your paw never was much hand with a pencil."

Hub got the paper and pencil and maw called the list of groceries to him. He folded the list and put it in his pocket and left. When he returned he had two large paper sacks of groceries and maw took them and examined them and then pushed them under the bed.

Hub left again and as he crossed the yard he saw Buddy seated beneath the maple tree busy with his crayons and paper. Hub walked up behind him and stood looking down over his shoulder at the miniature City Hall with its loiterers spotted about the steps and yard and the cars parked in front.

Buddy became aware of someone at his elbow at last and looked up startled and threw a quick protecting arm over the sketch but grinned shyly as he recognized Hub and removed his arm and watched Hub's face for the inevitable pleasure and approval.

"I declare, Buddy," Hub said. "That's it, ain't it?"

76

Buddy nodded quickly and Hub ran a hand through his fine soft hair and said as he turned to leave, "How's the paper holding out?"

"Got over half of it left," said Buddy.

"You let me know when you need some more," said Hub.

He walked on across the yard and stopped at the corner to glance back at Buddy who sat with his head bowed again over his paper.

This time Hub returned with rope and a borrowed hammer and saw and a small sack of nails. He rummaged the back-yard for pieces of board and by nightfall had fashioned a swing for Reno with ropes to suspend it from the rafters in the ceiling of their room and a shorter rope to tie across Reno's chest to keep him from pitching out of the swinging chair. He tore strips from an old sack to pad the chest rope and with Jutland's help swung the chair from the ceiling and placed Reno and his pillows in the swing. When Hub tied the chest rope and swung the chair lightly, Reno mewled and gurgled happily.

"Well now," said paw from the door. "If that ain't fine."

"Yes sir," said maw. "I don't see how Hub done it. Hit's right narce."

Paw came on into the room and took his seat in his usual place tilted back against the wall and Buddy came in on his crutches and grinned at Reno who answered with a croak of delight and Buddy swung across the room and took his seat by Hub.

"This is right interesting work we are doing now," said paw. "But there's some dissatisfaction with the water-boy. Ever' body chips in so much fer ice and he claims he had to put in four cents of his own money this morning to git the ice and some of the men claims he should of had enough fer this morning and one cent left over. He says he aims to quit if the men ain't got no more confidence in him but two or three of the rest of the men wants the water-boy job and they hadn't decided nothing when we quit this evening. I would kind of like to have it myself. He don't have to do nothing but come by the ice plant and git the ice and keep the bucket full of water. He don't have to handle no shovel a tall."

"Well, that would be right narce fer you," said maw. "I kind of hate to think about you out in this sun all day long. How fur does he have to tote the ice?"

"He gener'ly waits till the truck has a trip to town and gits the driver to take him by the plant."

"Well now. That would be narce," said maw. "Maybe he will git mad and quit and you can git the job."

"Well, I don't know," said paw. "They's too many older than me on the job that comes fust. We aim to hold a election tomorrow on our work hours. We can work just six hours a day and have a hour and a half fer dinner so we can all come home and still have time enough to git in sixty-five hours ever' fifteen days with working one Saddy."

"A hour and a half to give you time to git home and git hot dinner would be right narce," said maw.

78

"I don't know," said paw. "Some of the men don't much like that about working on a Saddy."

"Well," said maw. "They ain't none of 'em been used to it."

"Did Hub git our credit fixed up?"

"Yes, he did," said maw. "He got it fixed up just fine and the man was just as narce as he could be about it too. Said hit weren't no use fer you to even come by to stand fer it. Said to just come by when you git your check."

"Well, by Godfrey, I'll just do that," said paw. "I aim to be narce to folks as be narce to me."

"That's exactly how I feel about it," said maw.

"You 'bout ready to fix supper?" said paw.

"Just soon's I kin git my turn at the stove."

"Well, I believe I'll drop downstairs to Mr. Adamses room and talk to him some about this election tomorrow. He's on the same project I am."

"Why, that's real narce," said maw, "to have the men you are working with in the same house you are in. Makes it convenient, sort of."

Paw left the room and maw took her supplies from the dresser top and out from under the bed and sat listening for the sounds from the kitchen that would tell her that it was her turn at the stove.

The children had explored the place and the neighboring children and had become familiar with and used to their new surroundings and now they and the other children of the house were in the yard playing under the huge maple tree. Maw's turn at the stove came and she cooked supper and called them, and they trooped in to supper. She sent Harold back for paw and before he came in Hub and Jutland put in their appearance.

"Where's Virginia?" said paw as soon as he entered.

"She went up to town again late this evening," said maw. "It's so hot fer her to git out early she waited until it was cooler to go."

"What time did she git in last night?" said paw.

"Soon after you went to sleep," said maw.

"Did she say where she'd been?"

"Now, paw. Course she didn't. I didn't ast her."

"I don't aim to have no daughter of mine laying out at night," said paw.

"Virginia's a good girl," said maw. "She ain't up to no harm. She's just young, that's all."

Virginia did not come in late that night. She did not come in at all. She was absent the next day and the next and when she finally did come home she brought a husband with her. She stalked into the room ahead of him and her clothes were wrinkled and stained and she carried her hat in her hand. The husband followed along behind her, grinning sheepishly, fatuously, and she clicked across the floor on her high spike heels and flung herself on the bed and burst into tears.

The children stared at her, round wonder in their eyes, and paw watched her with drawn brows. Maw went to her and patted her on the shoulder and paw turned to the young man.

"We're married," said the young man.

"Well now," said paw, his face clearing. "Come right in."

"Virginia," said maw. "Virginia."

"I hate him," said Virginia. "I hate him. I'm going to have a b-b-ba-baby."

"Why, he done the handsome thing by you just like I did by your maw when Rinno was born," said paw. "What are you so wrought up about? You'll make him think he ain't welcome."

"Why, Virginia honey, that ain't nothing to worry about," said maw. "Here. Wipe your face off with this cold towel. Git me that towel from the cheer, Gwendolin, and wet it in that bowl of water. This'll make you feel better."

Maw wiped Virginia's tear-stained face and finally managed to pull her to a sitting position on the bed. Paw took the young man by the arm and pulled him into the room.

"You live in town, young man?" he said.

"Naw sir. I live 'bout ten mile out south. I come to town ever' day on the bus."

"You work for the WP and A?" said paw.

"Yes sir."

"Well, this is like meeting a old friend," said paw. "We're all just WP and A folks here," with a sweep of his hand that indicated not only the room but the whole house as well. "You kin just move right in here with us. You and Virginia kin have the bed in the corner to yourselves and maw kin fix the children on a pallet on the floor. Cain't you, maw?"

"I don't see why not," said maw.

"You're welcome right into the midst of your new family," said paw.

Virginia's new husband glanced slowly around the room, his gaze passing lightly over the children and Buddy's crutch, but when he came to Reno he paused.

"What's that?" he said.

"That?" said paw. "Why, that's Rinno."

"Rinno?" said Virginia's husband. "What's Rinno?"

"Why, that's your wife's oldest brother."

"Good God," said the husband and turned an indifferent back.

Virginia's first disappointment at having the new and partially tried fields of pleasure that town offered snatched away and replaced by the demands and caprices of one man and that man a type with which she had been raised and was thoroughly familiar was somewhat assuaged during the evening meal in which maw petted her and she received an unaccustomed condonement of her actions from paw, who grew expansive under the relief of turning his responsibility to the Lord for his daughter's conduct and upbringing over to younger and more willing hands.

By bedtime she was almost reconciled to her new lot and after they turned out the light and stripped off their outer garments and crawled into bed and these new and willing hands began stroking her breasts and thighs she forgot her loss entirely.

"Stop," she said. "They can hear us."

"Not if you keep still," he murmured.

"I can't," she said.

Silence and then the creaking of the bed.

"Wait till they get to sleep," she begged.

The room grew quiet and paw's snoring was the only sound.

"Now," she said. "Pull the sheet up over us."

The rickety old bed creaked and groaned, grew faster, more furious, then quieted suddenly and only their labored breathing punctuated by paw's snores filled the room.

Maw lay staring at the ceiling and then she reached over the baby and laid her hand on paw's stomach and paw groaned and turned over on his side.

This is the best one yet, the town said. This damned WPA don't work but sixty-five hours every two weeks and they had been working eight hours a day for eight days and one hour the last day and then lay off for about a week. Well, the project supervisor or whatever they call the ones that hang around the City Hall all the time and draw the big checks went down to one of the jobs here in town last Thursday to tell 'em to quit and go home for a week so he could quit hanging around the City Hall and go hang around the beer joints all day too instead of just at night and they told him they had three days left to work on this pay period and he asked them how come and they told him they had held an election and voted to start working just six hours a day instead of eight so they could take an hour and a half for lunch each day.

Five

Paw came in in a fidget of excitement one day in late June.

"Paw. Paw. What in the world's the matter with you?" said maw.

"I've got to git me a raddio," said paw. "We've got to have a raddio. Here Congress has done passed a law to give us WP and A men a raise and I never knowed nothing about it till this morning and they done it yestiddy. Ever' body else on the job knowed it but me."

"Well now. Ain't that just dandy. About that raise, I mean," said maw. "And about that raddio too. I've allus wanted one. I've heared some right narce singing come outen 'em. Well, I do know."

"Where's Hubbard?" said paw.

"He went into town after dinner and he ain't got back yit."

"I better git him to see about that raddio in the morning," said paw. "I don't reckon there's nothing open to town this time of evening."

Hub came in just then and paw said, "Hubbard, your

paw has just got his fust raise. Or least ways we are all going to git one pretty soon."

"I heard it uptown," said Hub. "The Senator told them folks from up North he weren't going to stand fer them gitting more money than us folks down here and they come across."

"I tell you," said paw. "We've got just about the smartest man up there. And I've voted fer him ever' time he's run. I knowed he was the right man to send up there the fust time I ever seen 'im. Hit was about him me and Tom Able's boy fit in the school bus that evening last fall. Tom was agin the Senator and course his boy was too. I wisht the Senator knowed that. I wisht he knowed I fit fer 'im."

"He'd be right proud, I bound ye," said maw.

"And I'd do hit agin," said paw. "Anytime. Like the Bible says, A man ought to be ready to fight fer his own connections."

"I was listening over the raddio—"

Paw had been tilted back against the wall in his cane-bottom chair but at the word "radio" the front legs of the chair hit the floor with a bang.

Reno, who had rolled his head to the door when Hub entered and was now mewling and whining in his hoarse idiot's impatience for Hub's attention, jerked at the sudden clatter of paw's chair against the floor and his expression changed to one of fear and his face contorted and an awful sound of tongue-tied anguish burst from his opened mouth.

"Great God-o-Mighty," said Paw. "Stop him. Git him quiet, Hub."

Under Hub's hand Reno soon grew quiet and mewled and writhed in pleasure at Hub's touch.

"He's the cur'ousest feller I ever seen," said paw. "Skeered the daylights outen me. Skeered me lots wusser'n hit skeered him. What was I talking about? Oh, year. Raddio. I most fergot. With all this new stuff coming out of Washington ever' day about raises and all, a man needs a raddio. He's most got to have a raddio so's he can keep up with his raises and such. You, Hubbard. Do a little trading around in town tomorrow and see ifen you can't pick us up a good used raddio cheap. Naw. I believe I'll just go with you. I ain't had a day off since the fust day I worked. With this new raise and all I believe I'd enjoy just sort of loafing around town fer a day. A body needs a day off ever' now and then."

"Yes, he does," said maw. "And you'll enjoy hit too, I bound ye."

"We couldn't quite pay our whole credit at the store this time," said Hub, "and the rent's due outen this next check."

"The man at the store didn't argy none about it, did he?" said paw.

"Well, no sir," said Hub. "I told him about you being off the day we moved into the house and he just said to try and git up the whole thing this time."

"Well," said paw. "We git our raise on the fust of July and ifen I wait until after then to take my day off hit'll cost more than hit will ifen I take hit off now."

"That's right," said maw. "A raise does make a difference, don't it?"

The man at the car lot said, Get those old cars
washed up and run them out here in front. Well, hell.
Fix 'em so you *can* crank them up. And get some black
paint at the dime store. We'll paint 'em every damned
one and sell 'em to these WPA workers. They got a
nine dollar raise. Boy, we'll get it all. Of course nine
dollars ain't enough to buy even one of these automobiles but four times nine dollars is a damn sight more
than I ever hoped to get out of 'em. They can chip in
four together and make the down payment— Hell, yes,
I said down payment. We ain't got enough old jalopies
to go around, so we'll just get about thirty or forty dollars and call it a down payment and sign 'em up on
stiff enough notes so's we can take the cars back in
about two or three payments and sell them right on
to the next one. Get going now and get them painted
so's we'll be ready for 'em when their first raise checks
come.

The man at the radio store said, Nine dollars a month
raise. Why, we can sell every old radio in the store. Get
'em all out and see that they'll play and we'll dust 'em
off and put on a used radio sale.
Yes, sir. Are you looking for a good used radio? Something not too expensive? We've just closed out a store
down the country and took over the whole stock of
used radios. My boy is back there now checking them

over to be sure they are in A Number One shape. Walk right back and look them over. Why, of course there's no use in a man buying a new radio every year. But you know how some folks are. See their neighbor with a new style radio or anything else new for that matter and they have got to have one too. You'll notice the smart folks in this world, though, get their money's worth out of what they spend. They buy good stuff and get the use out of it. That one? Why, it's a Thirty Seven model. No reason in the world for the owner to get rid of it except his wife saw a new model and from then on he didn't have any peace until she had a new model too. Price? Why, we are just about giving it away at fifteen dollars. The same model new costs you fifty. Only difference is the case it's in. Fifteen dollars. Five down and two and a half out of each check. You work on the WPA, don't you? I thought so. You haven't got the five dollars now? When will you have it? Next payday? Well, now you come back in next payday when you get the five dollars. No, we can't hold it for you. We have to turn our money quick in a cut-price deal like this. We'd like to let you take it on now but you know how it is. We have to get the money from the Bank to swing a quick deal like this one we made for these radios and the Bank won't like it if we let the radios out without getting a Contract on them and we can't give you a Contract until you pay the five dollars. You come back when your check comes. We've got our eyes on another stock we intend to have here soon in case we sell these all out.

Boy, I wish I knew where I could get some more used boxes. I'd sell every WPA man a radio. Throw those old Four-fifty signs out the back. I'll fix up enough of these Reduced to Fifteen Dollar signs to plaster this whole store.

"Well," said paw that night, "the feller was right narce to us. He wanted to let us have a raddio now but the Bank won't let 'im let one of them go outen the store without a contrack and them contracks costs five dollars. He had some right narce-looking raddios too. Some costs fifty dollars new and he offered to let us have one fer fifteen dollars. I'll just let enough of our credit at the store ride this time to git us a contrack. A man's got to keep up with his job."

"You don't reckon the man at the grocer store will mind?" said maw.

"I don't hardly see how he could," said paw. "With us good regular customers of hisn. He'd oughtn't to mind doing a little favor fer a man that's just got his fust raise. I guess maybe the news about them raises will be all over town in a few days. News like that's kind of hard to keep."

"I feel real good over it," said maw. "We kin maybe git the chilluns some good warm clothes this winter. I felt right sorry fer Gwendolin last winter going back and forth to school in them little cotton dresses. The boys though made it pretty good in them CC shirts that Hub give 'em."

"Yes sir," said paw. "A nine dollar raise ought to fix

us up in pretty good shape fer the winter. Pretty good shape."

"We going to git a car, paw?" asked Jutland from the edge of the bed where he was sitting.

"Well now, son," said paw. "That'll take a mite of thinking about. A man don't want to be too hasty about buying anything. He needs to do some figgering fust to be shore he can see his way out in case things don't turn out just like he thought they would at fust."

"That's right," said maw. "That's right."

"Where's Virginia and Fred?" said paw.

"They won't be here this Saddy and Sunday," said maw. "They druv out to Fred's paw's fer Saddy and Sunday."

"I wonder ifen Fred's heared about the raises," said paw. "I would like to drive out there tomorrow and tell 'em. I sort of wisht we had a car. Hubbard, you go down in the morning and price a few good used cars. We ain't just ready to plunge in and git one yit but I don't see's it would do no harm to know about 'em. Just in case."

"In case of what, paw?" said Jutland.

"Oh, just in case," said paw.

Virginia and Fred came in on the truck that hauled the WPA workers from the southern part of the county Monday morning and Fred went straight to work. Virginia came into the room to find maw sitting in conversation with one of the neighbor women.

90

"Come in, Virginia," said maw. "Come in and set. You look a mite pale."

"I'm sick," said Virginia. "Christ, I'm sick. I vomited all the way to town."

"Well now," said maw. "You mustn't talk like that. It ain't becoming in a girl."

"But I'm sick," said Virginia.

"That ain't but to be expected," said maw. "Ain't that right, Miz Jackson?"

"That's right," said Mrs. Jackson. "I recolleck when I had my firstborn—"

"Oh, Lord. Oh, Lord," said Virginia. "Get the pot."

Maw brought the pot and stood holding it under Virginia's bowed head and Reno mewled and croaked and twisted in his swing at the unusual disturbance.

"Now," said maw. "Now. You'll feel better."

"It looks like Fred might have stayed with me this morning," said Virginia crossly.

"Why, Fred's got work," said maw.

"With this new raise he's got he could lay off a day or two ever' now and then," said Virginia.

"He got one too, did he?" said maw. "Well now. That's real good."

"Fred's got a rating," said Virginia with a tinge of pride in her voice. "He gets forty-two ninety, now."

"Well, I do know," said maw.

"We are going to get a car," said Virginia.

"Well now. Won't that be narce," said maw. "Paw was just saying last night he wisht he had a car. He would have liked to have rid out to Fred's paw's place yestiddy and been the fust to tell Fred about the raises. I don't reckon he knowed Fred knowed it."

"He heard it on the raddio," said Virginia.

"Rinno!" said maw. "Fer pity's sake git still fore you wear some more of them sores on your chest. I declare. He gits excited and gits to twisting and squirming around and hits hisself or rubs agin something and starts them sores in spite of all I kin do."

"I notice them sores on his arms seems better," said Mrs. Jackson.

"Yessum," said maw. "They do. I managed to cyore them up with some powders a feller give paw the other day but hit looks like as fast as I cyore up one of 'em another one breaks out."

"Pore feller," said Mrs. Jackson.

"Yessum," agreed maw. "He is kind of pitiful, ain't he?"

That night paw came in with new news of the job. The water-boy was on strike.

"Well, I'll tell you," said paw. "They's two sides to it. Here-in-before they ain't been no difference between a water-boy and just a regular WP and A man but when they give us these new raises they must of overlooked the water-boy somehow. Instid of thirty-five ten like the rest of us is gitting they done made him a rated man but they cut him to thirty-one twenty. He don't know just exactly what to do. I felt real sorry fer him this evening. He's got him a shovel now but the poor feller cain't git his mind on working fer worrying about whether to give up the water bucket or take a chanct on them having made a mistake in that rating and mean forty-one twenty instid of thirty-one twenty. Ever' rated man on the job gits more than just us regular WP and A men. I don't hardly see how they could dis-rate a man. I ain't never heared of that. I've a mind to take the bucket in the morning, myself."

"Well, I do know," said maw. "What about them other fellers that's been wanting the water-boy job?"

"They're of about a mind with me," said paw. "It's got us all kind of undecided like."

The next night when paw came in he confirmed the rumor about the water-boy rating.

"They was right up to the office," he said. "We went up there this morning to find out and shore enough they had our cards. Our new ones. A water-boy is rated all right but he don't git but thirty-one twenty. We ain't got no water-boy now and I'm plumb tard out tonight with having to walk over to the ice plant ever' time I want a drink of water. It looks like the Supervisor would do something about it."

"Looka here," said the Supervisor to the Area Engineer the next morning. "What the hell are we going to do about a water-boy? With these new ratings the water-boy gets four dollars a month less than common labor and there ain't a damn one of them that will take it. Can't we just let one of the common labor carry the bucket?"

"Hell, no," said the Area Engineer. "We can't work a man out of his classification. That's as bad as padding the payroll. You'll be paying somebody for something they are not doing."

"Well, what are we going to do then? The men spent all day yesterday walking back and forth between that ditch they are supposed to be digging and the ice plant. I saw one bunch turn around and go back for more water before they ever got back to the job from the first trip."

"Do they have to have ice water?"

"Hell, yes."

"Why not make that one-armed nigger a water-boy?"

"Hell, he's the best worker I've got down there."

"Well, why not just haul a barrel of water down on the truck every morning?"

"I'll try it but it won't be fit to drink standing in the sun all day."

Paw got his radio on payday and the first night he got news about his job. A man couldn't work but eighteen months on the WP and A any more. Except veterans, that is.

"Well," said paw. "It's lucky I went ahead and got this raddio. Here I might of just went ahead working right on past my eighteen months and not know a thing about it. I reckon I best start looking around some, being's I ain't got but seventeen months left on the WP and A."

"Well, I do know," said maw. "Now I wonder what made them do a thing like that. And us just got good settled in town too."

94

Paw turned the radio dial to a different station and the nasal twang of a blues yodeler accompanied by the strumming of a guitar filled the room.

"Look at Rinno," suddenly shrieked Gwendolin. "He's trying to dance."

They all turned to Reno and they became aware of his hoarse croaks of pleasure even above the noise of the radio. His eyes glittered and his head rolled from side to side on the dirty pillow. He mouthed ecstasy and drooled into his beard in his pained effort to put into words the pleasurable instinct the music fomented in him.

"Well, I swan," said paw. "The pore feller likes the music."

"Well, I do know," said maw. "Maybe that'll be a good way to keep him content enduring the day."

"Ifen he just don't git to flopping around too much and hurt hisself agin the side of that swing," said paw.

"That's right," said maw. "He might fer a fact."

And the job seethed and simmered and the men drew garbled accounts from their radios and their newspapers and they said—

That's a damn dirty trick to fire some of us that have families and leave some bastard on that ain't got nothing but a good dose of syph just because the draft caught him twenty years ago. I wonder when they'll start firing us. I wonder how many of us they'll fire the first go round.

Hell, they ain't going to let anybody go.

95

Ed heard over the radio that it's just the American Legion they are going to fire every eighteen months.

Ed ought to clean out his ears. What the radio says is they are going to shut the whole WPA down in eighteen months.

I read that in the paper too.

And the merchants said, What about our cars we sold them on the installment plan? What about our radios? Who can tell us who is going to get fired and who isn't? How can we find out when they will be fired?

And the Supervisor said, I wish to God they would just shut the whole thing down.

The first layoff for eighteen months came the first of August and a new word became familiar in the WPA vocabulary. Four Oh Three. A discharge slip.

"A bunch of them got laid off fer eighteen months today," said paw that night. "They done it with a piece of paper they call a Four Oh Three. They got our foreman too and now we ain't got no foreman. The men aim to hold a election on a new foreman in the morning."

"Well, that's right narce of them to let you all elect your own boss," said maw.

"Some of us is got a right good man running, too," said paw. "The other crowd is behind the truck driver but I don't hardly think they got a chanct. I want to go down to Mr. Adamses fer a while to kind of talk it over with him tonight. Ain't hit about time fer supper?"

96

"Miz Jackson is fust on the stove tonight," said maw. "She said she'd call me soon's she gits her vittles dished up. We done moved up to second place at the stove now. Hit makes hit a lot better too. We don't have to set around so long waiting fer a chanct to cook our stuff."

"Well, I just believe I'll just go down to Mr. Adamses fer a while before supper since hit ain't ready yit," said paw. "You can send one the chillun in fer me soon's you git hit ready."

Paw tramped out of the room and passed Hub and Buddy on the way up the stairs, Buddy astride Hub's back and the crutch dangling from one of his hands. Buddy's eager flow of words ceased when he heard paw cross the hall above them and they moved to one side of the steps to let him by and then the rapid confidential flow started again as soon as paw was out of earshot. They entered the room with Buddy silent again and his shy grin fixed on Reno.

The next morning the Supervisor said to the Area Engineer—

Looka here. I went down to the job this morning to appoint a temporary foreman to take the place of the one that got the eighteen-month Four Oh Three and there wasn't anyone there but the timekeeper and he said the men had held an election this morning and elected that sorry son-of-a-bitch of a water-boy foreman and the first thing he did was to declare a holiday and now the men have all gone home. What can I do about it?

And the Merchants came in and said, Looka here. We've brought a list of the WPA workers that owe us money. We know some of them have got laid off and we want their checks ordered turned over to us.

And the Area Engineer said, We can't turn them over to you. Those are relief checks and no one can touch them but the ones whose names are on them.

And the Supervisor said, About these men leaving their jobs today. Can we fire them?

And the Area Engineer said, You not only cannot fire them. You cannot even dock them for today. You will have to let them make up this time they are losing at the end of the period.

Six

Paw waked and turned on his side. Maw was already awake feeding the baby. The first gray light was fading the stars from the windows.

" 'Bout time to git up, ain't it?" said paw.

"Hush," maw said. "You'll wake Virginia and Fred. They was out till late last night."

"Ever' body ought to be ready to git up come daylight," said paw.

"But this is Sunday, paw, and Virginia's allus so cross and sick to her stummick in the mornings I almost hate fer her to git outen bed. If Virginia does wake up before I git breakfast fixed turn the raddio on and leave the door open so's I kin hear. Turn hit up loud. I hate to miss them yodelings since I done got used to hearing 'em ever' morning."

Maw closed the door softly behind her and paw shut his eyes against the light.

Paw roused next to Gwendolin's hiss.

"Git away from there. Git away. You know maw don't 'low you to fool with that raddio."

Then he heard Gwendolin's bare feet thump on the floor and the light splat of her hand as she slapped the baby's wrist and the baby's surprised squall.

"For heaven's sake stop that and be quiet," came from Virginia's bed. "Can't a body sleep a little late on Sunday morning without you have to yell and squall till ever' body has to wake up?"

"Now, Virginia," said paw. "Now, Virginia."

"What is it?" said Fred. "What is it?"

"Now we're all awake," said Virginia. "We might just as well get up."

"Well, if ever' body's awake we might's well turn the raddio on," said paw. "Turn hit on, Gwendolin."

Gwendolin held the baby, squirming and whimpering to get at the radio, at arm's length behind her and flipped the switch below the dial. The light came on behind the black markings and numbers and the baby stopped its struggles and stared fascinated at the tiny yellow glow. The radio hummed as the tubes warmed, then suddenly burst into ear-splitting fury before Gwendolin, who was standing with her hand still on the control knob, could reduce the volume.

"God-o-Mighty," said paw.

"For Christ sake turn that thing down," said Virginia.

Gwendolin turned with a silly grin on her face.

"Looks like hit beats me ever' time," she said.

The baby stood petrified for a moment, then added its wails to the din.

"Hush," said paw. "Hush."

Reno let forth a hoarse bellow and now he lay on his dirty pallet on the floor mouthing horrible sounds into the new day.

"Great God," said paw. "Somebody call Hub. Quick."

But Hub was already in the door. He stood a moment surveying the room, and the occupants became frozen in their poses as Hub's eyes followed around the circle of faces and came to rest on paw. Then without a word he crossed to Reno's pallet and lifting Reno in his quilts and pillows, and with Buddy trailing, descended the stairs and walked out the front door and placed Reno in a chair on the front porch.

As Hub's footsteps died out down the lower hall, paw slid across the bed and slammed his feet to the floor. The baby stood hushed with its thumb in its mouth and paw rose erect in his stretched and worn-thin union suit and reached his overalls and jumper from the floor by the bed and donned them.

"Turn the raddio up a mite and leave this door open," he said to Gwendolin as he walked out into the hall.

Fred stretched with the luxuriousness of not having to get up until it pleased him and his foot touched Virginia's leg. He lay still a moment, then his searching hand found her thigh.

"Stop," she said sharply.

"Aw, the kids ain't nothing," he said, his hand sliding up on her stomach.

"It ain't the kids," she said. "You know ever' time I move I get sick as a dog."

His hand became still, lost its warmth, and slipped from her stomach to the mattress beside her. It withdrew further and he heaved over on his side with his back to her and closed his eyes.

Paw called to them from the foot of the stairs.

"Maw said fer you to come on down to breakfast. And set the raddio in the door and turn hit up a mite. We cain't hear hit good from way back here."

Eugenia rose from the pallet and she and Gwendolin dragged the chair with the radio in it across to the door and turned it on full. Gwendolin picked up the baby and set it straddle her out-thrust hip and they sidled around the blaring radio and passed out of sight down the hall toward the stairs.

Fred sat up on the edge of the bed and turned to Virginia, who lay watching him with resentment and accusation plain in her gaze.

"You going to git up?" he said.

"No," she said.

"You better eat something."

"I'd druther be hungry than sick to my stomach."

He turned his back and lit a cigarette and smoked half of it, then pinched the fire off the end. He placed the stub carefully back in the pack and rose abruptly and jerked his clothes on and walked out the door without a backward glance.

Virginia heard the family trooping back upstairs from breakfast and she lay watching the door as each one entered the room.

102

"Where's Fred?" she asked when they were all in the room.

"Why, he left in that car of hisn without no break-fast," said paw. "I thought you knowed he was going off."

Virginia turned her back to them and the slow tears welled out of her eyes, ran down her cheeks and made a dark splotch on the coverless pillow beneath her head.

After the family had finished eating, Hub picked Reno from his chair on the porch and took him back to the kitchen.

"Maw," said Hub when they had finished eating, "that raddio gits Rinno all tore up."

"Well," said maw, "hit's such purty music I kind of hate to miss hit. Long's Rinno's on the pallet hit don't seem to hurt him none. They ain't nothing fer him to hit hisself against then."

"The children oughtn't to laugh at him like they do," said Hub.

"Well," said maw. "Rinno 'pears to enjoy hit 'bout as much as the chillun do. Miz Jackson was a-talking about hit the other morning. And seems like they's so little the pore feller kin enjoy."

Hub gave up the useless argument and rose from his place and taking Reno from maw went back upstairs and placed him in his swing.

"Don't play that raddio while Rinno's in his swing," he said to the children and turned and left and they fol-lowed him with their sly, secretive eyes.

By eight o'clock the men were all out in the yard

grouped beneath the huge old maple tree. One or two were in cane-bottom chairs but the majority of them were squatted on their heels, a position they could maintain indefinitely but which no town-born man could even achieve.

The children made an outer circle around the men, standing first on one foot, then on the other, pot-bellied, their faces sunburned but of a sameness of dead color even in the cheeks that told not of insufficient food but of a repetition of soggy biscuits and sorghum molasses.

Virginia spent the morning in bed and came down to dinner cross, petulant, and nervous. She ate in silence and got up and left the table. When the men resumed their circle beneath the maple tree she was sitting on the porch and her expression and attitude was one of resentfulness and apprehension.

Maw finished washing her dinner dishes and stacked them on her allotted section of shelf and drew a pan of water and took it to her room. She bathed in the pan and put on a fresh calico dress and black patent leather pumps and smoothed her hair into a knot on the back of her head. She poured a fresh dip of sweet snuff into her lip and came and stood in the door behind Virginia, looking down at her. Virginia was aware of her mother standing behind her but she continued to stare out into the yard, refusing to acknowledge her mother's presence.

"Virginia," said maw, "you'd ought to git out and take more exercise. Hit'll help you when your laying-in time comes."

Virginia grew sullen and continued to stare into the yard.

Buddy sat farther down the porch bent over a drawing board that Hub had brought him. Maw walked on down the porch and stood looking at the almost finished picture on the sheet of paper.

"Well, I declare," she said. "Hit looks just like one them Christmas cards cep'n hit ain't got no snow on it. And I ain't never seen no water oaks on no Christmas card."

Buddy looked up at her with one of his shy smiles then turned again to his sketch. He raised his head to stare across the street and maw followed his gaze. She looked down at the picture again and said, "Well now. Ifen hit ain't the spitten image of that church acrost the street. Steeple, cross and all. Well, I declare. Ifen you ain't the beatin'est child."

And Reno slept on his pallet upstairs where maw had been careful to place him on his left side.

The men in the yard settled their cuds of tobacco and took out their knives and whittling sticks and waited in deference to Mr. Adams who sat in the center chair tilted back against the tree. Mr. Adams was not only the oldest man in the group, he was a deacon in the London Church. He sat with his hat tilted over his eyes and his heels hooked in the rung of the chair as he chewed gravely and spit into the center of the circle and whittled down between his bony knees.

"Now, this eighteen months," he said. "I seen one of them letters the gove'ment sent along with the Four Oh

Three's. Hit said the men were eligible for re-certifying again in thutty days. So I guess it will be just in the nature of a thutty-day vacashun."

The men sat quietly spitting into the dust and waiting and the children stood wide-eyed and still and pot-bellied behind them.

"You don't reckon, Mr. Adams," said paw, "that the gove'ment aims to fire us men with famblies, do you?"

"I don't hardly think so," said Mr. Adams. "The gove'ment aims to ack reasonable. They ain't fired no fambly man yit."

"Well now," said paw. "I knowed all along even the gove'ment wouldn't hardly fire no fambly man."

"I wonder ifen they'll pay us straight on through our little vacashuns," said the man squatting next to paw.

"Well, I don't hardly think so," said Mr. Adams, "but I heared they was going to put us back on the 'moddity list just soon's we git our Four Oh Three's."

"Ifen I do git a Four Oh Three you can just bet your boots I'll be the fust man down to the City Hall the next morning."

"Well, that wouldn't be no bad idea," said Mr. Adams. "Ifen a man could just catch Mr. Will he mought could git his thutty days cut down some."

"Yessir. Mr. Will is the man to see. He knows who to touch on the shoulder over to Tupelo."

An hour before sundown the women called the men and children in to supper. Virginia walked back to the kitchen, ate, still wrapped in sullenness, and got up and walked out. When the family came upstairs she was already in bed with her back turned to the room. Maw spread the children's pallet and placed Reno for the night and she and paw undressed in the twilight and soon the only sounds in the room were paw's snoring and Virginia's restless turnings. Fred came in about nine, staggering and smelling of beer. He sat heavily on the edge of the bed, stripped off his pants and shirt and kicked off his shoes and flopped back on the bed and began snoring almost at once.

There were two eighteen-month Four Oh Three's on the job the next morning and one of them was for Mr. Adams.

"Well now. I weren't hardly looking for this," he said. "I didn't hardly think the gove'ment would fire no fambly man. Soon's I work this period out I reckon I better go see if I can get aholt of Mr. Will."

"Did you tell the Supervisor about you being a fambly man?" said paw.

"Yes, I did," said Mr. Adams. "But he said that didn't make no difference. Said the reason they weren't no fambly men in that fust batch of Four Oh Three's was it just happened so."

"Well now," said paw. "What do you know about that?"

Seven

The building-length hall upstairs in the City Hall was a babel of sound and smells and restlessness. The farmers filled the one bench and squatted against the walls in their clean faded overalls with their old sweat-stained felt hats tilted low over their eyes. New arrivals came and nodded to acquaintances and milled up and down the long hall. The older ones, familiar with WPA procedure, found convenient places to sit or squat and patiently waited their turn with the Social Worker but the newer ones moved restlessly about and finally sifted down the hall to join and merge with the close-packed crowd in front of the Social Worker's door. They blocked the hall and the entrance to the offices opposite the Social Worker.

"What in hell are all those folks doing out there in the hall?" said the Area Engineer.

"That bunch up in the front sitting against the wall are some of these men that have gotten these eighteen-month Four Oh Three's, but that mob outside the Social Worker's office must be the farmers. It's about time for them to start coming in now."

The Social Worker stuck her head out her door and said, "Are any of you among the men who just got laid off for eighteen months?"

There was a rush from the front of the hall and the mob at the door divided to let them through.

"Just a minute," said the Social Worker. "You will be just wasting my time and yours to try to get an interview before your thirty days is up. The law requires that you wait thirty days before I can interview you again. I will be notified from Tupelo when your time is up and as soon as they notify me I will send you a card. Now the rest of you—"

"But, look here. Why cain't I just git my interview now and have it over with so's I'll be all ready to git to work when my thutty days is up?"

"The law requires that you wait thirty days before being interviewed again."

"Well, ma'am, I was listening on the raddio last night and it said we couldn't git no work fer thutty days but hit didn't say nothing about we had to wait thutty days just to be interviewed again."

"That's my instructions from Tupelo. That you wait thirty days. Now the rest of you—"

"Where's Mr. Will?"

"I don't know where Mr. Will is. Now the rest of you line up like you came in. I'll give each of you a number beginning with the first one and take you as you came in. I won't give but sixteen numbers as that is all I'll have time for today. The rest of you might as well go on home and come back tomorrow."

The disappointed men went back up the hall to squat patiently against the walls waiting for Mr. Will.

A lookout saw Mr. Will get out of his car at the front and enter the building.

"Here comes Mr. Will," he said.

They rose to a man and stood right inside the door and stopped Mr. Will as he entered the door from the hall below.

"Look here, Mr. Will. That lady back there won't even give us no interview. Says she can't give us no interview fer thutty days. Says Tupelo told her not to give us no interview fer thutty days."

"Well, I'll tell you, men. I'm going to Tupelo day after tomorrow and I'll get your cards for you then. You come around again day after tomorrow and I'll have your cards."

They went away happy, content.

"I knowed Mr. Will could fix us up."

"What the hell did you want to tell them that damn lie for, Will?" said the Area Engineer. "You know you can't get those men back on in less than thirty days even if you can get them back on then."

"You've got to keep them satisfied," said Mr. Will. "You don't want to get them mad at you."

"Mr. Will will have us back on day after tomorrow," said the men to their wives. "We knowed Mr. Will would take care of us."

"While we ain't got nothing else to do, we might's well git our names back on the 'moddity list, hadn't we?"

"Done already got mine on. Got hit on the day after my Four Oh Three come."

The boxcar loads of government commodities rolled in and the City truck hauled the boxcar loads to the commodity warehouse and the workers on the commodity project opened the sacks and bales and portioned out the apples and celery and grapefruit and oatmeal into equal sacks.

COMMODITY ROOM
OPEN
9 to 3 Sat.

The white farmers and the black farmers lined up at the door of the commodity room and elbowed and pushed and joked and laughed.

Heah come ol' Unc' Ned. Whut dey give you dis time, Unc' Ned? Unc' Ned git a big sack dis time. Dey mus' be runnin' heavy on de 'moddities dis time. I hopes I gits me a big sack uh 'tatoes and some 'lasses. Wouldn't keer if dey gimme some dem appuls in de winduh. Don't scrouge me, boy. Don't scrouge me. Dey got plenty to go 'roun'. An' heah come de truck wid mo'. Come ovuh heah, boy. Lemme see whut dey give you dis time. Whut dat stuff? Look like cabbage, kinder. Dem's big ol' oranges. Don't scrouge me, boy. Dey's plenty to go 'roun'.

And the town talked.
Lord, did you hear what the WPA's done now? They

ship these big boxcar loads of apples and celery and grapefruit and oatmeal and stuff in here and call it commodities and when a man gets fired off the WPA or can't get on the WPA they put him on the commodity list and give him a sack of this stuff every Saturday. Well sir. They give out apples and celery and grapefruit and oatmeal last Saturday and I wish you could have heard them down there this morning. Old man Browning was the only one who knew what celery was and he took his, two big bunches, and stood right by the celery rack in the corner grocery and waited till somebody come in wanting celery. The corner grocery asked fifteen cents a bunch for theirs and he butted right in and offered the man wanting the celery both his bunches for a dime and took the dime and went into the City Café next door and bought him a big beer with the dime.

But did you hear what that nigger woman said? Said she didn't want no more of them long cabbage. Said she boiled it and stewed it and fried it and cooked it every way she knew how and she never could get it so her family could eat it. Then she said, How does you cook de stuff, anyhow?

And these grapefruit. One woman said they were the biggest oranges she ever saw but she put hers up on a shelf over the stove to ripen and they never changed color at all. Just set there and rotted.

And this oatmeal. Some of them remembered the oat part and some the meal. Old man George said his wife walked out the door with a pan of them oats and give 'em to the mule and now every time she goes to the back door with a pan in her hand the old mule brays and comes a-running. And Old Uncle Ned. He thought it was meal and made him up a batter and put it in his stove to cook like a hoe cake and he called some of the niggers in to see how he cooked his meal and when he opened the oven door the patty had swelled up so he couldn't get the oven door shut again. And Ol' Payne. Said they give him about half a peck of that meal and his wife started cooking on it soon's he got home and by Sunday night he had two bushels and he believed by next month he ought to have at least fifty. Oh, Lord. Oh, Lord. Oh, Lord.

The building-length hall filled with the men in patched and faded overalls before seven each morning. The farmers who had come to town to get on the WPA stood in a knot in front of the Social Worker's door and the farmers who already lived in town and had already been on the WPA sat on the one seat and squatted against the wall with their eighteen-month Four Oh Three's in their pockets and their form letters saying that they were not eligible for re-certification for thirty days in their hands.

Where's Mr. Will? Have you saw Mr. Will? That lady back there won't talk to us but Mr. Will's going to Tupelo to git our cards. Said he was going to Tupelo and git our cards. Where's Mr. Will? Said he was going to Tupelo to git our cards today. Have you saw Mr. Will? Girl back there in his office said he was too busy to go to Tupelo yestiddy but he's going to Tupelo to-morrow to git our cards.

Will, why don't you go out there and talk to those men you promised cards?

Hell. Tell 'em I ain't here. Tell 'em I'm going to Tu-pelo tomorrow. Tell 'em I couldn't get off yesterday.

Where's Mr. Will? Is Mr. Will in yit? Mr. Will's going to take care of us.

Well now, you see, we ain't got just all that little account right now. We're on a vacashun right now. It ain't like gitting fired. It's just kind of a little rest fer us. And it ain't but only thutty days anyhow. Mr. Will, he's taking care of us. Said he was going to Tupelo to git our cards tomorrow.

Why, that lying Will can't get you a card in Tupelo. There ain't anybody can get you a card in Tupelo. Or in Jackson or Washington or anywhere else. The only way you can get a card is through that Social Worker down at the City Hall and she can't give you one until the government tells her to.

Mr. Will's going to git us a card. Said he was going to Tupelo to git us a card tomorrow. We need just a little more stuff till about next pay period. We'll git back to working soon's Mr. Will gits back from Tupelo with our cards. Well, yes sir. We got on the 'moddity again but a body needs something else sides them apples and grapefruit and stuff. Well now, that's right kind of you. We'll be back on soon's Mr. Will gits back from Tupelo with our cards.

How about some of you men going over to the Delta to pick cotton? Furnish you transportation and a house when we get there. Got a bumper crop this year. Plenty for everybody. Pay you six bits a hundred.

Well now, we cain't rightly leave here just now. We're liable to git back on the WP and A most any time now.

The building-length hall upstairs full of men. Farmers trying to get on the WPA and men who were farmers trying to get back on the WPA. Where's Mr. Will? Mr. Will's taking care of us. He couldn't git off to go to Tupelo yestiddy but he's going to git off and go tomorrow. He's going to git our cards tomorrow.

Cotton pickers needed. Got a bumper crop in the Delta. Plenty for everybody. Stuff's ruining right there in the fields. Transportation and houses free. Paying ninety cents a hundred.

Well now, we are liable to git back on the WP and A most any day now. Mr. Will's going to git us back on the WP and A.

Will, for God's sake go out there in that hall and tell those men something. We cain't even get into our offices there are so many of them out there.

I've got to go down to the doctor's this morning. This neuralgia's killing me. Maybe I better go to Hot Springs for about a week and take the baths.

You better go out there in that hall and tell those men something.

Are they still out there?

Still out there? Hell, they're backed plumb out on the walk in front.

Lock that door. Don't tell anybody I'm back here.

Mr. Will's going to take care of us. I was down to his house last night and he told me he was going to take care of us. Going to Tupelo tomorrow to git our cards. Mr. Will's going to take care of us.

Hub waited diffidently until the sales woman was through with the customer she was waiting on and then made his purchases and stood patiently beside the counter while they were being wrapped. He paid for them, selecting the exact change from the few coins in his hand, and tucked them under his arm.

He moved on out the door and down the street toward the brown house in which they lived and just past the City Hall he glanced through the areaway and saw Buddy with his drawing board under his arm swinging along on his crutch. Hub waited on the walk and as Buddy neared him he called, "Hey, feller."

Buddy looked up quickly from his intent scanning of the ground beneath his moving crutch and his face lighted.

"What you been drawing this evening?" asked Hub.

"Look," said Buddy, coming to a halt at Hub's side and extending the board with the paper thumbtacked to it.

"That's better'n the last one," said Hub.

He held the picture at arm's length and studied it while Buddy stood flushed with pleasure at his side.

Hub lowered the board and took the package from underneath his arm and held it out to Buddy.

"More paper?" said Buddy.

"Look inside," said Hub.

Buddy's excited fingers solved the knot and stripped the paper off.

"Paints," he said. "Paints."

"I'll fix you a thing to put your board on tomorrow," said Hub. "One them three-legged things with pegs in 'em. And a stool."

"Will you, Hub?" said Buddy.

"You bet," said Hub. "Just you watch me in the morning."

Side by side they moved on down the walk and turned into the path that cut across the yard, Hub carrying the board and supporting Buddy by one arm and Buddy with his glowing eyes fixed on the box of paints.

"Like 'em?" said Hub.

"Boy," breathed Buddy.

It wasn't yet time for paw to come in from work and Hub noted subconsciously the absence of shrill-voiced children in the front yard. It was after he and

Buddy had entered the hall door that they became aware of the hilarious screams from upstairs and the beat of the radio. They both became aware of its portent at the same instant. Buddy's face whitened and Hub's flushed with anger.

"Wait here," said Hub, handing the board to Buddy.

He crossed the hall in quick strides and raced up the steps. In the door to the room he paused and one of the children in the midst of paroxysms of mirth saw him and quieted suddenly and a hush spread as rock-made ripples on a pool except for the beat of the radio and Reno's contortions and mewlings.

Hub cut the switch on the radio and Reno's rage became awful in the stilled room. Two neighboring children slipped past Hub with quick furtive steps, then Hub blocked the door.

Jutland sat defiantly on the edge of the bed on which he had been rolling in glee at Reno's antics, and Harold and McKinley cringed back in a corner, their eyes big with fear. Eugenia peered from behind Gwendolin, who sobbed openly, the tears of fright running unheeded down her smudged cheeks.

"Harold done it," she wailed. "Harold done it."

Hub's eyes went to Jutland as the oldest and Jutland smirked self-consciously.

"I didn't have nothing to do with it," he said in smug satisfaction.

"You could have stopped it," said Hub, turning then to Harold.

118

"They dast me to," said Harold.

"Who did?"

"They did," said Harold.

"Who is they?" asked Hub.

"All of 'em," said Harold, "and they're dirty liars ifen they say they didn't."

"You oughtn't to have let 'em done it, Jut," said Hub.

"Why, I didn't have nothing to do with it," said Jutland.

"Except let 'em do it," said Hub.

Reno had somehow quieted, possibly realizing or sensing the difference in the atmosphere of the room or possibly he just forgot about the music, and now his eyes were rolled toward Hub and he whined and mouthed small impatient sounds.

"That boy from across the street was the first one that dast him to," said Gwendolin. "He was bragging about what his folks had and Eugenia told him about us having Rinno and he give Harold a slingshot to let him see Rinno and when we got up here in the room that boy said, Huh, Rinno weren't nothing. Said he couldn't even talk. And McKinley said he was something too. What ifen he couldn't talk. He could dance. And that boy said he couldn't neither and McKinley said he could so. And that boy said let's see him and McKinley said he wouldn't without the raddio, and when McKinley wouldn't turn the raddio on that boy dast him and said he was a fraidy cat and Jut said even Harold would take a dare like that and Harold said he bet he wouldn't and that boy dast Harold and he done it."

Hub walked over to Reno and placed him straight in his pillows and adjusted the breast ropes and that was when he noticed it. The rope was damp and Hub looked quickly at Reno's shirt and saw the two damp splotches, one on either side of his chest where the rope had rubbed, and he unbuttoned the shirt and held it back while Reno mewled delight at him. There across the skin-covered cage of bones were the two long blisters, not red like a burn but white and worn-looking like fat meat from which the grease has been cooked, with the rolled slivers of dead skin at the edges and the blister water shiny against the sallow skin below the burns.

"Mr. Will is a fine man," said paw one night a week later. "That there Social Worker she won't even talk to the men what got Four Oh Three'd but I tell you about Mr. Will. He stops and talks to 'em ever' time they kin catch 'im. He would of already been to Tupelo to see about their cards but he's been right busy. I feel right sorry fer him sometimes. With ever' body trying to see him about gitting on and him with that neuralgy. I've seed him up there talking to the men and his neuralgy a-hurting him so bad he had to just stand there and hold his face in his hand. But he ain't never too busy to stop and talk to 'em ever' time they kin catch 'im."

"I ain't never seen him," said maw, "but he must be a right narce man."

"I was talking to Mr. Adams down to the job this

120

morning. He's looking to git back on most any time now. Soon's Mr. Will can git off to go to Tupelo."

"Miz Jackson was telling me this morning her man done got one them Four Oh Three's."

"Well, they ain't nothing more than just a little vacashun," said paw. "All he's got to do is see Mr. Will."

"Miz Jackson is a mite worried over hit though. Poor thing."

"They was another one of them fellers from the Delta with a truck when I come through town this evening. Looking fer cotton pickers. Tried to git some of the men to go to the Delta with him to pick cotton but they didn't none of them feel just right about leaving right now with expecting to git back on the WP and A most any time."

"Yes. I heared they was looking fer cotton pickers over to the Delta. Hub went back with him. Said he thought he might go over fer a week or two and pick some."

"I've saw Hubbard pick as high as four hundred a day," said paw. "He ought to do right well over there."

"Hub was telling me 'bout being over in Arkansaw last fall and picking right 'longside the Arkansaw champeen. Said hit beat anything he ever seen. But Hub said he didn't pick clean. Said he told him you couldn't afford to fer what they was paying. Said to come out on it a body had to just pick what was in easy reach and keep a-going."

"Well, Hubbard ain't the fastest picker in the world, I reckon, but I've taught my children to pick clean. If a body is going to do a job he'd ought to do it right or not do hit."

"That's right," said maw. "That's right."

The thirty-day period was up and the hall was still full of the overall-clad men. Their number had increased, for new Four Oh Three's had come in.

"My thutty days is up today," said Mr. Adams. "I'll just go down early and git my interview over with."

Mr. Adams got to the City Hall before the doors were even unlocked. Two men were already sitting on the outside steps and he took his place by them.

"Well, my thutty days is up today," he said. "I guess I'll be gitting back on right away now. I won't mind gitting back to work neither. Gits kinder tiresome sitting around when a man's got nothing else to do but sit."

"Yes, hit does," agreed one of the men. "I'll be right glad to git back on, myself."

By the time the janitor came to unlock the doors there was quite a crowd on the steps. They filed up the stairs behind the janitor and took their places on the bench and against the walls. By eight o'clock the hall was full.

The Social Worker came in and pushed and wormed her way to her door.

Mr. Adams was right behind her as she inserted her key and slid the bolt back. Before she pushed the door open she turned and said: "You men who have not received cards to report for interviews needn't come in today. I can't possibly see you all today and I have sent out cards to everyone I will be able to see."

"I ain't got no card," said Mr. Adams, "but my thutty days is up today."

"That makes no difference," said the Social Worker. "As fast as they send the files to me from Tupelo I send out cards and unless you have a card it won't do a bit of good to interview you."

"But I'm one of the ones what got Four Oh Three'd fer eighteen months. It says here on this letter they sent me with that Four Oh Three that I can be interviewed again in thutty days."

"It says you can't be interviewed again in less than thirty days."

"But what about my fambly? I done been off thutty days. I got to take care of my fambly."

"What about these other men with families that haven't been on WPA at all? You'll just have to wait your turn like the rest of them."

"Where's the Area Engineeer?" said Mr. Adams. "I'll just see why I cain't git back on since I done already been off my thutty days."

"The Area Engineer can't help you any, but if you want to see him he's back there in that office at the end of the hall. Now, the rest of you, if you haven't appointment cards I won't be able to see you today."

"What about me? My card said fer me to come yestiddy."

"Why didn't you come yesterday?"

"Well, it was kind of disconvenient."

"Could you have come?"

"Well, yessum. I reckon I could have."

"Why didn't you then?"

"Well, they was a bunch of us had made it up to go grabbling yestiddy."

"You'll have to take your place with the rest of them then and if I possibly can I'll see you the last thing this evening."

Mr. Adams finally succeeded in pushing his way through the crowd to the Area Engineer's office. It was full also with the overflow from the hall.

The Area Engineer was saying: "There's no way anybody can get you back on right now. Congress tells us how many men we can work. They tell us how much money we can spend. If we put on more men than we have money to pay them with then nobody will get paid for working. Right now we are looking for another quota reduction and I doubt if anyone will be put back on before winter."

Mr. Adams stood in the outside of the circle around the Area Engineer's desk and listened intently, then when the Area Engineer was through he pushed his way up to the desk.

"Is this the Area Engineer?"

"Yes?"

"I want to know why that lady in the next office won't interview me?"

"Have you got an appointment card with her?"

"Well, no. But my thutty days is up today and this

124

letter here says I can be interviewed again in thutty days."

"It says you can't be interviewed again in less than thirty days."

"Well, hit amounts to about the same thing. I done been off my thutty days now and I need the work. You can ast air man down to the job and he'll tell you there ain't a better, steadier, harder worker down there than I was. I can handle one them shovels just as good as air man on the job and better than some I knows. I've allus been faithful to my job and I've allus tried to give 'em a honest day's work and that's more than I can say fer some of 'em down there."

"I don't doubt that at all," said the Area Engineer, "but until Congress says to put on more men, we can't. It's not our say-so how many men we work. Congress tells us how many."

"But hit says here in this letter that I can git back on again in thutty days."

"Well, until Congress says to put on more men there's nothing we can do about it."

"Well, they's one or two down there that's been working fer more than eighteen months that ain't got no Four Oh Three that I'd like to know how they manages to stay on."

What's the use, thought the Area Engineer. I'll talk myself blue in the face and when I get through he'll say, But hit says here in this letter that I kin git back on in thutty days.

The group of men at Mr. Adams' back had stood silent, listening, and now one of them seeing Mr. Adams was through pushed his way up to the desk and held out the familiar creased and grimy form letter and said, "I got one them letters too and that Social Worker lady won't interview me neither."

"Well, there's nothing anybody can do right now," began the Area Engineer again. "Congress sets the number of men we can work and—"

Eight

The grocers called their clerks and said, Take these bills down to those big houses where all those WPA workers stay and see if you can collect some on them. They haven't been by here in over two months now. By George, I didn't know these bills were running up so high, either. Here's one for fifty-six dollars and thirty cents and here's one for forty-nine and here's a couple for better than forty. Take 'em down there and see if you can get something on them.

And the radio men said, Go down there where those WPA workers stay and see about the payments on those radios we sold them.

And the finance companies said, You had better get some of these payments on those old cars coming in or we'll be calling on you for them.

And the collectors went down to the big houses and said, Does Mr. Jones live here? Is this where Mr. Smith lives? They've done moved? Do you know where they moved to? Well, are they still working on the WPA?

✦   *127*

"Mr. Adams moved this morning," said maw.

"Well, I swan," said paw. "Now I wonder what he went and done that fer."

"I didn't talk with him none," said maw. "He just come and got his woman and their bedstid and left. I kinder hated to see 'em go too. Miz Adams was a right narce neighbor. A right narce neighbor."

"Well, I swan," said paw.

And the next night at supper paw said: "Mr. Adams ain't left town. He just moved over on the other side of town in that house where Steve Joe and his woman lives."

"Well, I do know," said maw. "Now I wonder why. And they was a real narce-looking feller here to see him this morning too. Seemed right put out when I told him Mr. Adams had done gone."

"The lady from acrost the street was over here this morning and ast us not to play our raddios so loud no more," said maw. "Special early in the morning."

"What did you tell her?" said paw.

"I was to the back of the hall listening," said maw. "I never talked to her none. But Miz Jackson told her hit was her raddio and she aimed to play hit loud as she pleased."

"Well now," said paw, "I don't know whether she ought to have told her that or not."

"Well, I was right glad she did," said maw. "I don't aim to disturb nobody but I'm right glad I ain't got to miss them yodelings ever' morning, special since Rinno

128

cain't use his swing no more since he got them blisters on his chest and just has to lay on his pallet all the time."

"Them sores ain't gitting no better?" asked paw.

"Hit don't seem like they are," said maw. "I allus said a burn was the worsest kind of a sore to heal."

"One the men was telling me about some stuff a old nigger woman fixes up that might cyore Rinno," said paw.

"Did you tell him to git some of hit fer us?" said maw.

"Well, he ain't likely to see the feller soon what knows the old woman. Seems like he don't come to town regular on Saddys. But I told him next time he seen the feller to git him to tell the woman to fix us up some of it."

"That last powder you got to the drug store didn't seem to help much. Didn't do as much good as that sa've that feller give you. Hub 'peared to be right stirred up over Rinno fore he left. Kind of like he wanted to git a doctor to come see him."

"Doctors is fer rich folks," said paw. "Sides, I ain't got much confidence in doctors. The only time we ever had a doctor was with Rinno when he was born and I've allus been kind of disappointed in Rinno."

"Well," said maw. "I wisht we knowed something to do."

"The men down to the job seems right interested in how Rinno's gitting along," said paw. "I'll ast all of 'em again tomorrow and maybe some of 'em kin think up something we ain't tried yit."

"I wisht Hub was home from Arkansaw," said maw.

"Seems like he allus had a heap of influence over Rinno. Buddy's been a-moping around ever since Hub left too. Don't even draw as much as he used to."

"Well, Hub's likely to be back most any day now," said paw.

"I bound ye Buddy and Rinno will be glad to see 'im too," said maw.

The rent came due and the rent man came around to collect.

"Where's Mr. Adams?" he said.

"Mr. Adams ain't here no more."

"Well, who's responsible for the rent?"

"Well now, I just don't know. We ain't done no figgering on that."

"Somebody's going to have to be responsible for it."

"Well, our menfolks ain't to home now. I could ast 'em tonight when they git in and let you know some time later."

"Later, hell," said the man. "This rent's due today. You tell your menfolks I'll be here tonight after supper for the rent."

"Paw, what are we going to do about the rent?" said maw when paw came in from work that night.

"Well now, I just ain't never thought nothing about it," said paw. "Mr. Adams, he's been attending to it."

"The rent man was here this morning and he says he'll be here right after supper for the rent."

"Well, hit looks like he's a mite anxious just fer rent."

"What are you going to do about it?"

"Well, I guess I had better see the rest of the men and see if we can figger out something."

Paw walked across the hall to the door opposite.

"Hello," he called.

"That you, Mr. Taylor?"

"Yes, ma'am. Is Mr. Jackson around?"

"Why, yes sir. He's here a-setting by the window. Did you want him fer something?"

"Well, yes ma'am. Ask him if he's got time to step here a minute?"

"Mr. Jackson, Mr. Taylor wants to see you ifen you ain't too busy."

"Why, come in, Mr. Taylor. Come in. What's the news down on the job today?"

"Oh, nothing new. Nothing new. Hit gits along about the same, I reckon. We miss you fellers a heap."

"I wisht my thutty days was up so's I could git back on."

They sat in cane-bottom chairs, silent for a while, patient, a little futile, a little bewildered, Mr. Jackson waiting for Mr. Taylor to state his errand, Mr. Taylor a little elated, a little diffident over having Fate thrust even for a moment the lead and the superior feeling of being a leader in one of the vital affairs of this unit of humanity into his inept hands.

"Maw—er—that is, Miz Taylor," he corrected to the more formal term as befitted the momentousness of the occasion, "says that the rent man come around this morning."

"Well, I didn't see him," said Mrs. Jackson, surprised into intruding herself into the affairs of her menfolks, where no country-bred woman ever dares raise her voice. She looked more startled even than they and she became flustered and said, "I best git on down to the kitchen. Hit's my time fust at the stove tonight."

"Miz Taylor," began paw again, "says the rent man was around this morning."

"Well," said Mr. Jackson, "we'll just have to git him to wait on us this time. Just until we can all git back to working again."

"Well now, that's just about what I had figgered. Course now, ifen a man wants to keep his share of the rent up that's up to him and won't none the rest of us hold it agin 'im. Fur's I'm concerned I just as soon let mine run fer a month or so just so's none the rest of the men that are on their little vacashuns won't think just because I'm still working that I think I'm any better than they are. Hit might embarrass 'em fer some to pay when they can't. I'm allus a feller that tries to git along with the crowd."

"Well now, that's mighty thoughty of you," said Mr. Jackson. "That away we'll all share and share alike and won't no man have air comeuppance over no other man."

"That's just the way I feel about it," said paw. "Like the Bible says, Live and let live."

132

"Yes sir," said Mr. Jackson. "That's just exactly what I say."

Paw made individual visits to the menfolks and out of the seven families left (Mr. Adams was now gone) only three of them including himself was working. The rest had received their eighteen-month Four Oh Three's. His attitude was unanimously approved by the entire house and paw returned to his room to await the advent of the rent man in a mental haze of martyrdom and self-righteousness and almost a glow of altruistic beatification.

The rent man came back while they were still at supper and paw took his hat from the floor by his chair and placed it on his head, then rose and went out into the hall to meet him. The men on the lower floor opened cracks in their doors and stood peering through them with their wives and children straining to see over their overall-clad shoulders and between their legs. The people from upstairs came halfway down the steps, men first, then the women and children. The men stopped and the women stooped to see beneath the upper floor and the children squatted to peer between the posts of the stair railing.

"I've come for the rent," the rent man said. "They tell me Mr. Adams has moved."

"Well now," said paw. "I heared that myself. We hated to lose him, too."

"Who's responsible for the rent now?"

"Well now, I guess the boys done sort of elected me."

"Well, how about the rent?"

"Well now, you see, they's some of the fellers ain't working right now. They're on little vacashuns sort of and we thought just until ever' body gets back to working again maybe the best thing to do is just to let the rent run until we all git back to working again. We don't want none of us to feel like they can't pay their part."

"Why, hell," said the man. "We can't do business that way. We've got to have the rent every thirty days."

"Well now," said paw, "we don't none of us aim to beat you out of no rent, but we're all just WP and A folks here and we don't want none of us to feel like they're taking char'ty."

"Charity!" said the rent man. "Charity?"

"Well, you know how it is," said paw. "Ifen some of the boys pays, then the ones that can't pay feels sort of like they ain't just doing their part. They don't just feel right about letting some of 'em do fer all of 'em."

"Look here," said the rent man. "How many of you live here?"

"They's seven famblies of us now," said paw. "That ain't counting Mr. Adams what's done moved."

"How many of you still working?"

"They's three still working all told. They's me, I ain't got no Four Oh Three yit, and the two fellers what lives downstairs here."

"How much do your checks run each time?"

"Well, they's supposed to run about Seventeen Oh Five but they gen'ly runs about a dollar or two short what with us having to wait around the post office up

134

until about eight fifteen to git 'em from the mailman and then the banks don't open until about nine."

"Why, even that don't make them two dollars short."

"Well, you see, they's always about a day or two's extry work about the place here ever' now and then."

"But don't you get three or four days off between pay periods?"

"Why, yes sir."

"Well, why don't you do your work around the house then?"

"Well, I'd thought some about doing that but hit looks ever' time like it just ain't convenient during them days off."

"Well, I'll just be damned," said the rent man. "How much of this rent can you pay now? It's forty dollars a month, you know?"

"Well now, we hadn't figgered it just like that," said paw. "We ain't been used to paying but five dollars a month apiece."

"Sure," said the rent man. "There were eight of you families here and that's all it came to apiece."

"Well now, I reckon us three that are working could pay you our five dollars. I had been holding back about five dollars fer something like that."

"That's not even half a month's rent," said the rent man. "Can't the three of you get up twenty dollars?"

"Well, I just don't know about that," said paw. "I hadn't figgered on paying but five dollars fer my rent."

"Look here," said the rent man. "This house don't belong to me, you understand. It belongs to some folks who don't even live here. I just collect the rent for them every month and send it to them. They say how much rent I've got to get for the house and if anybody lives in the house and I don't send them forty dollars every month then I've got to send them forty dollars out of my pocket."

"Well now, that seems like it ain't just right," said paw. "Making you pay the rent that way when you don't even live in the house."

The rent man stared at paw dumfounded for a moment, then he turned and walked to the door and back and stopped in front of paw again and he was still breathing heavily.

"I'll tell you what I'll do," said the rent man in a strained voice. "You get me up twenty dollars and I'll wait until two weeks from today for the rest."

"Well now, that's putting a heap on us three fellers just because we're working hit looks like," said paw.

"That's the best I can do," said the rent man, "and if the folks that own the house knew I was doing that they would probably fire me."

"Well now, I've got to go see them fellers about that," said paw. "We hadn't figgered on nothing like that."

"I'll wait right here," said the rent man. "You go get that twenty dollars and I'll wait two weeks on the rest and that's just about the best I can do."

Paw called to the two men who had been standing in the downstairs room doors listening and they followed him out the front door and around to the side of the house and squatted back against the wall and paw squatted before them and said, "Well, men. It begins to look like it's going to be up to us workers to take care of the full rent."

"That don't look just right to me," said one of the men.

"Well now," said paw. "The way I got it figgered we can pay hit this time, then the other fellers can pay hit next time."

"How do we know they are going to have it next time?"

"Well," said paw. "I know to a certainty two of 'em's thutty days is up this week and they'll be back on by next time."

"Hit seems like them thutty-day men ain't gitting back on so good," said one man.

"That's right," said the other. "I heard down to the job today that the Social Worker won't even interview 'em after their thutty days is up."

"Have they saw Mr. Will?"

"Hit looks like even Mr. Will cain't do much now. Some the fellers down to the job was saying that Congress has done took a hand in it now. Said the Areal Engineer told 'em."

"Well, I declare," said paw. "If Congress has done took a hand in it, that's bad. I ain't kep' up good lately. The baby pushed the raddio offen the bed and you cain't hear good over it no more. But this ain't gitting that rent proposition settled."

"How come that girl of yours' husband cain't chip in on the rent this time?"

"Well," said paw. "I kind of hate to mention it to him being's he lives in the same room with us."

"Well, I just ain't got but five dollars left," said one.

"I ain't got but about a dollar extry," said the other.

"Well," said paw, "since I done been elected kind of to tend to it, it looks like it's up to me to git it up. You say you got a dollar? Well, I got about a dollar and sixty-five cents I was intending to have that raddio fixed with but I guess maybe I better put hit on the rent now. That makes about two dollars and sixty-five cents and if Fred is of a mind to put in with about two dollars and thirty-five cents we kin make out. Let me go and see him."

Paw went around to the back of the house and climbed the stairs to his room. It was well past dark now and Fred and Virginia were in bed.

"Fred?" called paw. "Fred?"

"What is it?" said Fred.

"We're running kind of short on the rent, Fred, being's so many of the men ain't working just now and we need about two dollars and thirty-five cents to round it out and we wondered if you wouldn't maybe like to chip in on it just this one time."

Fred rose without a word and reaching his pants from the foot of the bed pulled his wallet out of the back pocket and handed paw three dollars.

"Well now, you done give me three whole dollars."

"Keep it," said Fred and dropping his pants back to the foot of the bed he sat down on the edge of the wheat-sack-covered cotton mattress and lying back

138

swung his legs over on the bed and turned his back on paw.

Well, thought paw, I bet he'd of give the whole five soon's not.

He returned to the men waiting against the side of the house.

"I got it now, men," he said.

They each handed paw a five dollar bill for their share of the rent and then one of them extended a one. Paw took the money and added his part and said, "Strike a match, one of you."

One of them struck a match and in its flickering light paw counted the money carefully and then folded it and put it into his breast pocket with the zipper on it and led the way back into the front door.

"Well," said paw to the rent man. "We made it."

"I thought maybe you would by the time it took you," said the rent man who had grown uneasy at their continued absence as well as beneath the constant stares from the doors and the hall steps.

Paw laughed abortively over the rent man's joke and unzipped the pocket and counted out the rent into the rent man's hand.

The rent man wrote out a receipt and said, "Remember now. The other twenty dollars in two weeks from today. And understand it ain't my house. I just work for the folks that own it."

Nine

Virginia grew heavy and cumbersome with child and, as her weight and her waistline increased, so increased her crossness and her temper. Fred began avoiding her more and more and she grew crosser and his appearances became later and later at night, for he sought pleasures elsewhere and at last one night he did not come home at all. And the next day Virginia sat sullen and repugnant and when he did come in at supper she refused to speak to him or notice him except that she was more sullen and angry and Fred ate his supper and left soon after.

Dog days gave way to cool nights and autumn and the first light frost came. The man in the front room downstairs was laid off and now only paw and one other was left to pay the rent and the lights and water. They had attempted to keep the rent paid up, but after two months of trying and scheming they, as well as the rent man, gave it up as hopeless. And then the City cut the lights off and last of all the water and now the women and children trekked back and forth with buckets to the fountain in the goldfish pool in front of the City Hall and brought water for their cooking and their baths. The commode was now useless, and the tub was used for a bin to store the coal in, of which they bought a dollar's worth at a time.

Looka here, said the man who lived next door. About these people who live in that big brown house next to me. Something has got to be done about it. They never have taken the trouble to go to the house when they want to wet. They don't even go around to the side. They just get on the side of the closest tree away from the biggest part of the crowd and let go and now they have started doing their business in the back-yard. We'll all die with typhoid or God knows what if something isn't done. Since cool weather has come and we can put the windows down so we can't hear their damned radios we have been able to move back on the side of the house toward them, but now when the wind blows from them toward us the whole end of town smells like a privy. What can we do about it?

We'll send the Marshal down right away. Don't worry about it. We'll fix it.

"Look," said Gwendolin from the hard-packed dirt of the front yard where they were playing. "Police."

"Ah-h," said Harold. "Who's 'fraid of a p'liceman?"

"You are," said Gwendolin. "Ever' body's 'fraid of p'licemen."

"I ain't neither," said Harold.

"He's coming in here," said Gwendolin.

Eugenia watched with popping eyes as the Marshal in his brass-buttoned blue turned into the yard, then she broke and ran for the shelter of the front porch. Gwendolin picked up the baby and slinging him across her hip began sidling after Eugenia. Harold stood his ground, though his knees started trembling, and McKinley stood behind him, poised to run.

"Say, you boys," began the Marshal. "Do you live here?"

"Yeah," said Harold, trying to keep the tremor out of his voice.

"Well, let me tell you something. From now on when you have to wet or do the other you go into the house. You hear me?"

Harold glared defiantly at him.

"I say, did you hear me?"

"I ain't deaf, you old lard ass son-of-a-bitch."

"Why, Harold. Why, Harold," sang Gwendolin, standing all ears on the porch steps. "I'm gonna tell maw. I'm gonna tell maw."

"That's right, little girl. You go tell her and I hope she wears him out," said the Marshal. "And as for you, you mind what I tell you about that other."

And the Marshal stalked off in impotent rage.

"I'm gonna tell maw. I'm gonna tell maw on Harold," Gwendolin sang again.

"Ifen you do, you're one too," said Harold.

Gwendolin ran screaming into the house.

"Mam—maw—Harold said a bad word and he called me one too."

"Harold," said maw. "You come here . . . What did you say?"

Harold remained stubbornly silent.

"He said—" began Gwendolin.

"Hush," said maw. "What did you say, Harold?"

"He said large ass son-of-a-bitch," popped out Gwendolin.

"I've a mind to scrub your mouth too," said maw.

"I didn't say that," said Harold.

"What did you say?" said maw.

"I said lard ass son-of-a-bitch. And he is too."

"Well now," said maw. "Who did you hear say any such words as that?"

"Virginia."

"Virginia?"

"Yessum. When Fred come in last night."

Maw held him by the scruff of the neck and wrapped her finger in the hem of her dress and wet it and rubbed it across the yellow cake of laundry soap and held him kicking and squirming while she swabbed out his mouth and tongue.

Buddy was sitting in the upper hall staring out the front window when Hub turned in at the cut-off path. He blinked his eyes and the blood receded from his face and he looked again. He tried to get up from the chair in which he was sitting and overturned the chair and dropped his crutch clattering to the floor. He heard

Hub's feet cross the lower hall and mount the stairs and he watched from hands and knees as Hub's head appeared above the stair well.

"Hub," he said barely above a whisper. "Hub."

"Hello, Buddy-boy," said Hub, hurrying across the floor to him and picking him up and swinging him high in his arms.

He lowered Buddy and Buddy clung to him, laughing and crying in turn.

"What's the matter, feller? Ain't you glad to see me?"

Buddy only clung the tighter to Hub's neck.

"Got something fer you," said Hub. "Let's go in the room."

He carried Buddy across the hall and into the room where Reno lay on his pallet with the dirty strips of salve-coated sacking on his chest. Reno rolled his head at the disturbance and Hub went and stood over him.

"Hello, big boy," Hub said and Reno recognized him and mewled and mouthed inarticulate sounds of pleasure through his drooling lips.

Hub placed Buddy on the bed and untied the neck of the crocus sack he carried. He delved into it and retrieved a clean paper parcel and handed it to Buddy.

"More paints, feller," he said. "See how you like 'em."

Buddy gazed ecstatically at the huge square box of water-colors with the two neat rows of colored clay blocks and the one middle row of tube paints and the three brushes in graded sizes.

"What you been painting since I been gone?" said Hub.

144

"Ain't done much, Hub," said Buddy, tearing his eyes away from the opened box of paints. "Been waiting fer you to come home."

"Don't you ever wait fer me," said Hub. "You keep on a-painting, you hear?"

Buddy nodded his head and dropped his rapt gaze to the paints again.

"Is Rinno's chest any better?" said Hub.

"Nugh-ugh," said Buddy.

"Did they ever have a doctor with him?"

Buddy shook his head.

"Well, by God, I'm going to have one," said Hub. "Ain't no sense in them letting him lay here like this. You stay right here with him and I'll go git one right now."

"Well, Hub," said paw that night, "we're glad you're home again. Yes sir. Glad you're home. I was just a-telling your maw the other day you mought be in most any day now. How did you come out in Arkansaw?"

"Not so good," said Hub. "So many come in they started cutting prices on us."

"Did you git back with any money?"

"Not much," said Hub.

"Well, hit won't take much," said paw. "With this old raddio and about five dollars fer the down payment we ought to git us a pretty good 'un. And since Rinno cain't sit in his swing no more hit don't disturb him none to speak of."

"I ain't got five dollars," said Hub.

"He spent hit on a doctor fer Rinno this evening," said Gwendolin. "I seen him from Miz Jackson's room."

"Well now," said paw. "He'd oughtn't to have did that. We're doctoring Rinno right along. I've made arrangements fer old man Duncan to git us some stuff from that old nigger that lives next to him the next time he sees him."

Hub kept from saying anything but sat staring at the floor.

"Well," said paw at last. "I'm right disappointed."

Autumn gave way to winter drizzles and the mist collected on the brown limbs and bent them low and hung on them in almost globes of liquid ice. The early neon signs reflected green and red snake tracks across the paved square and cotton sprinkled with tinsel and small, too perfect Christmas trees filled the windows. Hurrying crowds went past with coat collars upturned against the freezing mist.

And in the country the neglected fields lay drear and weeping beneath the falling mist. The mist on the gray weeds formed edges of ice along each drooping blade and the mist melted the ice and it dropped to the black earth like silver tears. The ground was visible through the weary weeds and water stood between the rows. The soft gray of the plowshares turned dark and merged with the gray dampness and the smooth luster of the handles grew dull and lifeless, like forgotten ashes where a fire has been. And the winter winds sighed through the pines and swept in through the empty window sockets of the cabins, swirling into the cold hearths and scattering the dead ashes farther still into the empty rooms and whispering out past the open doors in their sagging frames.

Paw turned the collar of his threadbare coat higher and hunched his shoulders against the biting wind. He took his shovel from the box and blew on his numb fingers and straggled with the rest of his threadbare coated fellows over to the huge fire beside the ditch. He thrust first one foot, then the other toward the roaring logs and washed his hands in the flame.

"Hit's cold this morning."

"Wisht I had me a hog to kill."

"Wusht Ah had me a hawg t'eat."

"All right, you men," said the foreman. "I don't want you to get sick but we can't stand around that fire all day."

The men straggled over to the ditch and made a few half-hearted attacks on the hard ground with their shovels and returned one by one to the fire.

"Git some more wood, somebody. Git that plank we throwed outen the ditch yestiddy. Wisht we had us a good tree."

"We done cut down ever' thing in two mile."

Lord, the WPA. They make those old men go out on that ditch bank and stand around a great big fire eight hours every day and they have burned up every tree and piece of loose wood on that side of town. They even pulled those pieces of plank out that they use to keep the ditch bank from caving in and burned them and now they have done burned up old man Jones's barn and all them little privies behind them nigger houses of Mr. Brown's that the Board of Health made Mr. Brown build and they even pulled one of them down with a nigger setting in it.

Ten

Christmas had come and gone. The red-striped sticks of peppermint candy had been licked pink and dropped on the dirty floor and picked up brown-spotted and licked again, pink to white to nothing. McKinley and Harold and Buddy each had a knife, the girls each a cheap doll and the baby three ten-cent store toys. The commodity room had had an overplus of supplies and, after those on the regular list were doled out to, the Supervisors sent in the names of the workers and they lined up in the drizzle and each received a sack of apples and oranges which were put in the children's stockings hanging by the fireplaces Christmas morning.

Now Christmas was gone, the toys were stepped on and broken, the dolls neglected, and the knives rusting in the drizzle outside.

Maw came in the room after supper was cleared and the family was hovering about the remains of the meager dole of clinker coal. Paw sat with his feet outthrust to the grate and his wet shoes steaming. The children grew drowsy with the quietness of after supper and their pot bellies loaded again with badly cooked biscuits and sorghum molasses. Maw scrouged in between the children and bent over to the fire and pressed her red, roughened hands between her knees. Virginia lay back huge and uncomfortable on the bed with her legs dangling over the edge. Fred was out again.

"I declare," said maw, "hit's mighty nigh cold up here as it is in the kitchen."

"Hit was cold on the job today. We ain't gitting much done this kind of weather."

"I don't know how you stand it out there," said maw. "Hit's enough to make a body sick."

"Some of us has got right bad colds," said paw, "and I heard today that old man Black has done come down with the flu. Heard he was right sick too."

"Hit's a blessing you ain't come down with nothing," said maw. "What with ever' body done got Four Oh Three'd 'cep'n you and Fred hit would make it right worrisome trying to feed ever' body without nobody working. Them 'moddities don't help much."

"No sir, they don't," said paw. "A man cain't do no work on apples and celery and such. A man needs bread and molasses and stuff."

"That's right," said maw. "And thank the Lord ain't none of the chillun come down with nothing too. And I been kind of worried about McKinley. He ain't been any too peart the last few days. Seems to me he's gitting kind of peaked like. Thank goodness Hub's here again to take Rinno offen my hands. Hub's right good about staying up here with Rinno. Hangs around over Rinno amusing him near all day and course Buddy's right clost to Hub as he kin git."

"How does Rinno 'pear to be doing since I got that last stuff from old man Duncan?"

"Hub ain't never used none of it. He's been using some more of that sa've the doctor give him."

"Is hit doing any good?"

"I ast Hub this morning and he said he believed hit was but hit was mighty slow. He said the doctor told him the stiller Rinno kept the sooner he'd git well."

"Where is Hub?"

"Him and Buddy done already turnt in out in the hall, I guess," maw said. "He greased Rinno up right good just before you come in and Rinno went off to sleep. I ain't seen him and Buddy since supper."

"Well," said paw, "I believe Hub's making a mistake spending all that money on Rinno."

"He ain't spent much money, now," said maw. "He's been a-working some fer that doctor and the doctor gives him the sa've."

"Well, that's some different," said paw. "Still and all hit looks like ifen he's bound and determined to work he could git some money outen it."

"Hit looks like Rinno is staying right quiet anyhow," said maw.

"We don't want none of us gitting down sick," said paw. "We ain't gitting to work but about half the time now and we ain't got no money fer no sickness."

"Money does seem to be right sca'ce," said maw. "And

151

with us having to help out the rest of the folks here with flour, a sack don't last any too long neither. I don't think we need to worry none about the chillun though. Soon's I seen McKinley gitting sort of droopy I got some turpentine from the store and wormed 'em all good. I aimed to do it a little later on anyhow and since he was already ailing I thought I just might as well go ahead and do hit now and git through with it. Virginia too. I just took her right in with the rest of 'em. She needs to be in good shape ifen she aims to have a easy time with that baby. Hit ain't long off neither. How long off is it, Virginia? How fur did we count the other day?"

"Oh, I don't know," said Virginia, heaving herself clumsily over on her side, "but I'll be so damn glad to get rid of it I wish it would come right now."

"Now, Virginia," said paw. "Now, Virginia."

"I don't care," said Virginia. "I don't care. You try carrying one of them around in your belly for nine months with it trying to pull the muscles loose from your backbone."

"Now, Virginia. Now, Virginia."

"Where is Fred, Virginia?" said maw.

"I don't know," said Virginia, "and I don't care."

The fire burned down and they inched in closer and closer to the hearth.

"We better git to bed fore hit goes plumb out," said maw. Then to Virginia, "How come Gwendolin and Eugenia cain't git in the bed with you, Virginia, and then the boys could move in from the hall and git in the girls' bed and we could all have some extry cover?"

"With me and this baby this bed's full," said Virginia. "There ain't even room for Fred in it any more. Maybe that's the reason he quit coming home at nights."

And she sat up on the edge of the bed and sullenly removed her outer clothes and then lay back down awkwardly and pulled the cotton quilts over her.

The children rose, except McKinley, and he continued to sit staring listlessly into the fire.

"Git up, McKinley," said maw. "You git on to bed."

McKinley raised his too large eyes to maw.

"My head hurts, maw," he said.

Maw stooped and felt his hot forehead.

"Hit feels like you got fever," said maw, "but I cain't tell with you setting right up in the fire. You go on to bed and you'll feel better in the morning."

McKinley rose and dragged out into the hall and crawled into bed between Harold and Jutland after removing only his shoes.

"I'm right worried about McKinley," said maw as she settled herself in bed. "I'm beginning to be afeared he's fixing to git took sick."

McKinley was sick the next morning and maw brought him into the room and put him on the girls' pallet. He was flushed and feverish and his lips were dry.

"I'll keep him wropped up good," said maw, "and I speck he'll feel better tonight."

McKinley lay on the musty-smelling pallet on the floor throughout the day and his fever subsided somewhat, leaving him beaded with sweat and a pasty greenish color.

The women from the other rooms came in and sat and dipped snuff and spat into the smoldering coals in the fireplace and the room stank of unwashed bodies and snuff spit and fever.

"I mind one time when my oldest born was sick," said Mrs. Jackson. "He turnt the curiousest color, 'bout like McKinley is now. That was about two weeks afore he died with them convulsions. He were a right bright little feller too until he was took with his last sickness."

The other women sat and nodded their heads in solemn confirmation. Maw sat on the edge of the bed and said, "Well, I do know."

"That oldest boy of Miz Perkinses had a spell some similar to McKinley's. When he were a little mite of a feller. I believe the doctor called hit the yellow johndice. He got over hit all right but he ain't never been just right since."

"Well, I do know," said maw.

"Them yellow sicknesses always has a kind of peculiar smell," said Mrs. Jackson. "I rec'lect when my boy passed on. We could smell hit almost down to the barn."

They sat and nodded and spat and McKinley lay on the pallet and sweat beaded his face and dampened the filthy bedclothes.

"Have you tried oil yit, Miz Taylor?"

"Well, no, ma'am. Not just yit. I told paw to stop by the grocer store this evening and git a bottle."

"That's the best thing fer a sickness like McKinley 'pears to have."

"Or any other kind of sickness fer that matter. I rec'lect when that second girl of Miz Wesley's had that appendicitis. She was a-laying there drawed up in a knot with her stummick a-hurting fit to kill and Miz Wesley a-standing there wringing her hands. I come in about that time and took right a-holt. Got that bottle of oil and warmed hit and give that girl the whole bottle at one dose. I told the doctor when he finally got there that ifen I had of been there at the start we never would of had to send fer him and he said that was right. If he had of knowed I give her that castor oil he wouldn't have bothered to come a tall."

The women sat the morning out and at noon rose and stood over McKinley in peering inspection.

"I believe he's a mite greener," said Mrs. Jackson, "but I don't believe his fever's quite so high."

"I believe just a-laying here quiet-like is the best thing fer him," said one of the other women.

"We'll be back in this evening to set with you again," said Mrs. Jackson.

"Well, that'll be right narce of you," said maw. "I just don't know what I'd do without you all. A good neighbor is a sight of comfort in times of trouble."

Dinner. And then the women came back to sit again and nod and spit onto the hearth.

"I do believe his fever's mountin'," said one of the women.

And they all rose and went and stood over McKinley

and watched him shiver and shake beneath the dirty cotton blankets.

"Hain't you a-feared Rinno will ketch whatever hit is McKinley's got, Miz Taylor?"

"Well now," said maw. "I ain't never just thought about hit that way. Hub's been a-looking after Rinno."

"I seen Hub going out early this morning. He working some'ers?"

"Well, yessum. Leastways he's working out a doctor bill fer Rinno."

The women all shook their heads ponderously.

"I don't take much truck in them citified doctor ways. The old-fashioned tried and proved remedies is best," said one.

"That's what paw 'lows," said maw.

"Ain't you feared fer Buddy to be a-setting out in that cold hall all day like he done today?" queried another.

"Well now," said maw, "when Hub's out seems like they won't nothing do Buddy but he must set out there a-watching fer him. He'll be in soon's Hub gits home."

"He's allus been pow'ful peaked," said Mrs. Jackson. "I believe ifen he was mine I'd bring him in forcible."

"Well, hit looks like hit hurts him wusser to not watch fer Hub then hit does to set out there. I got him wropped up good in a quilt."

The women left soon after and paw came in with the bottle of castor oil and maw gave McKinley half the bottle and smoothed the blankets around him and he dropped off at last into a fitful, nervous sleep.

156

"Now, I just ain't going to let McKinley sleep out in that cold windy hall tonight," said maw as they prepared for bed. "I just ain't a-going to do it and that's all they are to it."

"Well now, maw," said paw, "when you git your head set hit ain't no use argying with you."

"We'll just move the girls' pallet up in front of the fire and put the boys' pallet here agin the wall."

She stumped out into the hall and gathered up the ragged clammy-feeling bedclothes that the boys slept on and came and dumped them on the floor by Virginia's bed and sent Jutland and Harold back for the lumpy cotton mattress.

"I'll just make the boys' bed here by the fire and the girls can have it and Jut and Harold kin just git in with McKinley and we won't even have to disturb him."

"What you going to do about Hub and Buddy?" said paw.

"I ast 'em ifen they wanted to come in here and they said they'd just stay out in the hall. Hub's done greased Rinno fer the night and turnt him on his off side and he won't need to be disturbed."

Virginia was already in her bed on her side with her back turned to the room and Fred's pillow stuffed under the burden she was carrying in her belly. Gwendolin and Eugenia slipped off their worn shoes and their thin worn cloaks and slid in under the covers of the pallet in front of the fire and Jutland and Harold ripped out of their woolen CCC shirts and overalls and heavy shoes and raised the cover on each side of McKinley and hunched themselves under it. Paw's snores already filled the room and maw had given the baby his night's feeding and was about asleep when Jutland raised up in the dying glow of the fire and kicked out from under the cover. Maw waked to full awareness instantly.

"What is it?" she said.

"Me and Harold cain't sleep in here with McKinley. He smells so we cain't even git to sleep. Why cain't Gwendolin and Eugenia git in the bed with Virginia? They ain't no use in her taking a whole bed."

"Well now," said maw. "Virginia's got to be took care of in her condition."

"I don't care," said Jutland. "We cain't sleep here."

"I can't sleep with them in here," came from Virginia's bed. "They'll kick me."

"Well, we cain't sleep here," said Jutland, getting to his feet and moving close in to the fire.

"Virginia," said maw, "hit looks like you might make a little allowance just fer tonight. Let Jut and Harold git in with you. Maybe by in the morning McKinley will be feeling better."

"Oh, all right," said Virginia. "Come on in then if you're such a big baby."

"Being a baby ain't got nothing to do with having to sleep with that smell," said Jutland and he crawled in by Virginia, and Harold, who had been awake and listening, slid out from beside McKinley and came and crawled in by Jutland.

"Now, for the Lord's sake, keep still," said Virginia.

The next morning when maw shivered her way down

the cold dank stairs to the kitchen she met Mrs. Jackson in the lower hall.

"How does McKinley 'pear to be this morning, Miz Taylor?" she said.

"Well now," said maw, "hit's most too dark to tell right good yit but I hope he's better."

"Yes sum, I hope so too. I feel right sorry fer the little feller."

She thought a moment, then said, "Rinno ain't caught it yit, is he?"

"Well, no'm. Not yit. They all 'peared to have a right restful night."

"Us women folks had a prayer fer you in your trials and tribulations last night in my room, Miz Taylor."

"Well now," said maw. "That was right narce of you and I thank you kindly."

Maw went on into the kitchen and cooked the breakfast and while the rest of the family ate she took a bowl of soup, made of chipped-up commodity cabbage and a small piece of fat back and greasy water, up to the room to McKinley. She brought the unappetizing broth back untouched.

"I declare, I wisht McKinley would eat a little something," she said. "I allus heard, Stuff a cold and starve a fever. McKinley ain't rightly got no cold, but I might of broke his fever with this soup."

"He cain't eat nothing a tall?" said paw.

"He 'pears to kind of shrink from it," said maw.

"Maybe Rinno would like that soup," said Buddy from his place beside Hub.

"Well now," said maw. "I never thought of that. I been use to feeding him after ever' body gits through. He were already awake too. And kind of fussing."

"Maybe Hub better go see 'bout him," said paw.

"I will 'fore I leave," said Hub.

"You working fer that doctor again today?" asked paw.

"Yes sir," said Hub.

Paw's check came that morning and he cashed it and took five dollars and had the radio fixed.

"I most got out of touch with my job here lately," he said that night. "Ain't been able to keep up with the news and stuff since we busted this raddio. How does McKinley 'pear to be today?"

"McKinley ain't perked up none to speak of. He's turnt a curiouser color even than he was yestiddy. Kind of purplish like. I just don't know hardly what to make of it."

"I do believe he smells a mite stronger too," said paw.

"Yes sir," said maw. "Miz Jackson was speaking of hit this morning. Said they could even smell hit right plain downstairs."

"I wonder ifen we couldn't move him out into the hall just until he gits better," said paw.

"I'm a-feared to, paw. With them window lights gone that the chillun knocked outen the front door sash hit's too cold out there."

"Well," said paw, "maybe he will be better tomorrow if we kin just last it out."

"I hope so," said maw.

160

But the next morning McKinley was not better. He lay flushed with fever, his eyes overbright and his cheeks almost red.

"I just declare," said maw. "He's turning red now. Paw, I'm gitting right worried. You reckon we better have a doctor?"

"Well now, maw. Doctors is fer rich folks. You know we ain't got no money fer no doctors."

"Well," said maw. "I wisht we could have one. I give McKinley the last of them aspirins. You better git me another box from the grocer store. Maybe Gwendolin better go along with you and bring 'em back now."

"Let's open the door, maw," said Virginia. "That smell's awful."

"That's what I say," said Jutland.

"Well," said maw, "I don't just know whether that's the right thing to do fer McKinley or not, but I reckon hit won't hurt him just fer a minute."

"I believe I'll move back into the hall," said Jutland.

"I believe we're all going to have to," said paw, "ifen McKinley don't kind of simmer down some."

Paw left and Gwendolin got her cloak and hurried after him. Jutland stood at the door and fanned it back and forth until Virginia said, "That's enough. Do you want to freeze us all out?"

"I'd druther be cold as to set here and smell McKinley much longer."

Gwendolin came back with the box of aspirin and maw started giving the small white tablets to McKinley at spaced intervals. His fever broke and as the red faded it left his skin with a yellowish tinge beneath the beads of sweat.

"Well, I just declare," said maw. "I never seen anything like McKinley. He turns a different color ever' day."

Fred came in that night after the family was in bed. Maw waked at the first creak of the door.

"Who is it?" she said.

Fred made no answer but felt his way across the fire glow to Virginia's bed. He sat down on the edge of it to take off his shoes and Jutland squirmed under him.

"What the hell?" he said, rising quickly to his feet and turning to face the bed. He stumbled over Gwendolin's foot and she cried out, startled.

Maw walked on familiar feet between the pallets and lit the lamp by the door. Virginia lay on the far side of the bed watching Fred. Maw stood in her knit unions and her hand on the wick adjuster and Jutland and Harold stared up at Fred with blinking sleep-filled eyes.

"What is this?" said Fred.

McKinley stirred uneasily in his sleep.

"And what is that I smell?"

"Get out of here," said Virginia. "Go back to your beer and your jook houses and your girls. I know where you've been."

Fred turned to maw.

"What is that I smell?"

"Hit's McKinley," said maw. "He's sick."

"He smells like he's dead," said Fred.

"Get out of here," said Virginia again and she threw

back the covers and started crawling over Jutland and Harold.

"Get back in that bed, Virginia," said maw. "You get back there 'fore you strain yourself."

"Get out of here," repeated Virginia and she stooped for one of the heavy shoes by the bed.

Fred fled across the room and through the door and the shoe hit the jamb by his head.

Virginia stood as she was when the shoe left her hand, a puzzled expression on her face. Then sweat beaded her forehead and a soundless scream burst from her distended lips.

"Maw," she said. "Maw."

And she slumped to the floor by the bed.

That bunch of WPA folks in that big house below the City Hall. It's— They— The damnedest— Well, I'll tell you. It just beats anything I ever heard of. The man that lives in the house below them was going home the other night about ten o'clock and some fellow come running out the door and he heard this screaming coming from inside the big house and he stopped and the screaming stopped and pretty soon the screaming started again and he could see the folks inside running up and down the stairs with lamps in their hands and the screaming would stop and start again and he went up on the porch and opened the door and he said it was the damnedest smell he ever smelt. Like to have knocked him over and the women were running in and out the kitchen with tin buckets of water in their hands and running up and down the stairs and he caught one and said, What the hell's going on in here? and the one he caught said, She's a-having it. She's a-having it, and he said, Having what? and she said, Having that baby, and he started then to go on home, the damn place smelled so bad, and then he thought maybe he better find out a little more about it on account of that smell and he caught another one by the arm and said, Is that her I smell? and she said, No. That's that boy you smell, and he said, What boy? and she said, Miz Taylor's boy, and he said, Is that Mrs. Taylor having that baby? and she said, No. That's Miz Taylor's daughter having the baby, and he said, Then what is Mrs. Taylor's boy smelling so for? and she said, That's the one that turnt all the different colors, and then he turnt her loose and started to leave again and then he sort of pulled his hat on tighter and started up the stairs and the screaming going on and off all the time and he said the higher up the stairs he got the worse the smell got, and when he got to the top of the stairs he seen all them women with the buckets of water running in and out one of the rooms and these men all standing in the door looking into the room, and every time one of the women would run in or out the men would make a path and watch the woman run through and then close the path back up and look into the room again, and nobody saying a word except this screaming that would start and stop, and he elbowed his way up in the knot of men and they thought he was another one of them women and they made a path for him and he walked into the room and there on a pile of old

164

quilts in front of the fireplace was this girl having a baby and some old woman helping her have it, and these two little girls hunkered back on their knees on the same pallet the girl was having the baby on crying—the little girls crying, not the girl having the baby, she was too busy screaming and trying to catch her breath between screams so's she could scream again—and these two boys leaning over the edge of a bed right above the girl watching her with their faces all white and scared-looking and another boy—the sick one, he said he reckoned he was because he was kind of greenish yellow and the smell was stronger the closer you got to his side of the room—and a old man—one of them WPA-ers, he said he looked like—on the other bed—they was two beds and two pallets in the room—with even his hat and jumper still on and the covers all throwed off of 'im and his head stuck under a pillow with the curled-up brim of his hat sticking out and some kind of a man, he said he reckoned it was, half rolled up in a old torn quilt and pushed up under the edge of the bed the old man was on. This thing, whatever it was, was about seven foot tall even all crumpled up like a bundle of old sticks and had a big dirty white head about as wide as it was long and a black beard right around its mouth and looked like pig bristles sticking flat out from the top of its head. He said he never seen anything like it. Arms and legs sticking out the holes in the quilt looked like match stems. And all that excitement must have made it mad 'cause it was bellering and croaking and rolling its head, and this little crippled boy all scrouged back in a corner with his face all white and scared-looking, and crying, and just about then here come some feller in, hollering, God damn it, get out of the way, and pushing folks to the right and left, and he had a doctor by the hand dragging him along behind him.

Eleven

A Citizens' Committee called on the Mayor early the next morning.

Looka here, they said. About these WPA people in that big brown house below the City Hall. Something has got to be done about it. They lay around on pallets on the floor and get sick and turn different colors and have babies and smell to the high heavens and we want something done about it.

And the Mayor said, Sure. We'll take care of it.

And the Citizens said, See that you do.

And the Mayor knew the Citizens meant what they said and so he called a meeting of the Board of Aldermen and the Public Health Department, and he said:

Looka here. A Citizens' Committee came to see me this morning and they said we must do something about this bunch of WPA workers that live in that big brown house next door.

And the Board of Aldermen said, Sure. We'll take care of it.

And the Mayor was scared and said, You don't understand. They mean it this time.

And the Board of Aldermen said, Oh.

And the Board of Health said, Why are we called in here?

And the Mayor said, They had a baby over there last night.

And the Board of Health said, They had a baby over there last night.

And the Mayor said, They had it on the floor. On a pallet. With a boy sick on another pallet, turning different colors and smelling bad.

And the Board of Health said, I see.

It was Friday night that the baby was born and since no WPA projects are scheduled to operate on Saturdays paw was at home when they came. They came down from the City Hall in an important group, the Mayor and a committee of two from the Board of Aldermen and two from the Board of Health and they turned in at the path across the yard. They mounted the steps to the porch and the Mayor knocked at the door. They heard the stealthy movements inside the house and caught glimpses of the surreptitious heads in the edges of the windows. The Mayor knocked again.

"Who is it?" whispered a woman in the front room to one of the heads in the window.

"Some them fellers from up to the City Hall," said the head in the window, who was her husband.

"What they want?"

"I cain't tell yit."

"Want I should send Junior out there?"

"I guess you might's well. Looks like they ain't going to leave."

Junior came out into the hall and opened the door and stood with his hand on the knob.

"Sonny, is your daddy at home?" said the Mayor as they entered.

"Yessir. Paw's to home."

The inner hall doors cracked open and the men in the rooms peered at the committee in the hall through the cracks.

"Well, can we see your—er—paw?"

"Yes sir. I guess you kin," said Junior, continuing to stand with his hand on the knob.

"Well, go call him for us," said the Mayor.

Junior turned and walked to his room door and opened it and disappeared inside. After about five minutes his father came out of the room.

"Good morning," greeted the Mayor in forced good humor.

"Morning," said the man.

"Er—I'm the Mayor of this City and these men are a Board of Investigation. We've come down to—er—sort of look around."

The man stood watching them, waiting.

"Er—how many of you families live here?"

"About seven now," said the man.

"You mean some new families have moved in lately?"

"No sir. Some has left lately."

"Good God," said the Board of Health.

169

"Did you have any trouble with your water works this last cold spell?" continued the Mayor.

"No sir."

"Well, that's fine," said the Mayor. "Some of the people here in town had trouble with theirs freezing. Yours didn't freeze?"

"No sir. They weren't no water in it."

"Good God," said the Board of Health again. Then, "Do you mind if we look at your toilet room?"

"Our which?"

"Your toilet—your wash room."

"Oh. No sir. Hit's right off the back-porch."

They followed him through the stale greasy smell of the kitchen and across the biting north wind of the back-porch and into the small cupboard off the back-porch that was added on after the house was built to contain the commode and bathtub. The man opened the door and the committee peered in. The stained toilet-bowl was empty and dry and the tub was black with coal dust and a few forlorn lumps of clinker coal lay in the bottom of it.

"What in the world do you use for a toilet?" asked the Board of Health.

The man included the back-yard in a sweeping gesture.

"We just uses out in the back here."

"Good God-o-Mighty," said the Board of Health.

They walked back into the kitchen and the Board of Health paused at the dry sink piled with dirty dishes

170

and littered with scraps of food. A pan of biscuits burnt to black cinders sat on the small wood range.

"What do you do for water to cook with?" asked the Board of Health.

"We gits it from over to that little concrete trough in front the Hall with them little fishes in it."

"You mean every time you want a bucket of water you have to go over there?"

"Well, no sir. We fills them two barrels up and just uses outen them till hit gives out, then goes and fills them again."

The Board of Health walked over to the two oil drums sitting behind the stove and peered down into them. One was empty save for an inch of rust flakes and purple-scummed water and the other was nearly half full, but it too had its scum of stagnancy.

The Board of Health raised their heads and looked at each other and then at the Mayor and the rest of the Committee who stood waiting in the door and then the whole Investigation Committee walked back into the hall followed by the man.

"Where did that girl have the baby last night?" said the Mayor.

"Upstairs in Miz Taylor's room."

"Is she still up there?"

"No sir. They come and taken her to the hospittle."

"Well, thank the Lord for that."

"How about that boy that turned all the different colors?" said the Mayor.

"They taken him too."

"Well, God bless the hospital," said the Board of Health fervently.

"Where is the father of the girl?" asked the Mayor.

"He's upstairs I reckon," said the man.

"Would you mind calling him for us?"

The man turned without a word and mounted the stairs. They heard his footsteps cross the upstairs hall and stop at the door, then heard the door open and the unintelligible sounds of a conversation, then two pairs of feet crossing the hall. They watched first the brogans, then the length of blue denim-clad legs grow longer and longer and merge into blue jumpers and swinging hands as the two men descended the stairs. Then two brown faces appeared below the upper hall floor. Two faces unlike save for identical expressions of bewilderment and diffidence and mild resentment.

"Are you the father of the girl that had the baby here last night?" asked the Mayor when they stood on the floor with them at last.

"Yes sir," said paw.

"I'm the Mayor."

"How do," said paw, extending a limp hand that the Mayor took.

The hand was hooked and rough and nebulous as dried and rotting twigs and the Mayor had a vague sense of discomfort as paw pumped his hand twice and stopped. The Mayor released paw's hand and rubbed his own hand against his leg.

"These gentlemen and myself came down here this morning to see something about the sanitary conditions of the house," said the Mayor. "We're proud of our City, Mr. Taylor, and like to keep it clean and healthy. We notice that you have been using the back-yard for a toilet and that the water in your bathroom is cut off."

"Well now," said paw, "since a bunch of us have been Four Oh Three'd we ain't been able to keep the place in just the shape we would like to. About keeping the lights and water on and stuff."

"You mean some of you are not working now?"

"Well, yes sir. Quite a few of us have got Four Oh Three's."

"How many of you here in the house have been laid off?"

"Well now, about six of us."

"You mean to say that there's only one man out of the seven living here that has a job?"

"Well, yes sir. That's just about right."

"Are you still working?"

"Well, yes sir. I'm about the only one that ain't been Four Oh Three'd."

"How long have these other men been off?"

"Well now, that's hard to say just exactly. Some since last summer and then they's some that ain't been off but only about two month."

"And the ones that are not working. They just sit here?"

"Well, yes sir," said paw.

"How do you eat? How do you pay rent? You surely can't pay the whole rent with just one man working."

"Well, not just exactly all. Of course maw gives the

173

other womenfolks here the loan of a little flour and coffee and stuff ever' now and then, and as soon's the men gits Four Oh Three'd the lady at the employment office puts 'em on the 'moddity roll."

"But how do you pay rent?"

"Well now, the feller that used to come fer the rent has been right nice about it. We all worried a whole lot about it when we fust started gitting Four Oh Three'd. He seemed like he was right worried at one time too but he ain't been around in quite a spell now."

"Why do these men keep staying in town when they get fired? Why don't they go on back to the country? They all moved in from the country, didn't they?"

"Well, yes sir," said paw, "but they are ever' one expecting to git back on the WP and A most any day now. Mr. Will is kind of looking out fer 'em."

"Mr. Will? Who is Mr. Will?"

"You know. Mr. Will over to the Hall."

"Well," said the Mayor, "I tell you what I'm going to do. You tell all these men to come over to the City Hall to the Social Worker's office the first thing Monday morning and I'm going to see myself if they can't be put back to work. And I'm going over to the City Hall right now and tell them to cut this water back on. I don't care what you keep in that tub, but you all use that commode and stop er—using—in the back-yard. I'll send the City truck down here this morning to clean up. Is there anything else?" he said to the Committee.

"We'd better come in here and fumigate this whole house," said the Board of Health, "and if the City has any sort of a contingency fund, why in the name of the Lord can't we give them about five dollars apiece to get them some coal and something to eat besides those damned stalks of celery the Commodity Room gives them every Saturday morning?"

"Well," said the Mayor, "that's as good a place to put the City's money as any place I know but we will have to call a meeting of the Board to allow it."

"Here," said the elder member of the Board of Health, pulling his pocketbook from his pocket. "Here's ten dollars to start the pot."

"And here's ten," said the Mayor.

"And five."

And the thirty-five dollar pot was made up.

"You take this, Mr. Taylor, and give five dollars to each man in the house."

"Well now," said paw. "I don't know whether we could just rightly take money like that."

"Why not?" said the Board of Health.

"Well, we're all just WP and A folks and we ain't none of us never took no char'ty."

"Why, the whole WPA is for relief."

"Yes sir. But we work for what they give us."

"Haven't any of you ever taken any of the commodities that they give?"

"Well, yes sir. But them's just apples and celeries and stuff that the folks what raised 'em had too many and give 'em to the gove'ment and the gove'ment gives 'em to us."

"Just take it as a loan then," said the Board of Health.

"Well now," said paw. "Just wait until I can sort of talk it over with the men."

"You take this and just tell the men it's a loan and they can pay it back out of their first checks," said the Board of Health.

"Well now, on a proposition like that I believe the men will be glad to git it, sort of. You can make some papers out on it and the men kin sign up fer it when they come to the Hall Monday morning."

Paw stood in the hall with the money in his hand and watched the Committee leave. As their steps died away down the walk the hall doors opened and the men all came out of their rooms.

"Well, men," said paw. "The City has done loaned us all five dollars apiece just until we kin git back to working again. I figgered we could all use a little spare change since most of us ain't back at work yit so I completed the deal fer the five dollars apiece and we kin all go by the Hall fust thing Monday morning and sign up fer hit."

Paw issued each man five dollars and stuck his own carefully folded bill in his pocket.

Now, he thought. Now, I kin git that big raddio that feller tried to trade me the other day.

The Mayor was waiting on the front steps of the City Hall the next Monday morning when the men came up.

"Are you the men from that big house over there?"

"Yes sir."

"You all follow me then."

176

He turned and mounted the steps and walked down the long hall to the Social Worker's office and opened the door without knocking. The Social Worker, breakfastless and with her toilet not quite complete, was seated behind her desk and the Mayor held the door open while the six men filed in and then shut the door behind them and slipped the bolt to.

"These are the men I called you about this morning," he said to the Social Worker. "Will you see if they're all certified?"

"Just give me your names please," said the Social Worker.

"You'd ought to know our names by now," said one of the men. "Much as we been up here."

"I know your faces well enough," said the Social Worker, "but I don't know all your names."

They gave their names shyly, defiantly, and she riffled through her files and said to the Mayor, "Yes sir. They are all certified."

"Follow me then," said the Mayor and they followed him back down the stairs and into the clerk's office.

It was too early for the Tupelo office to be open yet so the Mayor called the District Engineer at his home.

"Look here," he said. "I've got six men here that I want to put on the WPA today . . . Quota reduction? . . . I don't care what kind of reduction you got from Jackson, I want these men put to work. . . . You send work cards for these men and I'll take care of you in Jackson. . . . I don't care what the Placement Officer or any other kind of officer told you yesterday or any other time, I want these men put to work. . . . All right, I'll call Jackson. I'll call Washington. But you have those cards in today's mail. I'll get you the authority to issue them. I'll have it there by the time you get down to your office. Have you got a pencil? . . . All right. Take these names . . . Got 'em? Much obliged. I hated to have to call you but this is one thing that has to be done and that's all there is to it. Good-by."

He turned to the men.

"All right, you men. Your cards will be here tomorrow. And for my sake, keep that house from getting back in the mess it was."

"You can count on us fer that," they said. "Now about that paper fer that five dollars . . ."

"Just forget about it. You can pay it back when you get your checks."

"Well now, we'd druther sign that paper."

"Well, I haven't made it out yet. I'll get the clerk to fix it up some time today and you can come in late this evening and sign it."

"Well now, ifen hit ain't too much trouble, we'd druther sign hit now."

"Oh, Lord. All right. Let me type it out for you."

He typed the note and each one signed it.

"Well, I guess that fixes it," said the Mayor.

"Yes sir. Hit makes hit a heap more businesslike that way."

"I guess I got the date on this right. The twenty-first. That's the day you get your checks, ain't it?"

"Well now, these checks will be pretty short being's

we ain't going to git the full period in. Maybe we better just fix out two of them papers and then ifen we cain't pay the whole five dollars the fust check we kin ketch hit up next time."

"No," said the Mayor. "No. Just pay it if you can and if you can't pay it we'll just—er—catch the whole thing up some other time."

"Well now, ifen hit's all the same to you we'd druther—"

The doctor and Hub and maw stood beneath the dim glare of the one yellow ceiling bulb in the reception hall of the hospital. Hub was facing the doctor and maw stood to the rear and a little to one side of him. One of paw's old felt hats was perched on the top of her head, riding her brow in front and held up in the rear by the careless knot of stringy hair. The brim was turned up fore and aft and the rain that had fallen on her on her way to the hospital dripped from the lopped-down sides on to the padded shoulders of her man's coat. Her snuff stick dangled loose in the corner of her mouth and her face was sagged with bewilderment and pained concentration and her hands were clasped limply in the up-turned fold of her dress and water dripped and puddled to the floor from the hem of her dirty petticoat.

Hub's eyes, filled with dread certainty, were glued to the doctor's face, which was beaded with the sweat of foreseen disaster.

"You see, it's like this, Hub," said the doctor. "I have no connection with this hospital and the State only allows money from the Charity Fund to hospitals. Of course I could work it through this hospital if there was any money, but the Charity Fund has been exhausted for over two months now and no new money will be available until after July the first. This hospital is overdrawn on its allotment already. The doctor in charge is more than willing to give his time and you know I am and will gladly, but there's no money for ether and X-rays, the necessary things like that. I would let you have the money but I haven't got it. I'm still paying the bank back for the money I borrowed to go to medical school and I have to support my mother besides, and I'll tell you honest, I'm stripped clean."

"But I thought Virginia was gitting along fine," said maw as the doctor paused.

"It's not Virginia," said the doctor, not taking his glance from the mask of agony that was Hub's face.

"But McKinley 'peared to be all right," said maw.

"It's not McKinley either," said the doctor.

"Buddy," said Hub, and the flesh of his face drew taut against the bony substructure as his lips formed the word.

Now, he thought. Now, I've said it and it's so. Neither one of us would say it, to keep it from being so. But now I've said it. Buddy. Buddy. Buddy. Now see if anything can ever hurt again. It's Buddy.

"Buddy?" said maw. "Why, I never knowed nothing was wrong with Buddy 'cep'n he had a mite of fever from sleeping in that hall. I was mostly worried about Virginia and McKinley."

"You needn't ever worry about Virginia again," said the doctor. "If you all couldn't kill her the other night, she'll never die just from natural carelessness, and as for McKinley, all he needed was a complete sterilization."

"Well, I do know," said maw. "I would never have thought of that."

"No," said the doctor. "I don't believe you would," and his eyes returned to Hub's face.

"When does it need to be done?" said Hub, oblivious of everything but his own despair, which was mirrored in the doctor's face.

"The sooner we operate the better his chances are and they are slim enough at best," said the doctor, reaching out an understanding hand for Hub's shoulder.

Hub wheeled quickly from under the doctor's hand lest the friendly touch destroy what little was left of his innate, diffident reserve and he display to the doctor's kind eye the agony that was in his soul.

"O.K., Doc," he said with his hand on the doorknob. "You get him ready. I'll get the money. Maw, you wait here."

He whipped the door open and slipped through it and it slammed behind him on soundless shock cushions and he was gone into the night and the drizzle.

"Hub!" called the doctor, striding forward with his hand still outstretched. "Hub."

"Well," said maw, backing out of the doctor's way and collapsing on the leather divan next the wall. "Well, I do know."

The doctor turned to maw.

"Has he got any money?" he said quickly.

"Well now," said maw. "He went over to Arkansaw picking cotton last fall, but I never knowed he had none the money left. He didn't git back with much and he give you that about Rinno."

"Where has he gone, then?" said the doctor.

"Well now, I just couldn't tell you," said maw.

The doctor stood with arms lax at his sides staring at the floor and maw leaned forward and tugged at the sleeve of his white coat.

"What's wrong with Buddy, doctor? I never knowed he was sick."

"It's the result of the infantile paralysis he had. It's imperative that we operate if he is to live."

"Well, I declare," said maw. "I allus knowed he wasn't strong-like but he was allus so content with them colors Hub kep' a-giving him I thought he just liked to draw better'n play. Why, I never knowed he was sick."

"He's a pretty sick boy, Mrs. Taylor. His condition was already very delicate and the exposure he's gone through this winter topped off by the excitement the other night was just too much for him."

"Well, I do know," said maw, sinking back into the padded leather. The doctor squared his shoulders and turned on a brisk heel and went down the white tunnel of the hall, rolling up his sleeves.

Hub walked with quick, purposeful stride past the darkened store fronts until he came to the recessed entrance to the drugstore. He paused and cast a quick look over his shoulder back the way he had come, then ducked quickly into the alcové before the doors. He stuck his head cautiously past the line of store fronts and took one final survey of the sidewalks on each side, then turned to the door and hit the glass by the lock a quick blow with a sack-wrapped brick. The glass shattered and tinkled to the floor inside and Hub ran an exploring hand in through the jagged hole and worked the bolt and opened the door. He swung the door wide as he entered and felt his way along the soda fountain to the cash register and his extended hand found the partly open drawer and the sack of money and it closed over the neck of the sack and lifted it carefully. A small sound from the door caused him to whirl and the sack hit against the edge of the fountain with a muffled clink. A flashlight clicked on and its beam probed the depths of the store as Hub dropped quickly to the floor behind the fountain.

"Come out of there with your hands up," ordered a gruff voice from behind the light.

Hub listened to his heart hammering above the tense stillness of the store and he held his breath until his ears strained with its pent-up roaring.

"Come on out, now. I know you're in there. I heard the glass fall when you broke in the door. Come on out now, I say."

The apex of the light beam moved inside the open door. Hub watched the weaving slice of light—that he could see between the ends of the soda fountain and the cigar case on which the cash register sat—grow narrower and pick the minute unevenness of the floor into sharper relief. He held low to the floor and moved to the front of the store behind the fountain, slipping his feet carefully over the noiseless marble. The silhouette of a pair of sturdy legs was between Hub and the backward pointing beam of light as he rounded the end of the fountain and straightened up and stepped quickly and silently toward the door. The man with the flashlight turned his head and glimpsed Hub, and Hub saw the barrel of the pistol rise into the whirling light and saw the wide, flat, tapering shadow leap toward him along the floor. Hub jerked for the opening and his back framed by the door was outlined in black against the wet reflection of the street lights and the gun belched as he felt the hot band laid against his taut side. He staggered and caught his balance and whirled behind the protection of the outside store front and was gone.

Maw was still seated on the leather divan when Hub entered the front door. He came in breathless from his run with his left arm clamped tight against the burn in his side and his stomach striving to retch to the echo of the belching gun. His right hand was extended with the sack of money with dark splotches of rain on the dirty gray cloth and the fingers that gripped it white-knuckled and shiny with the dampness. His face was pale and twisted and beaded with the sweat of accomplished desperation and his breath rasped loudly in the stillness of the hall.

"Here," said Hub, coming closer and poking the sack

184

at maw. "Here. Give it to Doc. Tell him, here's the money."

"Hub," said maw. "Hub."

But Hub had been glancing fearfully over his shoulder as he talked and now he moved quickly back to the door and opened it and slipped into the outside shadows.

Maw was still sitting forward on the edge of the seat with the sack of money in a loose hand in her lap and her mouth hanging open in bewilderment when the doctor came briskly up the hall. He stopped in front of her, his eyes riveted on the sack.

"What's that?" he said sharply.

Maw looked up at him, then down at the sack. She raised the sack slowly and stared unseeing at it and her hand dropped back into her lap.

"Where did you get it?" said the doctor.

"This?" said maw, attempting to raise the sack again.

"Yes," said the doctor. "That sack. Where did you get it?"

"Hub," said maw. "Hub brought it. Here," she said, extending it to him. "He said to give hit to you."

The doctor took the sack and turned it over in his hand.

"Mitchell Drug Store," he read aloud from the label.

He kneeled on the floor and took the sack by the bottom and dumped the pennies out and maw watched him while he counted them.

"Two hundred and fifty," he said. Then again softly, "Two hundred and fifty pennies."

He scooped the copper coins back into the sack and rose and wheeled to go back down the hall, but stopped and turned again to maw.

"Dr. Mitchell is ready to operate," he said. "I'll let you know as soon as we can tell anything."

Maw's eyes followed his retreating back until it turned and disappeared through the door to the operating room.

Buddy's terror-filled eyes watched the needle as it pierced his quivering flesh and watched the lump on his arm as the doctor rubbed it smooth with a piece of alcohol-soaked cotton after withdrawing the needle. He raised his eyes to the doctor's face and his lip was quivering.

"Is Hub here yit?"

"Don't you worry about Hub," the doctor said. "He's mighty anxious for you not to worry about anything so you can get strong and well again."

"Will he be here soon?" persisted Buddy.

"You know Hub would do anything for you, don't you, Buddy?"

Buddy nodded.

"And wouldn't you do as much for Hub?"

"You bet."

"Then you stop worrying about Hub. That's the last thing he wants."

The dope began to take effect and Buddy's brow cleared and his finely etched features relaxed.

✦

They worked swiftly with machinelike precision beneath the shadowless glare of the tiered lights. A muffled "Huh?" came through the ether cone, then the small figure relaxed completely on the white operating table and the malformed leg quivered once.

The knife sliced delicately into the pale flesh and was cast aside and rehearsed hands placed new tools and ties into the doctor's swift-moving fingers.

"Respiration?"

"Weak."

"Pulse?"

"Sixty."

Another knife. A swift clamp. Quick silent feet across to the steaming cabinet and back.

"Respiration?"

"Weaker."

"Pulse?"

"Forty-seven."

Faster. Faster. There. There it is. Now. Quickly.

"Respiration?"

"Very weak."

"Pulse?"

"Thirty—almost too weak to count—twenty-five—twenty—"

The doctor paused abruptly and taking the gauze cone from the small pinched face pushed the lid of an eye back with practiced thumb and gazed into the sightless depths. He straightened slowly and allowed the lid to close and pulled the sheet gently over the small, twisted form and turned abruptly and walked across to the wash basin, stripping his rubber gloves off as he did so.

Spring came. Virginia and McKinley were home from the hospital and Fred was home for good. An eighteen-month Four Oh Three had caught him and the blue Model A Ford with the rumble-seat sat in the yard behind the house and gathered dust. He lazed about the house and took his place at table regularly and played with the baby. He and Virginia, though not completely reconciled, were at least easy in each other's company again and Virginia's greatest regret was not Fred's derelictions but her own no longer lissome figure. Her mouth, once petulantly attractive, was now definitely drooped at the corners and the sparkle in her eye was no longer a sparkle. It was a glint.

"I tell you," said maw, "hit takes a baby to change a body. Virginia ain't near the spitfire she used to be and her and Fred seems to git along better since the baby come."

"Yes sir," said paw. "A baby does make a heap of difference sometimes."

"Hit kind of reminds me of when Hub was a baby," said maw, and then, "We ain't hearn from Hub since the night Buddy was operated on. I kind of wonder how he's a-making it sometimes."

"Oh, Hubbard will make it," said paw. "Hubbard is a right thriving kind of feller."

"Yes, he is," said maw. "Yes, he is."

"Hubbard was allus a feller to git things done," said paw.

"Yes, he was," said maw. "I've wondered lots of times where he got that money that night. A whole sack full of pennies. Just walked in and put 'em in my lap and said, Here, and turnt around and left. He was all out of breath with the rain a-shining on him."

"I rec'lect the next day," said paw. "Some fellers up to town said something about the drugstore done been robbed and I kind of thought about Hub then, him being so wrought up over Buddy, but later on the same day I heared Doc Mitchell hisself say they weren't no robbing going on. Said somebody started hit when they seen the door glass busted out early that morning, but he said he broke hit out hisself. Said he come down early fer some medicines and slipped on that slick floor where the rain done blowed in on it and busted that glass with his shoulder."

"Well, I do know," said maw. "And hit didn't cut him none?"

"He never mentioned hit," said paw.

"That other doctor has been right narce about coming to see Rinno since Hub left," said maw. "The one I give them pennies to. I told him we would likely git around to paying him something some day, but he said he owed hit to Hub."

"I never knowed Hub did that much work fer him."

"Seems like he must have."

"How's them sores of Rinno's gitting along?" said paw.

"I git turrible outdone about 'em," said maw. "He ain't gitting no wusser but he ain't gitting no better. I seen the doctor kind of shaking his head over Rinno the other day too."

"Pore feller," said paw. "Pore feller. And he did enjoy that swing."

"He done got so's he don't pay much attention to the raddio no more. Done got sort of listless like."

It was Sunday evening and they were all sitting out in the front yard when the big car with the Tennessee tag on it drove up in front and stopped. The rent man got out first and turned and handed a gray-haired lady to the sidewalk and held her by the arm as they came into the yard.

"This is Mr. Taylor, ain't it?" said the rent man.

"Well, yes sir," said paw. "That's about who I am."

"This is Mrs. Austin, Mr. Taylor. The lady that owns the house."

"Pleased to meet you," said paw. "Won't you set?"

The lady looked with distaste on the assembled group.

"Mrs. Austin came down from Memphis to see about the rent," said the rent man.

"Well now. We was just talking about that the other day," said paw. "Since we done all got back on the WP and A we 'lowed as how we might's well take up the rent again. We 'lowed we'd start about next payday."

"But what about all this back rent that you owe?" said the rent man.

190

"Well now," said paw. "We ain't got around to fig-gering on that yit."

"Look here," said the gray-haired lady. "I haven't had any rent from this property for over six months and my taxes go on just the same. You get my rent for me or get out."

"Why, Miz Austin, they ain't no call to git all stirred up about it. We aim to pay our just owings."

"Aim to?" snorted the lady. "I want my rent paid in full by the first of next month or I'll have the law on you."

She wheeled away and walked rapidly to her car and the rent man trotted along after her.

"Well now," said paw. "They weren't no call fer her to ack that way. We ain't harming her proppity none. Just living in it."

The rent man came back on the first but the door was swinging wide and the WPA people were gone.

Twelve

Paw had taken the entire household and moved them to the other side of town. His new landlord was unfamiliar with the WPA workers and their problems and he saw only the blue government checks that paw would draw every two weeks and he was glad to get tenants in the white elephant of a house that he owned. Even then he would have thought at length before he closed the deal had he known that paw's household consisted of seven families and each family blessed or burdened with children.

They arranged with one of their former country neighbors to use his truck one Saturday and they loaded their scarred and bent iron beds with their rusty coil springs and lumpy mattresses and their sleazy cotton blankets and ragged quilts and their rickety dressers and cane-bottom chairs and stoves with their rusty pipes and pots and pans and placed the rocking chair on top of the load. Reno lay on the pallet of quilts that Gwendolin and Eugenia had bundled up and dragged down to the porch while maw gathered up Reno and, holding

192

him to one side, made her cautious way down the stairs and out on the porch and deposited him in the dirty folds of the quilts where he lay like a bundle of sticks too knotty to even burn and too brittle to even waste the time to stoop and pick up.

"I reckon we ain't fergot nothing, have we?" said paw.

"Well, I don't guess so," said maw. "Leastways I sent Gwendolin back up to see and she didn't mention nothing we had fergot."

They were all standing around the truck and the driver was sitting impatiently beneath the wheel.

"I guess we might as well git started then," said paw and he walked up to the cab and opened the door and raised one foot to the running board and mounted to the seat.

The children scrambled up over the tail-gate of the truck and fell kicking and squealing on the stacked mattresses. Virginia, with her baby in her lap, was already in the cab between paw and the driver and maw climbed up over the wheel and fender and on up the side of the stake-bodied truck and down on the inside, where she seated herself on the mattress with her legs stuck flat out before her.

"Well now," she said. "I done fergot Rinno."

Paw turned and looked back at Reno lying on his pallet on the porch and paw looked at the driver with apology in his face.

"Maw fergot Rinno," he said.

"Well," said the driver. "Hadn't you better git 'im?"

"I guess we had," said paw.

He clambered down from the cab and stood with his hand still on the door handle looking toward the porch.

"We got to git Rinno in," he said into the empty yard.

The children were kneeling on the packed goods in the truck, peering at paw over the edge of the truck's side. Maw sat patiently looking at paw over her shoulder.

"You reckon you and Jut could maybe git him up here?" she said at last.

"Well, we might could," said paw. "Is Jut up there?"

Jutland climbed slowly down from the top of the load and stood at the rear of the truck looking at paw.

"Well, are you going to get him?" said the driver.

"Hit looks like we are going to have to," said paw.

He walked slowly past the truck under the interested stare of the children and on toward the porch and Jutland fell in behind him and stopped when paw halted at the foot of Reno's pallet.

Paw looked down at Reno then back at the truck and maw.

"I guess we might could lift him on the pallet and git him out to the truck," he said, turning to Jutland.

Without a word Jutland moved opposite paw and stooped and grasped two handfuls of the quilt and straightened up and maw called, "Be careful. Don't spill him out on the floor."

And Jutland promptly released his hold and the quilts slumped back in dirty folds at his feet.

"Are you going to bring him?" called the driver impatiently.

"Well," said paw. "We ain't never done this before. Hub, he allus 'tended to Rinno."

"Why don't you pick him up by the corners of the quilt and come on like Jut started?" said the driver.

Paw stooped and caught the quilt by his corners and Jutland stooped and came up with his and Reno folded down into the sagging pocket at the bottom of the sling.

"Lift him high so's you won't bump him against the steps," said maw.

They got him as far as the rear of the truck and there eased him down to the ground, where Reno lay in a twisted bundle in the folds.

"Now, how can we git him up to maw?" said Jutland.

"Well now," said paw. "I just don't rightly know. I doubt ifen maw could reach down and git him even ifen we lifted him high's we could in the quilt."

"Reckon we could kind of sling him up to maw?" said Jutland.

The truck driver rounded the rear of the truck and pushed them roughly to one side and in furious disgust scooped up Reno and lifted him into maw's lap.

"Here," he said and threw the quilts in and turned on an outraged heel and swung back around the corner of the bed and climbed into the cab and slammed the door.

Paw shuffled around to the cab on the other side. He clambered in by Virginia and the old truck wheezed into life and roared and shivered backwards into the drive by the side of the house and the driver jerked it savagely into low and it moved slowly, jumpily, down the drive and out into the street. They rattled across town.

At the new home the driver backed up to the porch and dropped lightly to the ground from the cab and swung around to the rear of the truck where he reached in, retrieved the quilts and spread them on the porch floor, and took Reno and placed him in the quilts. After this he returned to the truck cab and slid in beneath the wheel and sat waiting for them to unload.

"Well, this is right narce," said maw as she explored the new house. "I believe I like hit better'n the other'n'."

"Yes sir," said paw. "And being's they done made me the head of the community, sort of, we gits fust choice of our room."

"Well now. Ain't that narce," said maw. "And we'll be fust at the cookstove and hit ain't even our week yit."

"Well now. We best think about that some," said paw. "Even if we are the natural leaders of the community we oughtn't to feel called on to push ourselves too far forward."

"That's the rule though, paw. They done it when they moved to the other place. Mr. Adams, he was the head then and Miz Adams, she taken fust turn at the stove. Course I ain't aiming to just keep on being fust. But being's we're the head now, the fust week just naturally falls my lot."

"Well, how-some-ever you womenfolks sees fit to work hit out is all right with me. Like the Bible says, Fust come, fust served."

196

"This is just fine," said maw after further explorations. "It ain't so dark like with being gray 'stid of brown like the other'n', and the wash room in this house is inside instid of off acrost the back porch like in the other'n'. A body kin git his coal now without even gitting wet when hit's a-raining."

"Here comes Fred," said paw from the front door, "so I guess this must be the last load."

The old truck groaned up the driveway with steam hissing out the radiator and Fred seated in his car tied to the back of the truck. The truck stopped in the drive and Fred got out and untied his car and the truck pulled away from the car and passed the porch and out into the yard and then backed up until the end of the body rested against the top step.

The women and children of the last two families climbed down from the top of the load and the menfolks climbed out of the cab and stood talking to the driver while the women and children unloaded the truck. Fred came forward and stood with the men. When the load was emptied on the porch the children helped push Fred's car around to the back of the house.

"What you take fer your car, Fred?" said the truck driver.

"Ain't aiming to git rid of 'er just yit awhile," said Fred.

"You going to let her just set there behind the house?"

"Naw. I got my Four Oh Two this morning. Going back to work Monday."

"Well, ifen you git ready to git rid of 'er, just let me know. I'd like to do a little trading with you on 'er."

"I'll let you know before I git rid of 'er."

"Well, so long."

"So long."

And the truck driver drove on out of the yard.

The checks were due the following Thursday and paw had told the landlord he would pay the rent then. The checks came and paw as head of the house collected the rent from the different men and took it and gave it to the landlord. Fred was back working now, but before the end of the week the regular April quota reduction came in and two of the men were laid off and the commodity apples and celery began making their regular Saturday appearances at the house.

"I wisht they wouldn't give us so many of them celeries," said one of the men. "I just cain't learn to stomach 'um somehow. They don't seem to be much suption in 'em."

"That's right," said paw. "A man cain't put up a good honest day's work on just celery and apples. Hit don't seem to stand up well in his stummick."

"I went around to the Hall today but hit seems like they ain't aiming to put none of us back on yit awhile. Be 'bout the fust of July, Mr. Will says."

"You seen Mr. Will, did you?"

"Yes, and he was right nice about it too. Said they wa'n't nothing he could do about it right now but he'd have us all back on the fust of July. Said the gove'ment physical year starts the fust of July and it seems like

198

somehow they won't be no more money to pay us with until after the fust of July."

"Them folks up to Washington miscalculated again, I guess," said paw. "They tell me they have to lay a bunch of us men off ever' year about this time on account of the gove'ment is about to run out of money. They always manages to just skin by somehow though. Leastways I ain't never heared of no one not gitting paid yit."

"Yes sir. They're pretty smart about that. Feared some one will sue 'em, I guess."

"That's about it," said paw.

"We'll all git back on right after the fust of July though. I heared over the raddio last night that the President done give Congress, oh, I dunno, some big amount of money to give us next year. They got to give it to us in eight months too."

"I hate about we are going to have to wait till next year to git it though," said paw.

"Oh, them fellers don't use the same kind of years we do. Their kind is that new physical year I been talking about. They starts it the fust of July. I heared hit over the raddio last night."

"Why, I never heared about that," said paw. "Never knowed a thing abouten it. How-some-ever we was listening to them fellers give that thousand dollars away most of the time. Feller out in Dallas got it. A WP and A-man, just like us. He was setting right by the phone when they called him too. I've a mind to git us a phone next payday. I'd hate right bad fer 'em to try to call me and I didn't have no phone."

"A thousand dollars would come in right handy."

"Yes sir," said paw. "Hit would come in right handy. I've allus been a great believer in the Bible. Hit says, Make hay whilst the sun shines. I believe I'll just git us a phone next payday."

"I never was much hand to have things give me," said the man.

"I wa'n't neither," said paw. " 'Cep'n' one time. I rec'-lect it plain's ifen hit were yestiddy. I was a mite of a boy—'bout twelve year old I reckon—and paw had brung us all to town. Hit was in the fall and we had brung our cotton in to have it ginned and they was a crowd on the Square that day. Biggest crowd I ever seen. Paw was to the gin with the wagon and he had left me up on the corner by where that old store building was that burned down about twenty year ago so's I could just stand there and watch all them people. They was a-passing and a-passing and me a-watching. Well, sir, I looked down and there hit were. All folded up and dirty acrost one edge where somebody had done stepped on it. I couldn't even make out the green edge of it good but I knowed even before I stooped down to pick hit up, hit were money. I ain't never forgot how I just looked down and there was that money. Like that was what I come to town fer, and I might of knowed hit were there all the time. Hit were like when Mr. Brown-ing found his saddle that time he went over to Uncle Mark's and drunk all that wine. He thought the mule throwed him but some of the folks 'lowed as how he just fell off. That old piece of plow line he tied his saddle on with was about wore out anyhow and some thought he just went to sleep a-setting on that mule and maybe thought he was to home in bed and tried to turn over and just fell off. The saddle come off too and when Mr. Browning got up all he seen was the mule a-standing there looking at him and I guess he must have thought the mule was trying to git away because he said he run to catch the mule and the mule turnt and run down the road a piece and stopped and looked back at him and when he would git most to the mule, a-whooping and a-hollering to the mule to whoa, the mule would turn and run a little farther. Mules is the orneriest critters when they takes a notion. He never caught that mule until they got plumb home. Mr. Browning allus thought that mule did it on purpose but some 'lowed the mule was trying to wait on Mr. Browning but Mr. Browning just kept on a-scaring it. And he never noticed the saddle was gone until he finally got home and he knowed ifen somebody else found that saddle before he did he never would git it back so he got his lantern and rid back over to where he thought the mule throwed him. He was kind of mixed up about just where he thought the mule done it, because after hit did, he had been too busy trying to catch the mule to pay much attention to just where he were and he had a awful time finding that saddle. He must have walked up and down them ditches on both sides of the road most all night and had about give up when he just crossed over the road right quick and walked up to a place in the ditch and looked down and there hit were just like he must of knowed hit were there all the time and had just forgot. Just found hit all at onct like. And that's the way I found that dollar. Just all at onct. I'll never fergit it."

"Some folks is just lucky and some ain't," said the man.

"Yes sir," said paw. "Yes sir. Some is and some ain't."

Maw was in the kitchen, first on the stove, cooking supper and she called Gwendolin.

"Gwendolin. Gwendolin. Leave the baby with Eugenia and go git me another bucket of water."

"When are we going to git water in here?" said Gwendolin. "I'm gitting tard toting water all the time."

"Paw ain't got around to having hit turnt on yit. You go on and git that water like I told you now and hurry. These 'taters is most boiled down."

Gwendolin took the empty lard bucket and went through the hall and out the front door. She crossed to the neighbor's yard-hydrant and filled the bucket and returned with the water splashing her and the ground and the floor at every step. She set the bucket on the kitchen shelf and splashed more water on the shelf and floor.

"Wisht paw would git the water turnt on here so's we wouldn't have to tote so far," she said again.

"He's sort of thinking about it next payday," said maw.

Maw soon finished cooking the supper of boiled pota-

202

toes and sorghum and biscuits and called them in to eat. Virginia left her baby on the bed upstairs and came down and Fred came in from the back-yard where he had been tinkering with his car.

"Maw," said Virginia as she came in, "it looks like since we had first choice of the rooms you could have taken one of the downstairs ones."

"Well now," said maw, "ever since I was a little girl and allus lived in a house without no upstairs I been a-saying if I ever did git the chanct to live in a upstairs house I aimed to do hit. Hit's a sight of pleasure to set in one them upstairs rooms and just rock. That's one the things I enjoyed so about that other house. We was upstairs."

Fred rose from the supper table first and said to Virginia, "Come on if you want to go."

Virginia laid her fork down and rose and followed Fred from the room on bare feet. She had taken her bath that evening and put on a wrap-around house-dress and now she followed Fred upstairs and while he shaved and bathed in a single pan of water beneath Reno's blank unrecognition she shrugged out of the wrap-around and slipped into her "good" dress and then slipped her feet into her spike-heeled, open-toed shoes. Fred put on his blue pants and a clean white shirt and his two-toned sport shoes and powdered his face and slicked his hair back with pomade.

"Let's go," he said.

Paw and the children had come into the room and Virginia turned to Gwendolin.

"Tell maw to listen for the baby," she said. "And tell her if it cries to give it that old piece of fat meat to suck on."

"Hit's a pity maw has done dried up from our baby," said paw, "or she could handle yourn easy. Maw allus did have more milk than she knowed what to do with. I rec'lect when Hubbard was a baby. Maw scoured him fore we knowed what was wrong."

As Fred's and Virginia's feet died out down the stairs they heard maw's heavy, rubber-soled, subdued thumps come into the lower hall from the kitchen and mount the stairs. She gripped the rail with a reddened hand as she heaved each weary step upward.

"I'm tard tonight," she said to the room at large as she entered the door and flopped down on the bed. The springs gave forth a rusty screech in protest.

"Virginia said to tend her baby ifen hit wakes," said paw. "Her and Fred have done went out."

"Well, I'm glad they did," said maw. "Seems like Virgina has been right restless lately. I'm glad they went out."

Reno's head rolled toward the door at each new entrance and each time he rolled it back and mewled his indignation and disappointment.

"I wonder what's done got into Rinno lately," said maw. "Ever' time anybody comes into the door he rolls his head towards hit and then makes a face and starts a-fussing."

"I just don't know," said paw. "He's a monst'ous cur'osity."

204

"I done used the last of that sa've what the doctor give Hub," said maw.

"Hit weren't a-cyoring him anyway," said paw. "I'll see some the men tomorrow and maybe they kin git up something fer him. Likely old man Duncan kin git some more of that stuff from that nigger out by his place."

"I'll just leave them bandages on till you git that stuff since we ain't got no more sa've," said maw. "I disremember which side I turnt him on last night. Do any of you chillun rec'lect?"

"On his left," said Jutland. "I remember him looking at me when I come in the door just fore dark last night and making a face."

"I declare," said maw. "I wisht I knowed what was wrong with him. He et all right when Hub was here even after he cut hisself on that rope that day."

"I don't reckon he could be missing Hub, do you reckon?" said paw.

"Well, I don't hardly think so," said maw. "Leastways he never done this way before when Hub was gone away."

"He was right cur'ous about Buddy," said paw.

"He never taken no particular attention about Buddy though," said maw. "Just kind of looked at him ever' time Buddy come in. He never carried on over him like he did Hub."

"Well, maybe this stuff I'm going to git from old man Duncan will fix him up," said paw.

"I hope hit will," said maw. "I do hope hit will."

✦   *205*

Fred had borrowed two dollars against his next payday and after buying fifty cents' worth of gasoline he had a dollar and a half left for beer and whiskey and to put in the nickelodeon.

He and Virginia drove out north to the jook house and parked in front. It was early yet. Scarcely dark and only one empty car stood in front besides their own. They sat in silence watching the reflection of the changing red neon sign in their windshield. The hard, bright ceiling lights were already on inside and they saw the owner occasionally cross the bare floor and in the back corner was visible a section of green-curtained booths.

"Be back in a minute," said Fred and he slid out from under the steering wheel.

Virginia sat with legs crossed, ignoring him, and he disappeared inside the house and returned soon with a half pint in his pocket. He got back under the wheel and broke the seal on the bottle and drank and passed the bottle to Virginia.

"You know I can't drink without a chaser," said Virginia.

Without a word Fred slid back out from under the wheel and went and got a Coca-Cola.

"Here," he said, extending the cold drink to her.

She tilted the chaser and swallowed once, then filled her mouth and taking the chaser down lifted the whiskey and quickly swallowed three times. She shuddered and took another swallow of chaser.

It was almost dark now and another car drove in beside them and stopped. Giggles came from it and swift movement and muffled protestations, then the occupants got out and walked, still laughing and talking, into the jook joint.

Soon the nickelodeon started and Fred and Virginia saw the couples dancing on the floor.

Fred took another drink and handed the bottle to Virginia and she drank and shuddered again and took a swallow of chaser.

"Let's go in," said Virginia abruptly.

She got out of her side of the car without waiting for Fred and walked quickly in the door. The two couples were now out of sight in the back booth and she walked over to one of the center booths and tucked the curtain wide behind the back of the bench and slid in on the slick worn seat. Fred watched as she left the car and walked in the door. When he saw her legs silhouetted through her thin dress he took one more drink and followed her inside. He stopped a moment just inside the door and glanced at the sounds from the back booth, then walked across the floor and slid in opposite Virginia.

"Give me a drink," said Virginia, and Fred took the bottle from his pocket and passed it openly across the table to her.

She tilted the bottle to her lips and drank and Fred snatched it away, spilling whiskey on her dress. Surprise gave way to anger and she half rose from her seat.

"Sit back down," said Fred harshly. "What are you trying to do? Get drunk?"

"What's it to you if I do?" said Virginia, already feeling the drinks in her.

"You just try it and I'll show you what it is to me," said Fred.

One of the couples came out of the back booth and the boy dropped a nickel into the nickelodeon and stood watching as the record slid out of the evenly racked pile on its brass tray and lifted to the phonograph needle. The preliminary chords boomed out deep and rich and resonant, incongruous in perfection of tone to the bright hard glare of the lights overhead and the flimsy appointments of the plain unpainted building, yet its mad rhythm startlingly appropriate to the unnatural glitter in the eyes of the poised and waiting couples and the aura of unrestriction and license and the smell of alcohol in the room.

"There's a man that comes to our house every single day.
 Then papa comes home and the man goes away.
 Papa does the work and mamma gets the pay.
 And the man comes around when papa goes away."

Two more couples came in the front door with whiskey bottles half empty carried openly in their hands. The other couple from the rear booth moved out onto the floor. Two overall-clad workers unbathed after a day's work came in and leaned against the beer box by the door.

"The man that comes to our house, he comes to take the trash
 In a little white jacket and a little black mustache."

208

Fred tilted the bottle and drank and Virginia took the bottle from his unresisting and unnoticing hand and tilted it to her lips and drained it. Fred was watching one of the couples on the floor and he felt for the bottle with his hand and finding it raised it to his mouth. He swallowed and took the bottle down from his lips and looked at it. He turned in his seat and stared at Virginia and she returned his stare defiantly.

"It's always very strange but it always seems to me
    He's a little more familiar than a trash man ought to be."

"Get up," said Fred. "Let's dance."

"There's a man that comes to our house—"

"Who is that that came in with that boy right behind us?"

                                    —"every single day.
    Then papa comes home—"

"What do you care? Ain't you got me?"

                            "—and the man goes away."

"Ain't that Mr. Taylor's girl that had that baby on the floor?"
"She could have one on my floor. Let's git a beer."

"Papa goes to work—"

"Ain't that boy with her the one that's been hanging around here all spring?"
"Uh-huh. Her husband. Leastways they say he is."

209

"—and mamma gets the pay."

"He ain't been acting like no husband."

"And the man comes around—"

"I'd like to act like her husband fer a while."

"—when papa goes away."

"Somebody must have already did it onct anyhow."
"Let's git another beer."
Other nickels in the slot. Other records moving out
and up to the needle. Half pints of whiskey over the
counter.

"I'd never be a doctor with an office downtown—NO—"

Fred swayed drunkenly against the beer box and
tried to focus his eyes on Virginia in the arms of a
stranger, dancing, swaying, eyes closed, with stray locks
of hair falling across them, lips half smiling. His eyes
wandered to the light in the ceiling, focused, and returned to the dancers. He singled out Virginia and
started to her. She and her partner stopped dancing
abruptly and arm in arm, oblivious of the crowd on the
floor and swaying against each other as they walked,
started for the door. Fred's eyes sharpened and his skin
drew tight over his cheekbones and his mouth hardened
to a thin slit. He moved over quickly and barred the
door, shocked sober by this public affront to his pride.
They tried to step around him and when he moved over
and barred them again they noticed him and Virginia

saw who he was. Her glassy eyes fixed on him and she pushed at the fallen locks of hair. The man's eyes showed no sign of recognition. He swayed against Virginia. Fred hit him with all his strength and as the man fell, caught Virginia by the arm and spun her to one side. The man lay still for a moment on the floor, then pushed himself up on one elbow and gazed up at them in bewilderment and blood ran from the corner of his mouth in a thin stream and spread over his chin.

Fred stood for a moment looking down at the man, then he raised his eyes to Virginia who was watching not the man but Fred. The dancers had stopped and the workmen by the beer box stood with frozen leers on their faces.

"I'd rather be just the man that comes around."

"You bitch," said Fred. "You God damned whoring bitch. I'll fix you so's you'll know who to go out in a car and park with."

A month later Virginia knew it. She stormed and cried and cursed Fred. Then she grew sullen, then listless and uncaring. She was pregnant again.

Thirteen

"I most fergot," said paw as they sat around the room after supper.

He hunched to one side in the cane-bottom chair and delved his hand deep into the recesses of his hip pocket and withdrew it with his fingers clutched around a small snuff-box pocket-worn to the soft luster of old silver.

"Here's them powders that old man Duncan got fer me. Said he got that old nigger to make 'em up a mite stronger this time since the others didn't do much good. Said the old nigger told him this stuff ought to have a good scab on them sores in two-three days."

"Well, I'm glad to git a-holt of 'em," said maw. "I'll pull them bandages off tonight and sprinkle him good."

Maw took the box and went and knelt down by Reno and lifted the two weeks' old bandages off the two sluffed-out spots in Reno's chest and sprinkled the sores liberally with the powder and tore new strips from the flour sack hanging by the bed and patted them in place while Reno mouthed hoarse indignation at the disturbance.

212

"He don't holler as loud as he used to," said paw.

"You know, I been noticing that," said maw. "Maybe he's gitting more content like."

She turned Reno on his side and heaved herself erect by pulling against the head of the bed and prying against her knee.

Paw stripped off his overalls and jumper and placed his hat on the floor by the bed and kicked off his brogans and stepping between Reno and their bed lay back on the lumpy mattress and hunched himself over against the wall and turning his back on the room began immediately to snore. Soon maw followed him and the children went one by one out into the hall.

Rent time came and paw went to see the landlord.

"Hit's like this," said paw. "I ain't just exactly come to pay the rent yit. Some the men done been laid off till the new physical year. The gove'ment's running kind of short of money right now and some the men's on kind of a little lay-off just to kind of help the gove'ment git by till the new physical year. We'll all git back on soon's the new gove'ment physical year gits here. We could pay you, say, about fifteen dollars on the rent now and when we all git back to work we could ketch the rest of hit up without no trouble. Mr. Will over to the Hall is kind of looking out fer us and we'll all be back on after the new gove'ment physical year gits here."

"I guess that will be all right," said the new landlord. "I don't want to be hard on you men. You pay what you can now and we'll get the other straightened up when you get back to work. By the way, the man that lives next door to you has been to see me about you all using that hydrant in his front yard. Said his water ran over the usual amount about a dollar and a half last month. Are your pipes out of fix?"

"Well, no sir. I don't know as they are."

"I didn't see hardly how they could be. I had them all gone over after that freeze last winter. God knows that plumber charged me enough to have put in a whole new system."

"I noticed some the pipes was right new and shiny looking. We ain't used 'em none yit. I been laying off to go by the Hall and git 'em to turn the water on but somehow I ain't got around to it yit."

"Well, you better go see about it right away so you won't have to bother that man next door any more."

"I'll likely git around to it soon," said paw.

The landlord stood watching him as he made his shambling hesitant way down the walk and out the gate.

Paw came in from work the next night with his overalls stained with salt-marked sweat. His muscles ached and his hands were blistered.

"Land's sake, paw," exclaimed maw. "What in the world has happened to you?"

"They's a gove'ment man been on the job watching us all day and I'm just tard to death. So is the rest of the men. One or two of us burnt plumb out and had to go lay down in the shade."

214

"A gove'ment man?" said maw.

"They come around and checks up on us ever' now and then, some says, but don't nobody ever rec'lect one acting just like this feller does. He just drove up to the job in a big new shiny car and set down by the tool box and watched us all day. Ain't said nothing to nobody. I hope he got us all checked so's he can go on to some the other jobs tomorrow. I ain't never been so tard in my life."

"Well, I do know," said maw. "What do you s'pose he's looking fer?"

"Don't none of us rightly know," said paw, "but some thinks hit's on account of this war they're having over to Yurrup. We heared they was going to fire all the fellers that was too old to work good and just keep the young 'uns to build them fields them airyplanes lights in."

"And he ain't said what he was doing?"

"Not nair word. Just come in and set."

The government man was there the next day, sitting under the tree by the tool box, watching the men at work, saying nothing.

"I declare, hit just beats me," said paw. "My hands are so sore I cain't hardly pick up my shovel no more. Some of the men went to the foreman and tried to git transferred but the foreman said hit would take quite a spell to arrange fer a transfer. I reckon shorely he'll be gone tomorrow."

"Well, I do know," said maw. "You ain't going to work yourself into a spell, are ye, paw?"

"Well, I'm just about past going," said paw. "Steve Joe just give up today. He told the foreman, gove'ment or no gove'ment, it ain't right to make no man work like we are working."

"Ain't the man said nothing yit?"

"Not nair word," said paw.

"Ain't none of you been to see Mr. Will about it yit?"

"Well, by Godfrey," said paw. "We ain't none of us thought of that. We been so busy working we ain't hardly had time to think about nothing else. I'll just go by and see him in the morning."

Paw went by the City Hall and caught Mr. Will in front of the building just getting out of his car. He told Mr. Will about the government man and Mr. Will said, Good Lord, Good Lord, and ran into the Hall and took the stairs two at a time, hollering, "You all get to work. You all get to work. There's one of the FIB boys down on the job."

Paw went on down to the job now more scared than ever. That night when he dragged in home he was near the point of collapse.

"What did Mr. Will say?" said maw as soon as he got in the door.

"He acted like he was right worried about it too," said paw. "Poor feller. His neuralgy done come back on him too. Soon's I told him about the gove'ment man he grabbed his face like he allus does when one them pains strikes him and run in the Hall just hollering. I declare I don't know what we are going to do. Two more of

216

the men burnt out this evening and they had to take 'em to the doctor and old man Doyle said he was aiming to just quit. Said he'd druther be back on the 'moddity and eat them apples and celery and brown flour again."

"You ain't aiming to quit, are ye, paw?"

"I aim to keep going as long's I kin," said paw, "but they's a end to mortal endurance."

Maw rubbed paw's aching muscles with grease drippings from a piece of fat back that night and covered his hands with soda and lard and bound them in strips of old flour sacking.

When she stooped to place Reno for the night after she was through with paw, Reno mouthed a sound of pain as her hands touched his chest.

"Well, I declare," said maw. "I do believe the pore feller's chest is sore."

She raised the piece of flour sack bandage and looked long at the hard scabs over the sores with their pulled and inflamed edges.

"Now, I wonder ifen some of them grease drippings mightn't help, kind of."

Maw took the pan of drippings and dipped a corner of the bandage in and swabbed the sores and kneeled back, studying the results of her ministrations. Then she took the lard and coated the scabs with it and as an afterthought sprinkled them with more of the powder. She replaced the bandage and turned Reno on his side.

"I believe hit eased the pore feller," she said as she

clambered erect and slipped her dress and tennises off and, placing the baby on the edge of the bed, crawled across it and lay down with a heavy sigh. She raised to a sitting posture and took her forgotten snuff stick from her mouth and leaning over the baby placed it on the floor by the bed.

The next day at noon when the government man went to town for his lunch, paw and the men collected around the hydrant in a yard close by and ate their lunches in gloomy silence and scattered the paper sacks and pieces of bread over the grass.

"Fellers," said one of the men, "we just cain't stand this no more. We are ever' one gitting stove up."

"That's right," said another. "We are just gitting wore to a frazzle."

"What can we do about hit?" said another.

"We might just strike like them fellers up North do when things don't go to suit 'em."

"Well now," said paw. "We better not do nothing like that. I ain't just rightly shore the gove'ment would like nothing like that."

"We might do like Ed and Joe. Pore fellers. They just couldn't stand it no longer."

"What did you do with Ed?"

"We laid him over in that feller's back lot where he keeps that muley-head cow."

"Joe went to git him another pint. He's pow'ful worried about the whole thing. Just cain't seem to git that gove'ment feller offen his mind a tall."

The WPA. They've pulled the best one yet. There's a big-shot politician lives up in the next county that's got a no-'count bastard for a brother that told them to put him on the WPA and at first they wouldn't do it, so he went to Tupelo hisself and took the brother with him and they put him on all right but they knew he couldn't do nothing so they just made him a job where he couldn't bother nobody nor worry the folks at Tupelo neither. They made him a tool checker. I reckon they thought this would be a good chance to count all them shovels they had and see if maybe they hadn't finished a job somewhere and gone off and left some of the shovels with the men just standing there leaning on them. Well, they didn't nobody know to tell this feller how to check tools because they hadn't never tried it before so they just give him one of them Oh Two's and his brother bought him a new car and he started out. This was the first place he got to and he went down there on that job that morning when the men went to work and set by the tool box without saying a word to anybody because he was scared some of them would find out he didn't know how to count tools and try to count the tools the men was using but some of them was in that ditch and some was out on the bank and he counted and counted and couldn't never get the same number twice so he went back again that evening and tried it again and didn't have no better luck than he did that morning and the men all got to working fast and some of them burned out and some of the shovels got covered up in the sand they was throwing out of the ditch and it had done got so now every time he counted the shovels he got less and less. Well, sir, the longer he set there the harder the men worked. They blistered their hands and some of them burned out and had to be took to a doctor and that real old feller they had down there and that big fat 'un just give up and quit. Then yesterday he went back down there again to try to count the tools and two of the men got worried and got to drinking and one of them passed out and they just laid him over to one side and the other one got the DT's and thought he was seeing snakes and got down there in that ditch with his shovel and started fighting the snakes he thought he was seeing and run the men all out of the ditch just as them niggers come along with that big dairy herd of Mr. Brown's and the whole herd stampeded right over the feller that had passed out and not a one of them stepped on him. I tell you the Lord couldn't look after them WPA workers no better if they was his own children. And, oh, yeah. Just after all them cows got through running over that feller without stepping on him a car of WPA Safety Men drove up from Tupelo. They had come over to see how come so many of the men was burning out all at onct. Well, them Safety Men pitched in and helped catch the feller that had the DT's and after they got him quieted down they was all standing around breathing hard and looking at one another and one of the Safety Men saw the tool checker sitting over by the tool box and he said, Hello, there. You got the tools all checked yet? and the foreman said, What did you say?

and the Safety Man said, I asked that feller sitting over by the tool box if he had all the tools checked yet and the foreman said, Is that what he is doing? and the Safety Man said, Yes. What did you think he was doing? and some old codger standing there said, Well now. And we thought all the time he was one them gove'ment fellers.

"Maw," said paw that night, "it just ain't right fer the gove'ment to play no trick like that on us."

"Well, it 'pears to me like hit ain't just right. Looks like to me he could have told you he weren't no gove'ment man easy enough."

"That's what some the men 'lowed. Well, I'm glad we finally caught on anyhow. Another day or two and they wouldn't none of us been fitten fer nothing. I ain't never worked so hard in all my life. I'm just plumb wore out. I believe I'll send one the chillun over to Steve Joe's and old man Doyle's and let them know they can come on back to work now."

"Well now," said maw. "I bound ye they'll be right pleased to know it too."

The children trooped in and Reno rolled his head toward the door and even after they passed his line of vision he continued to face the empty opening.

"Rinno must be better, maw," said one of the children. "He gen'ally makes up a face when one of us comes in but he ain't done nothing yestiddy and today but just roll his head towards the door and look."

"Well, I hope he is," said maw. "I noticed he don't

'pear to git mad ever' time somebody comes in no more. Maybe hit's them powders and stuff I been a-putting on him."

Steve Joe and old man Doyle were back on the job the next morning and before noon another quota reduction came in. There was also a Four Oh Three there for the foreman for eighteen months' service. The Supervisor came down and brought the pink slips.

"They got you this time," said the Supervisor to the foreman. "It looks like every time I pick a man for foreman the eighteen-month thing gets him. Well, I've got to pick another one. Who do you suggest?"

"There ain't much pick between them," said the foreman. "The truck driver is a good boy. Quiet and he already has a rating. You might try him."

So the Supervisor called the truck driver and said, "We've got to have another foreman down here. Eighteen months caught the one we have now. How about you taking it? It will give you a thirteen-dollar raise and you seem to be about the best bet to handle the men."

"Well, sir, I guess I could handle it all right."

"Well, that's just fine," said the Supervisor. "I'll get your experience record fixed up and bring it down here in the morning for you to sign."

That evening when paw came home, maw and Virginia were sitting on the porch and the children were playing in the yard. Maw was in her mother hubbard with her legs spread about a tin pan into which she was shelling butter beans. The beans plinked into the pan and she dropped the hulls to a paper on the floor by her chair. Virginia was bathed and in a clean house dress but the permanent was no longer in evidence in her hair and the red fingernail polish had long since flaked from her fingernails and had not been renewed. She sat sullenly staring out into the yard.

"You'd ought to take care of yourself a little better, Virginia," said maw. "I allus thought you looked so pretty with your hair set and that red on your fingernails."

"I don't care," said Virginia.

"You'd oughtn't to feel that away about it," said maw. "It ain't but natural fer a body to have chillun after they gits married."

"Fred ought not to have done it this soon again, though," said Virginia, her eyes smoky with resentment. "He just did it for meanness."

"Why, I wouldn't think that about it," said maw. "Hit ain't right."

"Well, he did," said Virginia. "He wants to run around and have himself a good time and whenever I want to go and dance with somebody a little bit he's got to go get me in this fix again."

"Why, Fred's a good boy," said maw. "He's been right good about hepping out with the rent and such. All young men is wild-like. Fred might settle down into a real good husband some day."

"Well, I'm getting tired of having babies while he's waiting to settle down," said Virginia. "Fast as I have

223

one and get over it here I am with another. I'm getting so tired of being sick to my stomach every morning I don't know what to do."

"Here comes Fred now," said maw as Fred's blue roadster wheeled into the driveway.

Virginia rose from her chair and went into the house and up the stairs to their room and took her seat in a rocker and sat staring out the window, sullen, resentful, discontented.

"We've been right busy today," said paw as he took his seat on the top step. "We got to elect us a new foreman."

"I thought you just elected Mr. Brooks foreman not so long ago," said maw.

"Well, we did," said paw, "but somehow or other the Supervisor didn't take to the idea much and he just went ahead and made somebody else foreman. I think we'll git Mr. Brooks in this time though. We been studying some about it today. Seems like the Supervisor kind of leans towards the truck driver but some the men thinks Mr. Brooks will be the better choice fer it. That truck driver is too kind of stand-offish. Don't never have much to say to the men and all. He's a right good worker all right but he just ain't friendly-like. Don't never josh with the boys and carry on."

"Well, I do know," said maw. "I ain't never seen him but I know I'd druther have friendly folks around me."

"That's what the men thinks," said paw. "Like the Bible says, Friendly is as friendly does. Steve Joe sort of wants the foreman's place. He kind of stands around and di-rects the men ever' now and then. I don't know about him though. Not that he wouldn't maybe make just as good a foreman as Mr. Brooks, but then we done already run Mr. Brooks onct and him being a older man on the job most of the boys feel like they ought to sort of stick to him."

"Well now, that's right thoughty of 'em," said maw. "I allus say, Stick to them you been a-sticking to."

"That's just how I feel about it," said paw.

"Well, I guess I better be gitting supper fixed," said maw. "Miz Jackson give us these butter beans. Her and Mr. Jackson driv out to the country Sunday with some of their folks and she brought back a great big sack of 'em and divided with us. It was right narce of her, I thought."

"Yes, hit was," said paw. "Right narce."

Maw set the pan of shelled beans on the floor by her chair and rose and shook the hulls out of her lap onto the paper on the floor.

"Gwendolin," she called. "Come git these butter-bean hulls and throw 'em out in the road fer good luck. And when you git back go fetch us a bucket of water."

She picked up her pan of beans and disappeared in the direction of the kitchen. Paw continued to sit on the top step and Gwendolin ran up and got the paper of hulls and took them and threw them broadcast into the street. She came back up the walk running, with the paper waving from a hand extended behind her, and dropped it on the porch as she ran in the door. The door slammed behind her and paw got up and shoved the paper to one side with his foot and entered the hall. He mounted to their room and pulling a chair up to the radio twisted the dials to Amos and Andy and sat laughing and slapping his knee while Virginia sat without turning her head from the window and Reno lay without moving on his pallet.

Maw called them to supper and they wolfed their food in silence and got up one at a time as they finished and went out.

That night after supper maw squatted on the floor by Reno and chewed his food as usual and took the well-masticated mass from her mouth with a thumb and forefinger and tried to place it in Reno's mouth, but he grimaced without sound and turned his head aside.

"Well, I declare," said maw. "Rinno acts like he don't want no food."

Paw watched from his tilted-back chair and the children came and formed a half-circle behind maw and watched.

Maw tried again and Reno rolled his head away again.

"Lemme hold his head," said Jutland. "Maybe he's done already fergot about eating even from just last time."

"Be careful," said maw.

Jutland stooped over Reno and held his head and maw forced the mass of chewed food into his mouth and he tried to roll his head away and then repulsed the food with his tongue and it lay on his chin matted into the black whiskers. Reno clenched his hands and mouthed idiot rage and drooled from the corners of his mouth onto the pillow.

"Hit looks like he just won't eat," said maw with a puzzled frown on her flaccid face.

"He's a-gitting his voice back though," said paw.

"Hit did sound a mite stronger, didn't hit?" said maw.

"Maybe he's foundered," said paw.

"Well now, I hadn't thought of that," said maw. "Maybe he is. I'll just wait till morning and try him again. I allus say a child will eat when he gits hungry and they ain't no use a-forcing hit."

Maw scooped the mass from Reno's chin and scraped it off her finger into the bowl and rose from the floor.

"Turn him loose," she said to Jutland. "I ain't a-going to try no more tonight."

The men held their election the next morning and voted Mr. Brooks in unanimously and the Supervisor came down about ten o'clock with the truck driver's papers all made out and ready to be signed.

"Just sign these," he said, "and we'll get them right off to Tupelo."

"I done about changed my mind about that," said the truck driver. "I believe I'd druther not be foreman."

"Why, what's the matter," said the Supervisor. "You can handle the job all right. And it means thirteen dollars more a month to you."

"I'd just ruther not have it," said the truck driver.

"I tell you what you do," said the Supervisor. "I'll just hold these papers over until tomorrow and you think it over again tonight and let me know in the morning. You keep on acting foreman and we'll see how you feel about it in the morning."

The next morning the Supervisor came down to the job again but the truck driver was worried and stubborn in refusal.

"I'd druther be put back to just common labor than to have to take it," he said.

"Well, all right," said the Supervisor, puzzled. "If you just won't take it, you won't. You won't be put back to common labor for refusing it, but I do wish you'd take it."

"I'd druther be just common labor," repeated the truck driver.

"We got our man elected all right," said paw that night, "but the Supervisor just weren't agreeable with us a tall about it. All of us was glad to see Mr. Brooks git it too but somehow it looks like the Supervisor is just plain prejudiced agin 'im. I cain't understand it neither. Mr. Brooks is a good deserving man and one of the oldest men on the job too. I just cain't understand it. I guess we showed the Supervisor pretty plain we weren't a-going to stand fer that truck driver though."

"Well, I do know," said maw. "Have you got air foreman yit?"

"Yes," said paw. "They transferred a feller from another job that don't none of us know. I never knowed 'em to git a transfer through so quick before. I wisht we could of kept Mr. Brooks. He's a right friendly sort of feller. Likes to josh with the boys and all."

"Well, I do know," said maw.

They sat without talk or movement, then paw stretched and yawned and rose to go to bed and maw rose and got the bowl of food for Reno from the wash-stand.

"I declare," she said. "I got interested in the election and stuff and done set here and let Rinno's food git cold. Hit don't look like hit makes much difference though. The pore feller is just about quit eating."

"Well," said paw. "And I thought the other night when he bellered out so he was gitting better."

"Naw," said maw. "Hit just looks like he ain't doing no good a tall. He even done quit rolling his head to-wards the door ever' time somebody comes in."

"Maybe I better see ifen the men kin git up some-thing else to try out on him," said paw.

"Maybe you better," agreed maw. "This last is done about give out anyhow."

"Is he got a good scab on him?"

"He did have," said maw, "but the whole thing come off this morning, and I declare hit's a deep hole in his chest."

"Maybe that last stuff was a little too strong."

"Hit might have been," said maw, "then hit might have been that lard that I put on him the night I fixed up your hands and back. Maybe that made hit stick to the bandage and pull off. Hit looks like we ain't never healed hit up down inside a tall."

"Maybe ifen we had got to hit fust with that stuff before that doctor put that sa've on hit we could have cyored hit down inside."

"I wonder ifen hit would," said maw. "How-some-ever that doctor was right positive agin anything but sa've."

"I never had much confidence in doctors since that 'un made such a pore out of Rinno," said paw.

Fourteen

Rumblings from the War were becoming louder and more threatening and the government was turning an anxious eye on its navy in Mid-Pacific and its pitifully small army and its inadequate defense system.

"—and so," said the man from Tupelo, "it has become necessary that the government get a dollar's worth of work for each dollar spent. Those men who are too old to give us a day's work will be laid off and their names placed on the direct relief rolls and their places will be filled by younger and more able-bodied men. Do not Four Oh Three them, just suspend them indefinitely on a form Four Eighteen."

Paw got laid off and Steve Joe and old man Doyle.

"Hit just ain't right," said paw. "Here they done got us to move to town and promised us work and now they want to lay us off. Hit just ain't right. Us men needs the work too, just the same as the younger ones. And I bound ye I got just as big a set of dependents as air one of 'em. Hit just ain't right. I'll go see Mr. Will in the morning fust thing. He can keep us from gitting laid off."

"No, it ain't right," said maw. "A body cain't git used to white flour and meat agin afore they got to be thinking about them celeries and apples and stuff. It just ain't right. You git to Mr. Will early afore somebody else thinks about him and beats you to him."

"I aim to do it," said paw. "I shorely aim to do it."

Paw got to the City Hall shortly after day the next morning but a goodly crowd was already there. Seven o'clock came and seven-thirty. Mr. Will drove up and stopped before he noticed the crowd on the front steps.

"I'll be back in a minute," he called as he re-started his motor and drove off away from the City Hall hunched over the wheel of his car.

Eight o'clock came and the office workers commenced to arrive. The crowd on the front steps had increased and they followed the office workers upstairs. In faded overalls and patched overalls they sat on the one bench and squatted back against the walls.

Mr. Will's going to git us back on. He ain't here right now, but he said he'd be back in a minute. Mr. Will's going to help us.

They knotted in front of the Social Worker's door and stood staring at the scuffed concrete beneath their feet. At each movement inside her office they raised their eyes and stared in silence at the vague reflection on the opaque glass of the door. The door opened and the men straightened up and fastened their eyes on the Social Worker in the door.

232

"Is Mr. Moody out in the hall?"

Mr. Moody shuffled forward with a grimy and bent appointment card in his hand. The Social Worker held the door open as he entered and closed it behind him. The men in the hall settled back into their former positions and dropped their eyes to the floor. Patient, resigned, bewildered.

Steve Joe came into the hall and pushed his huge bulk through the crowd. His mouth drooped and brown tobacco juice stained it at the corners. His red-rimmed eyes glared balefully at the crowd in the hall as he pushed his way up to the Social Worker's door and opened it without knocking. The Social Worker was seated opposite the hunched-over drab little figure of Mr. Moody and she looked up not surprised but annoyed at this unannounced intrusion.

"I'm busy right now," she said to Steve Joe. "If you'll wait in the hall until—"

"I just got to say something," said Steve Joe, blocking the door with his balloonlike proportions.

"You'll have to wait your turn," said the Social Worker, rising and coming around from behind the desk.

"Hit won't take but a minute," said Steve Joe, "but I got to say it."

The Social Worker took the inside knob of the door in her hand and tried to swing the door to but Steve Joe was weighted too firmly in place.

"Mrs. Scott told my wife that her husband told her

that some feller told him that the foreman down to the job told him that the Supervisor said that I couldn't use no shovel. I just want to know ifen he did?"

"Even if he did, it wouldn't be on the record that I keep. And I would appreciate it if you would move back so I could close the door and the next time you want to see me about anything, please knock before you enter."

She pushed the door against Steve Joe, but he still stood firm as a rock.

"I just want ever' body to know that I can use a shovel as good as air body."

"I'm sure you can," said the Social Worker, "and now if you'll let me close the door—"

Steve Joe allowed himself to be pushed slowly into the hall but the baleful light glowed undiminished in his red-rimmed eyes.

One of the office men who had been standing in the hall grinning at the Social Worker over Steve Joe's shoulder said, "Steve, what's your trouble? Somebody been telling something on you that wasn't so?"

"You been hearing about this war in Yurrup, ain't you? Well, that war ain't nothing to the one I aim to start if I find out that feller told that on me."

Steve Joe turned and waddled down the hall and as he left an old fellow propped against the wall by the Social Worker's door said, "That's that fat son-of-a-bitch of a foreman that got my boy fired offen the WP and A."

✦

234

Boy, did you hear that one about that big fat feller with the funny-looking red eyes that's been working on the WPA that hangs around over to the Court House yard all day Saturdays? You know. That one that's always standing sort of bent ahead with his hands behind his back doing all the orating. Well, after they held that last election down there on the job the Supervisor finally had to transfer a foreman off of another job to be foreman because the men wouldn't let nobody on their own job be foreman except that sorry old Brooks feller and the Supervisor couldn't let him be foreman because he couldn't even hold one them shovels good, he was so old. Well, this new foreman hadn't been on the WPA long and he didn't know they was just supposed to stand around and lean on them shovels. He thought they was supposed to work. Well, this big fat feller just stood around trying to tell everybody else what to do and how to do it and they was one feller down there that talked so much he not only didn't have time to do no work hisself but he wouldn't give nobody else time to do none, they was so busy listening to him, so this new foreman sent the fat feller and the talking feller way off to theirselves so's they wouldn't worry the rest of 'em—when the talking feller would kind of stop to catch his breath then the fat one would have a chance to tell the men how to do whatever it was they was doing and he always told them wrong—and one day the foreman went over to where he had sent the fat feller and the talking feller to see what they was doing and there was the fat feller

setting on a stump talking and the talking feller standing in a ditch about ten foot in front of the fat feller
talking. The fat feller had elected hisself foreman and
the talking feller didn't care who was foreman and the
fat feller had got hisself a dollar watch and tied it onto
the front of his overalls with a wide red strip of cloth
so's they could tell easy which one was foreman and
every now and then he would pull about a foot of red
cloth and the dollar watch out of his pocket and look
at the watch and after a while he would pull it out and
tell the talking feller it was time to quit and then he'd
stuff the watch and some of the red cloth back in his
pocket and the talking feller would hide his shovel under some brush and they would go home. Well, they
started getting some of these quota reductions down to
the office and this talking feller got caught with one of
them and got one of them Oh Fours or whatever it is
they send out from Tupelo when they figger they've
got too many men leaning on what shovels they got
left and the talking feller's daddy thought the fat feller
was the foreman sho' 'nuff and had fired his boy. The
WPA. I declare.

Paw was sitting on the steps in front of the City Hall
when Mr. Brooks came shuffling up and dropped down
beside him. They sat in silence for several minutes and
then Mr. Brooks spoke at last.

"Hit looks like something ought to be done about hit,
don't hit?"

"Yes," said paw. "Hit does."

236

They sat and stared across the yard with their hands hanging limp between their knees.

"Yes sir. Hit looks like something ought to be done."

"Hit ought to, shore 'nuff. They got us to town and now they won't let us work."

Silence then for a few more minutes while two more of the overall-clad figures shuffled slowly and without purpose up the walk between the well-tended lawns and stopped in front of paw and Mr. Brooks.

"Won't you all set?" invited paw.

"Don't keer if we do," they said and sat on the steps.

"How's that boy of yours that had them sores?" one of them asked paw.

"Looks like he ain't doing no good," said paw.

They gazed with mild unhurried eyes out across the yard.

"Still a-running, air they?"

"Yes," said paw. "Seems like ever' time we most git 'em stopped they just bust out wuss."

"I knowed a old woman named Net what lived out by us what could cyore 'em."

Their eyes followed a truck past the City Hall and on down the street.

"She give my wife the knowing of how to mix up some stuff that I bound ye will cyore 'em."

Their hands hung limp between their knees and their hats were tilted against the light.

"I'll git some fixed up fer you tomorrow."

"Well now," said paw. "I'll be right obliged."

The next day paw saw the man in front of the post office.

"Here's that stuff I was a-telling you about," said the man, holding out a small used paper sack. "Just put hit on twict a day and he's bound to git well."

"Well now," said paw. "You fellers have been a sight of help with Rinno. Hit's a pleasure to have a sickness in the house when a body has good friends. I'll give this to maw tonight and I bound ye Rinno will be well in no time. I allus believe in home remedies."

"We are a great believer in 'em too," said the man. "I've knowed my old woman to even cyore risings with that stuff."

"Well, I know hit'll cyore Rinno," said paw.

That night paw gave the new medicine to maw and she removed the bandage from Reno's chest and applied the medicine and replaced the dirty pads.

"I'm proud to git this," she said. "Them sores 'pear to be gitting deeper and deeper. I hope this will stop 'em."

"Hit will," said paw. "The feller that give hit to me said hit'll even cyore risings. Said a old, old woman named Net give hit to his woman. Leastways give the knowing how to make hit."

"Well," said maw. "Hit was right narce of 'em to give this to us."

"He said his woman will be glad to make us some more when this gives out. I tell you, a good neighbor is a sight of help."

238

"Yes, he is," said maw. "A good neighbor is a comfort."

Reno lay without even rolling his head now. He did not repulse his food any more nor did he swallow it. It merely lay in his mouth until maw hooked a finger in and removed it and now she tried to feed him by dipping the end of a strip of torn cloth into a bowl of suet and placing the saturated end in his mouth, hoping that some of the liquid would trickle down his throat.

The next morning paw stood with his fellows waiting for the post office window to open—a long line of overalled figures in their cracked brogans, with their sweat-stained felt hats pulled low over their eyes. They stood not in resignation, for their lives knew no compulsions, but more in patient unhope.

The mail was up and as the clock boomed out the first of the eight notes the window slammed up to frame the neat, spectacled clerk with his fixed half smirk, smug in patent forbearance, and the nearest in the long line called his name timidly across the polished metal of the counter. The clerk riffled through the letters beneath one of the alphabetical slots and flipped them back expertly as he shook his head. The man moved away, not disappointed, for he had not been expectant, and the next in line moved up through the stillness of carefully shuffled feet. Paw's turn came and the clerk flipped a letter out to him.

"Fer me?" said paw in surprise.

"For some of your folks," said the clerk. "It's in your care."

"Well," said paw. "I weren't hardly looking fer nothing this morning."

"What did you come up here for then?" said the clerk.

"Well," said paw, "I thought I might somehow git a Four Oh Two. Some of us fellers is hoping we might git a Four Oh Two."

"Move over please," said the clerk. "There are some people behind you trying to get to the window."

Paw shuffled to one side, turning the letter over and over in his hand.

"Why don't you open hit, Mr. Taylor?" said one of the men at his elbow.

"Well now, I could do that," said paw.

He hooked a gnarled finger under the corner of the poorly stuck flap and inched it slowly along the length of the envelope. He spread the ripped edges open and peered into it.

"Well," he said. "A five dollar bill. Now I wonder who sent that."

"Look and see who signed the letter," suggested one.

"Well now," said paw. "Somehow I never had time to learn how to read. Kin any of you fellers make hit out?"

He partly withdrew the sheet of folded foolscap from the cheap envelope but paused as they all shook their heads. He smoothed the paper back into the envelope and put it in his hip pocket.

"Well, I guess some of the chillun kin read hit to me tonight."

240

But that night when paw happened to think of the letter he could not find it.

"I must have lost it," he said. "But anyhow I'm right glad I taken the five dollars out when I fust got hit. I'd of hated to not been able to git this new raddio."

"Hit's a sight purtier than the last one," said maw.

"Yes, hit is," said paw. "And the feller give us twenty months to pay fer hit in too."

"Well now. That was right narce of him," said maw.

And at the City Hall that evening the janitor swept up the letter along with the rest of the trash that littered the floor up in the long hall. Noticing the folded sheet of paper inside, he picked it from the trash basket and withdrew the letter hopefully.

"Shucks," he said. "Look lak they mought drop something with some money in hit sometime."

He unfolded the piece of foolscap and laboriously spelled out the words.

DEAR BUDDY—

I'm getting along fine and hope you are the same by now. I'm working out at a saw mill and can not get to town to get you some more paints and paper so you take this money and get you some. I guess Rinno is all right now with that salve the doctor give me for him. I will write to you again soon.

HUB

Another quota reduction came in and the last two men in the big house lost their jobs. Only Fred was left on. Rent time came again and paw went to see the land-lord.

"Hit looks like we ain't going to be able to pay no rent this time," said paw. "They done had to lay the last of us off this time to help the gove'ment git by till the new physical year. But Mr. Will says he will have us all back on soon's the new physical year gits here."

"Well," said the landlord, "that's in two weeks now and I guess there ain't much we can do about it until then. Did you get your water turned on?"

"Well, no sir," said paw. "We somehow just didn't never git around to it."

"Well, I don't know what you are going to do about water. The man next door has been to me about you using his water again."

"Well now, I just reckon we will have to see about having that water turned on," said paw.

That evening when Gwendolin went for the water she came back with an empty bucket.

"They ain't no more pipe over there," she said. "They's a new pile of dirt right where the pipe was."

"Well, I do know," said maw. "I reckon hit must have got something wrong with it and they just took hit up. Or maybe he needed hit to put in his house some'ers. Go over to the house on the other side and see ifen maybe they ain't got a pipe in their yard. We ain't never looked in hit."

Gwendolin went there and came back with her bucket empty again.

242

"They got a pipe in their yard but they ain't no water in it," she said.

"Well, I do know," said maw. "Maybe the waterpipe out in the street has done gone dry. Maybe we better try acrost the street anyhow. Hit might be somebody drawed up some water afore hit give out."

Gwendolin went to the house across the street and this time she returned with her bucket full.

"Well, that's fine," said maw. "I was beginning to be a-feared we might have to start going back up to that little pond in front of the Hall."

The landlord was talking to a group in the barber shop the next morning.

"It looks like the WPA could handle matters better than they do," he said. "I've got that big house of mine rented to a couple of old fellows with their families with 'em and they've cut both of them off from work. They came in from the country I guess. Old fellow looks like a farmer. Old fellow by the name of Taylor."

"Taylor? Why, that's the fellow they had such a time with in that big house below the City Hall. How much rent are they paying?"

"Well, we agreed on forty dollars."

"Forty or forty hundred's all the same. Do you know how much they get a month?"

"Well, no."

"After they take out for the time they stand around the post office waiting for their checks and then the time they spend in the beer joints when their checks

243

do come it amounts to about thirty dollars a month."

"Thirty dollars a month? Why, I don't see how they can pay forty dollars rent on that. With just the two of them that's twenty dollars apiece. And they both have families. I've noticed three or four men over there once or twice. Maybe they took in a couple more men to help pay the rent. I've noticed him talking several times like there might be more than just the two of them there."

"If you've got a five it'll get you ten that there are at least seven families in your house and maybe eight."

"There can't be. There are only five rooms in the house besides the kitchen and dining room."

"You go down there and count them."

"Good Lord," said the landlord.

"Have they paid their rent regular?"

"Well, they did the first month."

"You'll never get rid of them. The City will be cutting their water off pretty soon and when they do those folks will make the biggest mess out of your place you ever saw."

"Why, they never have been able to get it cut on yet. They borrowed water from the house next door until the man that lives there had to have his yard-hydrant taken up."

"You better get to work on them now. It took six months after they quit paying rent to get them out of that big house below the City Hall."

"Good Lord," said the landlord again. "How did they get rid of them before?"

244

"They had to put them all back to work so the lady that owns the house could start trying to collect the back rent they owed her and they all left then."

"Well," said the landlord, "this Mr. Taylor has been telling me that some Mr. Will down at the City Hall is going to put them all back to work on the first of July."

"Why, that lying Will will tell them anything. They ain't going to get put back on the first of July. Them old fellows ain't going to get put back on at all. The WPA is going to hire a bunch of young fellows to build roads and airports with on account of this war in Europe and we've got to train a bunch of soldiers and we've got to do it quick. How long do you think it would take Mr. Taylor to build an airport?"

"Well, I'll be damned," said the landlord at last.

They filled the long hall outside the Social Worker's door again, sitting and squatting patiently in their patched and faded overalls and spitting into the corners, stoop-shouldered from long years of digging and peering at the soil, thin-eyed from watching the long rows before the mule, brown from unprotected labor beneath the summer's sun, as eternal and uninviting as the very land that bore them, patient to resignation, diffident, self-contained, pleased with small considerations as children upon being noticed, wanting little and getting less, complaining among themselves because complaint was their universal language, not resentful of a world that scorned them, believing steadfastly in a guidance and a fulfillment, misunderstanding and misunderstood, shy of every man yet believing in them all, not immoral but unmoraled, trained through generations to unambition and canny greed, open-handed yet subversive, different in shape and form and fashion, yet with identical expressions and summations of vagueness and bewilderment and despair, as much a part of the land that bore them as the land itself that they tortured and desecrated with their half-hearted efforts at plowing, transplanted but unwelcome in an environment that their fathers made possible and that they themselves supported, incongruous and incomplete away from their ill-tended fields and the poverty of their disreputable shacks, untrustworthy and forgetful yet steadfast as faith itself in their devotion, bringing disaster on themselves with eager hands, tragic in their ignorance, and the ultimate tragedy was that they were unaware of the tragedy that they were.

From seven until five they sat and squatted in the hall, walked into the Social Worker's office when their turns came and repeated their identical stories of want and mouths to feed and willingness to work and desperation. The Social Worker listened patiently to the oft-repeated tale and shut her mind to the tragedy of it and carefully explained the rules and regulations that were final and unchangeable, and they protested half-heartedly and left with their shoulders a little more stooped, their eyes a little more bewildered, their minds still unconvinced.

I declare, hit looks like the WP and A could go ahead

and put us back to work, they said. Mr. Will said he was going to put us all back to work soon's the new gove'ment physical year gits here. Looks like they might's well put us back to work now.

Where is Mr. Will? Ain't saw Mr. Will this week. Been looking fer 'im too.

Have you looked back in his office?

Yes. That girl back there said he weren't in just now.

Maybe ifen we wait around awhile we could see Mr. Will.

I saw him passing through here the other day but his neuralgy had done took him bad again. He couldn't even stop and talk to none of us.

Mr. Will could git us back on ifen we could just catch him sometime when his neuralgy weren't a-hurting him.

Maw waked first that night drenched with the sweat of unconscious fear. She strained her ears into the darkness and caught paw by the shoulder and drew him awake.

"What is it?" said paw.

"Listen," said maw into the tense stillness.

They heard it again and maw rose trembling in bed.

"Hit's Rinno," she said. "Listen."

A gurgling rasp like an indistinct bellow heard through turbid water filled the room and then silence cut off the sound.

"Hit's Rinno," said maw again.

And now the children waked and were held in the

thick silence that followed the sound and the baby waked and shrunk close to maw's trembling side. Their breath burst across the darkness.

"Git up! Git up!" said maw and they heard her bare feet thump to the floor and heard her fumbling hands find the box of matches, then the rasp and sputter of the match against the doorjamb by the lamp. The chimney rattled against the burner prongs and was drowned out in Reno's next gurgling croak. The tiny flare of the match moved beneath maw's jutting cheekbones and touched the blackened wick and the wick flared into life. Maw replaced the chimney and adjusted the flame with practiced hand and turned to Reno's pallet. The children tiptoed in a close huddle in behind her and paw hung over the edge of the bed and Reno writhed and gasped for breath beneath their grouped down-stare.

"Rinno!" said maw. "Rinno!" And she dropped to her knees by his pallet.

Reno's mouth drew back from his yellow snags and his face contorted in awful effort to fill his clamoring lungs with breath.

"Look, maw," shrieked Gwendolin. "Look. His shirt's a-jumping up and down over his chest. They's something in it. Somethin's a-biting him," and her voice rose to a shriek of prolonged terror and Eugenia added her wails to Gwendolin's and the rest of the childen shrunk in a closer knot behind maw.

Maw lowered her gaze from the grimace of effort that was Reno's gargoyle face to the shirt above his chest. At each painful gasp the splotched cloth would flute as

248

from the stroke of a hand pump and at each exhalation it plastered flat to his skin. Maw stretched forth a trembling hand and raised the edge of the pad and as Reno gasped in the next lung full of air the hole in his chest bubbled a foamy froth and as the exhaled air whistled out through his distended lips the froth subsided and drew back into his lungs.

"Paw," said maw. "Paw. Hit's et plumb through his chest. He's a-breathing right on through his skin."

Paw's mouth hung lax and he gazed at the bubbling hole in fascinated horror.

Reno's gasps grew faster as his pumping lungs strove to replace the leaking air and he sucked the drool from his mouth into his throat and his lungs filled with it. His hands clenched and the sweat of agony beaded his flat forehead as he sucked desperately at the air that whistled and gurgled into the distorted snarl of his lips. And his lungs filled and he died with his eyes staring up into the cool dark air that he struggled for.

They left the lamp on and sat the rest of the night out and Reno lay on his pallet and stared up into the shadows.

Daylight came and maw went down and cooked breakfast and they trooped silently down the stairs and ate and came back up to the room and sat around and at last someone thought to turn the light out.

"Well, paw. What are we going to do now?" said maw.

"I just hadn't thought about it," said paw. "Seems like

we maybe ought to git some kind of a coffin together fer him."

"Hit won't take much a one," said maw. "He's so kind of wasted away."

"He ain't real what you might call hefty," said paw.

The neighbors from downstairs came in and stood awkwardly about the room and the women sat by maw and sniffled and wiped their noses on the hems of their aprons.

"Me and some the fellers might could scare up enough plank out in the back to knock together a coffin fer him," offered one of the men.

"Well now," said paw. "That would be right neighborly of you."

"Yes, hit would," said maw. "I know Rinno would like to know some of his own people done hit."

The men clumped out and down the stairs and while one of them went to his room for a hammer and saw and a small sack of bent and rusty nails the rest scoured the back-yard for plank.

"Plank is right sca'ce out here," said one of the men. "We might take up two-three them plank outen the back porch though, to kind of finish hit out with. We kin notify ever' body about the hole so's they won't nobody fall in hit."

"Won't likely nobody be coming out on the back porch after dark nohow," said another.

"That's right," said the first. "So hit won't make no difference nohow."

They ripped up planking from the porch and fash-

250

ioned a flat box and knelt back on their heels and surveyed it through their mild sweat.

"Well, she's finished, men. We might as well take her up and see how she fits."

Two of them lifted the light dry box and clumped heavily and solemnly into the house and up the stairs and set it on the floor by Reno with careful clumsiness and stepped back while two of the women lifted Reno in his quilts and let him easily down into the box and folded the corners of the quilt over him. The men hammered the top on and stood back.

"Well, that was a pretty good fit fer a quick job like that," said one of the men.

"Yes sir, hit was," agreed another. "Didn't have to do nothing but kind of bend his legs a little and that don't show under all them quilts."

"Where do you aim to put him to rest, Miz Taylor?" asked one of the women.

"Well now," said maw. "I just hadn't never thought about hit."

"The rest of Mr. Taylor's family is out to London Hill, ain't they?"

"Well, yessum," said maw. "They are."

"I guess then ifen Rinno could say he would want to be with his own people."

"Yessum," said maw. "I know he would."

"Ifen you want me to, Mr. Taylor, I could go down to town with you and see ifen we kin git a-holt of Frank," offered one of the men. "He don't come to town regular 'cep'n' Saddys, but he might be in today."

"Well now," said paw. "I'll take hit right kindly ifen you will."

So paw and the man departed for town and they hung around the Square until night without a sight of Frank and his truck but they sent word by roundabout verbal message that paw wanted to see him the next time he came to town.

That night when bedtime came the neighbor women were still sitting about the room solemnly morbid and spitting unhurriedly into the empty fireplace.

"I guess Miz Taylor had better rest tonight," said one of them. "We kin just take hit time about, setting up with Rinno, and she can git the rest she needs so bad in her time of trouble."

They nodded their heads in solemn agreement.

"Thankee kindly," said maw and she rose and lay down on the bed above Reno without even taking off her tennises and soon was asleep.

Paw took off his hat and shoes and crawled over maw and lay back and composed himself for slumber. The children crawled into their beds and lay down on their pallets and Virginia lay in her bed and watched with resentful eyes while her baby sucked at her full breast. The women rose and clumped heavily out, save one who sat stiff-backed in the glow of the lamp discharging her duty into the snore-filled room.

Frank failed to get the word and although paw spent the next day sitting on the curb at Frank's usual parking place he did not show up.

"I just don't know when we'll git word to Frank,"

,aid paw that night. "Likely I won't see him till Saddy."

So the neighbors gave up their death-watch and one of the men helped paw shove Reno's box out of the way under the bed and Reno lay beneath the quilts staring up into the blackness of his coffin.

Fifteen

It was the next day when the Board of Health called on the landlord.

Looka here, they said. You are going to have to do something about that big house of yours down on Mill Street.

I've already done something about it, the landlord said.

Well, you've got to do something else then, the Board of Health said.

What else can I do?

Make them move out.

How? In God's name.

That's up to you. It's your house and you must keep it clean. That's the law.

So the landlord went to see his tenants.

"Look here, Mr. Taylor," he said. "It's after the first of July and it don't look like you will be able to get back on the WPA for a while yet anyway. And besides that the Board of Health is complaining about this place. My taxes run right on whether I can collect any rent from this property or not and with you all here there is no chance for me to rent the house to anyone else. Can you all be out of here by the first of next month?"

"Well now," said paw, "we don't none of us aim to stay nowhere where we ain't welcome. I guess we kin git around to moving by the fust."

"Now, I don't mean it exactly that way," said the landlord, "but you understand how it is. A man has certain obligations that he has to meet and these days and times it takes all any of us can rake and scrape to keep out of the poorhouse. If you could pay even part of your rent it would help or even if you had any prospects of a job we might could work out something but the WPA is changing every day now. The government has got to get ready in case of war coming to this country and we've got to get ready in a hurry. It takes young hardy men to stand the kind of work the WPA is going to have to do from now on. Us old fellows can't stand the pace."

The landlord stood watching paw, and paw gazed out across the yard with a vague bewildered stare.

"Well, see if you can get moved by the first of August and we will just forget about the rent you already owe me."

"I 'low we kin git around to the moving," said paw, "but we ain't aiming to not pay no rent. We'll git back on soon's Mr. Will kin git around to it."

"Well, I hope you do," said the landlord. "I hope you do."

The landlord went by the Board of Health's office to report to them.

"They are getting out by the first," said the landlord. "Then I intend to tear the house down and put up an apartment house down there."

"I hope you are right about their moving," said the Board of Health.

"I'm sure I am," said the landlord. "I felt right sorry for the old codger. He and his kind are sort of pathetic. The WPA brings them to town on a mere pittance and then takes their jobs away from them when it's too late for them to make a crop or even a garden."

"Humph," said the Board of Health.

The landlord contracted to have the house torn down and included a ten-day time limit in the contract. The beginning date was August the first and there were penalty clauses and bonus clauses included. August the first, and the contractor moved his equipment in to start demolishing the house. They set up their ladders and scaffolds and nailed toe-boards to the roof and began ripping off the shingles. Paw and his people came out in the yard and craned their necks back as they watched the men tearing off the roof.

"I wonder ifen they could use any more help," said paw.

"I don't know," said one of paw's men. "We might could ast 'em."

They picked out the one who seemed to be boss. He

was standing straddled the ridgepole of the roof with his feet braced against the pitch on either side and paw, followed by the six men, started up the ladder. The men working on the roof were unaware of their presence until paw's head appeared above the edge of the roof.

"Hey," shouted the man straddling the ridgepole. "Get the hell back down that ladder before you fall and get hurt. Get on down, I say."

Paw strained around and leaning his head down as far as he could passed the word to the six men below him and they began their slow, unaccustomed descent of the almost straight up-and-down ladder. It swayed alarmingly under their combined weight and paw cautioned them to descend one at a time. The boss, seeing paw still with his head stuck above the roof and not knowing the other men were on the ladder below him, grew angry and slid from toe-hold to toe-hold down the roof towards paw.

"Get the hell on down there," he shouted again angrily. "You old gray-headed fool. You'll fall off that ladder and kill yourself."

Paw looked up with his mild eyes.

"We're hurrying fast's we kin, mister," he said. "Seems like if we all try to git down to onct the ladder pretty near throws us off."

"We?" said the boss. "How many of you are there on that ladder?"

"They ain't only seven," said paw.

"Seven? God-o-Mighty. It's a wonder that ladder

ain't broke before now. It's a wonder you ever got up this high. What do you want up here anyhow?"

"We 'lowed as how you might need some help gitting the roof off. Air ye fixing to put a new roof on?"

"Hell, no," said the boss. "We are tearing the house down."

"Well, I declare," said paw. "We all lives in it."

"Live in it? Why, the man we contracted with said the house was empty. Said there were some folks in it then—that was about two weeks ago—but that they would be moved out by the first. Are you the folks he was talking about?"

"Well, I guess we must be," said paw.

"Who are all the rest of those men on the ladder?"

"They are some of the folks what lives here."

"Haven't any of you got any womenfolks to look after you?"

"Why, yes sir," said paw. "Them's our womenfolks down there in the yard."

"And them children too?"

"Well, yes sir," said paw. "Leastways that's the most of us. All 'cep'n' what babies we got. They're mostly in the house."

"God-o-Mighty," said the boss again. "All those people live in just one house?"

"It is a mite crowded at times," said paw.

"I believe that," said the boss. "How many families do you put to the room?"

"Well, nearly ever' fambly has a room to hitself."

"Look here, grandpaw," said the boss. "We con-

258

tracted to tear this house down in ten days and every day over ten it takes us we got to pay fifty dollars to the man that owns it. I don't know what sort of arrangements you had about the house but unless we get orders to stop, down she comes. Can't you get the folks you work for to let you have a truck or something to move in and start moving?"

"Well, you see," said paw. "We ain't none of us working now. We aim to git back on right away but ain't none of us got no job just now."

"Well, can't you get whoever you've been working for to help you out?"

"Well, no sir. I don't hardly believe we could."

"Why, there ain't any boss that hard. Who you been working for?"

"We all been on the WP and A."

"Well, I'll be a son-of-a-bitch," said the boss. "Well, you get on down this ladder while I hold it and tell them folks down there they better move farther away from the house so's we won't hit any of 'em with these shingles and pieces of roof."

"You couldn't use no more help up here?"

"No, grandpaw. I'm sorry but we're full up right now."

He held the ladder at the roof edge while paw made his laborious way down.

The workers tore the roof off and when the splinters and dust started sifting through into the upstairs rooms the inhabitants of the rooms gathered their scant belongings and moved downstairs and paw and Jutland carried Reno in his box and placed him under maw's bed in its new place. The workers finished the roof and went to work on the upstairs walls. They finished these and tore out the upstairs floor and paw found a new home for the seven families.

A widow had moved to town and built a plain two-story house and taken in roomers and boarders to enable her to send her children to school. The children finished school and moved away and got jobs and sent for their mother and she went to live with them. The house had served its purpose but the payments for its erection had not all matured. The mother placed the house in the hands of an agent and he rented out the downstairs floor but the rent only amounted to half the payments. And paw heard of the vacant upstairs and contacted the agent and made his arrangements to move in. He came with his families and all their belongings and the seven families placed themselves in the four upstairs rooms. The occupants of the downstairs part stared aghast as the borrowed truck made load after chugging load, bringing the bent, iron beds and the rusty springs and the ragged quilts and the broken and spliced chairs.

The last load came and in it was Reno in his box and he was carried upstairs and pushed under maw's bed and the man from downstairs came out to meet paw as he climbed down from the cab.

"Is this all?" he asked paw.

"Yes sir," said paw. "I believe that just about winds hit up."

260

"I hope so," said the man. "How many of you are there?"

"About seven families not counting my daughter and her husband and their baby."

"I mean, how many people are there?"

"Well now," said paw. "You know we ain't never tooken the trouble to count up. I wonder, myself, just how many of us they are. We've got a right sizable crowd since you come to think about it."

"Yes, you have," said the man. "How are you all going to get in just four rooms?"

"It may be a mite crowded," said paw, "but I 'low we'll manage somehow."

"About the light and water," said the man. "I've got a deposit up for it at the City Hall."

"Well now," said paw, "we aim to pay our share. Whatever it comes to just let us know at the end of the month and likely we kin git it up."

The agent came around as they got the last of their furnishings moved upstairs.

"I see you got moved all right," he said.

"Yes sir," said paw. " 'Tweren't no trouble a tall. No trouble a tall."

"Place suit you all right?"

"Why, hit's just fine," said paw. "Just fine."

Finally the agent said, "You know it's customary to pay your rent in advance around here."

"Well now, we aim to do just like the other folks. This moving has took about all the money we had but we will have a little money coming in about next Saddy and we can catch the rent up without no trouble a tall then."

"Well," said the agent, "I guess that will be all right. We don't generally do that but since you've already moved in I guess it will be all right."

"You kin come by and git it," said paw, "or likely I'll be around on the Square next Saddy and I could just drop by and hand it to you. Save you the trouble of having to come way out here."

"Well, if it won't trouble you, just drop by my office with it. I'm always pretty busy Saturday evenings and don't like to leave the office unless I have to."

" 'Twon't be no trouble a tall," said paw. "No trouble a tall."

Sixteen

This new residence of paw's was of plainest frame construction. The walls were of stained ceiling and the floors were unpainted and of pine boards. The only entrance to the upper part was by a stairway that mounted from the lower front hall. Small noises resounded and echoed through the ill-proportioned bare rooms and the heavy workshoes of paw's people clumping through the hall and up the stairs created a clamor that disturbed even the people in the houses across the street and, when they dragged in after night-fall from the beer parlors and places of amusement uptown, sleep in the house itself was impossible. Eugenia had acquired a small dog which slept on the porch and greeted each individual arrival with vociferous and prolonged yapping.

From the habit of years maw waked the first morning in their new residence with the first gray light of dawn and stood in the window as soon as she slipped her mother hubbard over her head and gazed out over the gray still sleeping world as she combed her sparse hair and pulled it into a knot on top of her head.

Paw lay awake, but with eyes still closed as he followed, without having to look, the motions of maw's dressing as she slipped the mother hubbard over her head, shook herself into it as she smoothed it over her spread hips with her hands and buttoned the overlapped front as she moved on bare feet across the floor to the window. He saw her in his mind's eye as she picked the snuff stick from the right-hand side of the window-ledge and placed it in her mouth without withdrawing her gaze from the gray breaking dawn. He could follow the movements of her head, as she cocked it away from the cheap, scarred hairbrush to left, then to right, and almost count the strokes she gave each handful of hair. He heard her feet slipping over the bare floor as she crossed the room, then grow faint and fainter down the hall toward the kitchen, and then he turned on his side and opened his eyes. The children were not yet disturbed by the growing light on their pallet on the floor but he heard Virginia's irritable grunts as her baby pulled and sucked at her breast. Fred had not come in.

Soon the smells of coffee and fat meat frying drifted in from the kitchen and the children stirred uneasily in their dreams. Paw lay over on his back and closed his eyes for a moment, then pushed his feet over the edge of the bed and sat up, his bony wrists and thin shanks sticking past the torn and stretched ends of his union suit.

He pulled his shirt on as he sat on the edge of the bed

264

and slipped his feet into his overalls before standing up and pulling them up over his hips and hunching his shoulder into one still-fastened gallus. He flipped the end of the other gallus over and pulled it down and fastened it, then sat back down and slipped his un-washed feet into his heavy brogans. With no attempt at quietness he clumped across the floor and down the stairs and out the front door and crunched through the gravel driveway by the side of the house to the back of the garage. The dog followed him around to the rear of the house, then left him and returned to the front porch and barked shrilly at him on his return.

The people downstairs waked from their already dis-turbed sleep at the shrill clamor of the dog and, as the rest of the older people upstairs got up one by one and clumped across the floor and down the steps and crunched out to the rear of the garage and the dog's shrill yapping grew almost continuous, they gave up and rose from bed and dressed.

The children got up from their pallets in the rumpled clothes they had worn the day before and now they were all over the stairway and the hall and the front porch, and the ones whose mothers' time at the one stove had not yet come finally drifted aimlessly around out in the yard until one of them happened to see the people below in their dining-room at their breakfast. He moved slowly up to the ground floor window and pressed his face against the screen until the end of his nose and a spot on his forehead showed white, criss-crossed with the black hair lines of the screen, and stared at the food on the table and the people eating it and followed each mouthful from the plate to their mouths. Another head appeared by the head of the discoverer and soon the window was crowded with the pinched faces with their sallow complexions and their too large eyes. Gwendolin came out with the baby and she crowded up to the rear of the knot of children and held the baby a-straddle her hip so it too could peer into the window.

The people at their breakfast saw the children and kept their eyes lowered to their plates to shut out the hungry stares and finally put their forks down and got up and left the table.

The younger boys still slept on their pallets in the hall upstairs, for it was they who had been out late the night before and some of them slept the sleep of just not having waked yet but a few slept the heavy unresting sleep induced by alcohol.

By nine o'clock the men were all squatting in a ring in the front yard, hunkered back with their weight evenly distributed on their two heels, their hands and forearms hanging limply over their knees and their felt hats tilted down over their eyes. The children stood in a silent waiting outer ring and the women had usurped the rockers on the porch and sat and rocked.

"Well, men," said paw, "hit don't appear like hit does much good to go see the Social Worker no more."

They sat quietly, turning this over in their minds.

"No, hit don't," said one finally. "The Hall's been

266

right crowded the last two month. We cain't hardly git in to talk to her."

"If we could just of seen Mr. Will before he left."

"Yes sir. That was too bad about Mr. Will. His neuralgy must of took him turrible. Poor feller."

"Well, them Hot Springs might be the very thing fer 'im. I've heared that they was good fer a right smart different ailments."

"I knowed a feller what went over there onct. Leastways a cousin of my wife's mother's people knowed him. He was took pow'ful bad with the rheumatism. Had done tried ever' thing. Linimint and sa'ves of all kinds and seemed like nothing didn't do him no good. She had another cousin what worked in some shop over there and the feller what had the rheumatism had some kinfolks what lived next door to my wife's cousin and this feller stayed with the folks what lived next door and them baths cured him. They shore done it."

"Them things must be pow'ful stuff or I reckon them rich folks wouldn't all go there."

"I hope they help Mr. Will. I've seen his whole face hurt him so bad he would just have to stop talking to us and go back in that back office and stay back there some times all day. I've waited fer him, myself, sometimes all evening and he couldn't even git outen that back office. I shore hope them Springs help him."

"We lost a friend when Mr. Will left, shore."

"Yes sir. Ifen he could of stayed he would of gotten us ever' one back on. I seen him the morning he was leaving and them's the very words he told me."

"Have any of you men been out to the new road job yit?" said paw.

"Well, yes," said one man. "A couple of us went out there the other day and talked to the foreman but he didn't talk much encouraging about giving none of us work. I told him there was seven of us fellers and hit seemed like he knowed you, Mr. Taylor."

"Well now," said paw. "I don't rec'lect ever knowing nothing about him."

"When I told him they was seven of us all living here together in town he ast me if we was the bunch with a man named Taylor and we told him we was and he said he didn't have nothing we could do right now but ifen anything turnt up later he would know how to git in touch with us."

"Well, I declare," said paw. "I wonder how he knowed me."

When the Tupelo office opened for work that morning, Mr. Will was parked in his car in front of the building. He waited until the District Engineer drove up and then got out of his car and followed the District Engineer into his office. The District Engineer was hanging his hat on the rack when Mr. Will walked in.

"Why, hello, Will," he said as he turned and saw him. "What brings you over here this morning?"

"How about fixing me up a transfer?" said Mr. Will.

"Transfer?" said the District Engineer. "What in the world do you want with a transfer? I thought you were settled for life over yonder."

"Well," said Mr. Will. "You know how it is. A fellow needs a little change every now and then. Needs to see new places and new people. A little change does him good. He gets stale just staying in the same place all the time."

"Have a seat over there," said the District Engineer, indicating an empty chair with a wave of his hand. "As soon as the Placement Officer gets down we'll fix you up something. How are you all getting along over there?"

"Just fine," said Mr. Will. "Just fine."

And back in the City Hall the Supervisor was seated in the Area Engineer's office.

"What's become of Will? I haven't seen him in two or three days now. Is he sick or something?"

"His 'neuralgy' has got him bad," said the Area Engineer.

"I knew he was going to keep on telling all these folks he could get them work cards just a little too long. Why did he do it anyhow?"

"God knows," said the Area Engineer. "I asked him once and he said he had to keep them satisfied. Said that's what they put him up here for."

"Well, he did manage to keep them satisfied for a long time and most of these people still believe he's going to get them a Four Oh Two. They every damn one just know there's somebody up here that can get them a card if they just 'knowed who to tetch on the shoulder.' But it was a shame the lies he told 'em. He kept the whole building full of them all the time. Every time they came up here instead of just telling them there wasn't a chance for them to get back on even when he knew there wasn't he'd always tell them to come back day after tomorrow and he'd have them a work card. Then when they all would gang up on him he would grab his face and say his neuralgia was killing him and run back in that office of his and hide. I've seen him sit back there for whole days at a time just hiding. And I bet he's paid the hospital five hundred dollars when there wasn't a thing wrong with him just for a place to hide in."

"Well," said the Area Engineer. "He's gone now. Went over to Tupelo and got a transfer to the next county."

"Well, I reckon the hospital over there will be glad to see him coming in."

The next morning when paw woke Virginia's baby was nursing and Fred's place in the bed by her was still empty.

Two of the men spent the next day on the bank of the ditch talking to the men at work.

"That boy that married that girl of Mr. Taylor's has done left, ain't he?" said one of the workers.

"Well, I don't know. I ain't heared Mr. Taylor say nothing about it."

"I think he has," said the man in the ditch. "He sort of quit running around and hanging around them dance halls fer a while while he was laid off but he started back again as soon's they put him back to work. I heared some of 'em say that him and that girl of Mr. Taylor's was out to that place out north of town one night soon after that baby was born and him and some city feller had a fight. Leastways he knocked the city feller down and since then he ain't had her out there no more but he kep' on going out there hisself. Ever' time a feller passed out there you could see that A Model of hisn parked in front and most of the time him and one or two girls was in it. He took off from here last Tuesday soon's he got his check with one them girls with him and some one said he had done gone to Memphis."

"Well, I declare. I ain't heared that but he ain't been home in over a week, I know."

"He's gone then. Done left shore. He ain't been to work since he got that check."

That night at supper paw said, "Virginia, where's Fred?"

"I don't know," said Virginia.

"He ain't been around lately," said paw.

Virginia continued to eat her supper in silence.

"One the men heared today down to the job that he had done run off to Memphis with one of them dance-hall girls."

"Well, I'm glad he's gone," said Virginia. "He weren't any good anyhow."

"Didn't he say nothing to you about he was going?" said paw.

Virginia's chair crashed backward to the floor. She

raised her hand as if to strike paw, bafflement and the hurt of outraged pride in her face.

"You go to hell," she said and turned and ran from the room.

"Well now," said paw. "I never knowed I said nothing to make her fly out like that."

"You leave Virginia alone," said maw. "Ever' one of you. You hear?"

When they got upstairs Virginia was on her bed and her face was strangely calm and the hurt and bafflement and resentment were almost gone from it as the baby sucked and gurgled at her breast.

If I can just get you up to where maw can take care of you, she thought, and get rid of this little bastard in my belly, I'll bet you I never get caught again. He's gone for good now. He's gone for good. And I'm glad he's gone. Glad he's gone. But I hope some day I'll have a chance to get even with him for getting me in this fix I'm in.

And back at the supper table maw said, "That lady downstairs was a-talking to me this morning, paw, and she mentioned something about the smell."

"I had noticed that Rinno was gitting to kind of smell," said paw.

"Ain't you got no word from Frank yit?"

"Well no," said paw. "I intended to make 'rangements with that feller that hauled us around here last Saddy to take Rinno out to London Hill but somehow hit slipped my mind. Me being busy with moving and all."

272

"Virginia was complaining about hit today too," said maw. "Said hit disturbed her baby being right there in the same room."

"Hit disturbs ever' body," said Jutland. "Even us out in the hall. Cain't we put him out in the yard just at nights?"

"Well now," said paw. "Hit wouldn't be treating Rinno just right to put him out like that."

"No, it wouldn't," said maw. "Rinno wouldn't want nothing like that."

"Well, I wisht we could git a-holt of Frank," said Jutland.

"I'll most likely see him Saddy," said paw.

The people downstairs sat at breakfast the next morning. The shades were drawn and the single bulb in the ceiling shed its hard glare over the table. Their tempers were short for it was almost two hours before their usual breakfast time.

"Papa," said the son, "let's put the shades up. It's plenty light outside now and it's hot in here with the shades down and the windows shut."

"We just ain't a-going to do it, son," said papa. "That smell whatever it is has gotten so bad we can't stand it with the windows and doors open and when we put the shades up I just can't eat with all them children watching every bite I take. It makes me feel like I was taking it away from them."

"Let's go around there and run them away from the window then," said son.

273

"I've tried it," said papa.

"Go on and eat your breakfast, son," said his mother.

"You ain't eating yours," said son.

"She's saving it for them children out there," said papa. "I know what she's doing. Or else got the headache so bad from not being able to sleep at night she can't eat."

"What time was it they made so awful much noise last night?" said the daughter. "I got in about ten-thirty and it was after that. I had been asleep awhile and they woke me."

"I don't know which time you are talking about," said papa. "They start going to town as soon as it gets dark and as soon as the last one gets out the first one starts coming back in."

"That noise doesn't bother as much as that dog barking all night," said the mother.

"I'm going to town to see the agent about it this morning," said papa. "Something is going to have to be done about it."

So after breakfast papa went to the agent's office and the agent was seated behind his desk.

"Ain't there something we can do about all these people in our house?" said papa.

"All of what people?" said the agent.

"All of those people that live upstairs," said papa. "They are going in and out until midnight and we can't sleep and then they have a dog that barks all night and something is going to have to be done about it. We haven't had a decent night's rest since they moved in."

"Why, there's no one down there but one old man and his family."

"One old man and his family? Why, there are seven families living upstairs."

"Seven? Great God-o-Mighty. Where did they come from?"

"Why, you rented the upstairs to them."

"No, I didn't, either," said the agent. "I rented it to that old man."

"Well, he brought the rest of them in with him when he moved in."

"Why, I saw all those people down there that evening but I thought they were just friends and neighbors that came to help get them moved in and settled down."

"No," said papa, "and somebody told me that they're the folks they had such a time with in that big house below the City Hall last winter."

"The ones that had that baby on the pallet?"

"Yes sir."

"Hmmmm. Well, if that's the same bunch, none of them are working now. They were all on the WPA and got laid off because they wouldn't do anything but stand around down there and hold elections on first one thing and another."

"Well, is there anything we can do about them?" said papa.

"I'll tell you what," said the agent. "They haven't paid the rent yet. Said they would pay it Saturday. That's day after tomorrow and there is no way in the world they can get up any money by then. I'll just go down there and tell them if they don't have the money for me by Saturday they will have to move out. Are you going down that way now? If you are I'll take you."

So papa and the agent got in the car and drove down to the house. Paw as well as the rest of the menfolks was out but the agent left word for paw to come by his office.

Paw came in at noon and maw said, "They was a man here to see you this morning, paw. A real narce feller, too. Said fer you to come by his office over the hardware store to town. Said fer you to come by this evening."

"Well now," said paw. "I bet it's that foreman feller what knows me. Likely he's got jobs fer us. I'll just git the rest of the men and we'll all go up there directly after dinner and that way we won't lose no time. We can just go to work from there. I bound ye the men will be right glad to hear it too."

"I know they will," said maw. "I know they will."

Paw told the men after dinner and one or two of them demurred.

"I just don't know now," said one of them. "I set and watched them fellers out there the other day and hit ain't just like working fer the WP and A. I just believe I'd druther wait till Mr. Will gits back. I'd feel right bad ifen Mr. Will got back and got our cards and we had done took another job."

"That's about the way I feel about it too," said the other. "Hit wouldn't be treating Mr. Will just right."

276

"What do the rest of you men say?" said paw.

"I'll tell you what," said one. "You go down there and talk to that foreman and you can tell him you'll talk hit over with us tonight and then that'll give us kind of a chanct to study hit over."

"Just tell him you'll let him know in the morning," said another.

"Well now, that might be a good idea," said paw. "We won't be bound by nothing until we git a chanct to kind of think hit over like."

So paw went to town alone and the men squatted in a circle and drew marks in the dirt and the children stood pot-bellied behind them watching and the women sat on the porch and rocked.

Paw found the hardware store and the steps that led to the offices above them and he climbed the steps between the soft red brick walls with the weathered plaster crumbling from between the brick. He placed each hesitant exploring foot carefully in the center of the tread where countless steps before him had worn a hollow. At the top he hesitated, looking at the ranked doors on each side of the narrow hall and then moved down the hall peering into each open door. He saw the agent and stood in startled recognition as the agent looked up at the darkening of the door.

"Come in," the agent called.

"Well," said paw, "I didn't know you was up here."

"Weren't you looking for me?" said the agent.

"Well, not just exactly," said paw. "A feller sent fer to give me a job."

277

"What fellow?" said the agent.

"One the foremen out to the new road job."

"You must have gotten your directions mixed up," said the agent. "That road outfit hasn't offices up here. Their office is over on the other side of the Square over that drug store."

"Naw sir," said paw. "This is the place he told me to come. Right up them stairs by the hardware store and the—" he leaned back into the hall and checked the doors off with a gnarled and stiffened forefinger—"one-two—the second door down the hall on the right-hand side. This is it all right."

"When did he tell you?" said the agent.

"Well, he didn't just exactly tell me," said paw. "I wasn't to home when he come this morning but—"

"This morning? Why, that was me out there this morning. You weren't at home and so I left word out there with some of those women that I wanted to see you up here this evening."

"Well now," said paw. "What do you know about that?"

"Has that foreman promised you work?"

"Well, no sir. Not exactly. Some the men was out there the other day and he said he would git in touch with me ifen he ever had anything fer us. He knowed me."

"An old friend of yours?"

The agent was beginning to hope that maybe the man that lived in the downstairs part of the house was mistaken and that there was a possibility that he could get even more rent than the twenty dollars a month he had agreed on if all seven of the men could get road jobs. But another glance at paw's ineffectual attitude raised a doubt as to anybody wanting him for any kind of work and paw's next words wiped the hope clean from his mind.

"Well, not just exactly," said paw. "I don't rightly know him a tall but hit seemed like the other day when them two fellers was a-talking to him he somehow knowed me. Soon's them two fellers told him they was with Mr. Taylor—that's me—he called me to mind right off. Said he didn't believe he had nothing that us fellers would be interested in right then but ifen he ever did he'd know to git in touch with me."

"Well," said the agent, "I doubt if he's got anything for you yet. But what I wanted to see you about is this. Are you going to have the rent ready for me day after tomorrow?"

"Well now, we had been figgering some on it," said paw.

"Well, you'll have to get it up, that's all," said the agent. "You see, I don't own the house. I just handle it for the folks that do. I really shouldn't have let you move in like I did without you paying the rent in advance. And besides that, why didn't you let me know there were so many of you? I thought it was just you and your family."

"Well now, what do you know about that?" said paw. "Why, I never thought nothing about it. We're all just

WP and A folks and we been together might nigh ever since we got into town."

"But none of you are working now, are you?"

"Well, naw sir. Not just right now. Mr. Will has been kind of looking out fer us but his neuralgy done took him so bad he's done went to Hot Springs to take them baths."

"I'd like to be in Hot Springs with Mr. Will," said the agent. "I'd like to give Mr. Will just exactly two and one half baths. In and out, in and out, and in."

"Yes sir," said paw a little puzzled about the bath business.

"Well, anyhow. You have that rent for me Saturday," said the agent.

"Well now, we'll most likely do some figgering on hit," said paw.

Paw made his hesitant way back down the steps, stood for a moment in the doorway at the foot, then made his slow unurgent way on around the Square. He saw the Supervisor pull his car into the curb, get out and enter a store and he quickened his pace and stopped in front of the store the Supervisor had entered and watched him through the plate glass as he waited patiently for him to come back out. The Supervisor emerged and paw caught his attention with a half-raised diffident hand.

"You ain't heared nothing down to the Hall about none of us fellers gitting back on, have you?" said paw.

"Not a thing," said the Supervisor. "We are not looking for anyone to be put back on before the middle of October."

"I need to git back on bad," said paw. "I've got a wife and about six children to support and now my son-in-law has went and run off and left me with his wife and baby and it looks like I have just about got to git back on somehow."

"Well," said the Supervisor, "there's not anything any of us can do about it. There won't be another quota increase until October and until there is there won't be any way we can put anybody back on."

"I need the work about as bad as air man down to the job," said paw, "with my own folks and my son-in-law done left me now. I was a good honest worker down to the job. I give a honest day's work fer my pay."

"That's not the question though," said the Supervisor. "For every man on the WPA now there are about three waiting on the certified list to get on and most of them are in just as bad a fix as you. There just aren't any jobs for them."

"I need the work pow'ful bad," said paw. "I don't rightly know what I'm going to do ifen I don't git back on."

"I wish we could put every one of you back to work," said the Supervisor, "but there just ain't any jobs."

Paw stood on the edge of the sidewalk and watched the Supervisor get into his car and back away from the curb and drive away down the street toward the City Hall, then he too turned and followed on down the walk toward the Hall.

The long upper hall was full as usual now and paw took his place against the wall and squatted down on his hunkers, patient, silent, without aim or compulsion, just squatting there against the wall. When the Social Worker left at noon he rose with his fellows and they too descended the stairs and sat on the front steps of the City Hall with their hats pulled low over their eyes and waited her return. Paw stopped only a short while with the rest of them, then he rose and moved without purpose down the walk and across the street and slowly along underneath the shade of the overhanging water oaks toward home.

The men were still in the yard waiting for him and he walked in and took the place which had been held vacant for him and squatted there facing them but not looking at them, his limp listless hands hanging over his bony knees and his gaze fixed between the two mild ineffectual faces opposite him. The faces watched him for a moment, then lowered behind the felt brims of their hats and the men took up their interrupted tracing of hieroglyphics in the dirt at their feet.

"Hit wa'n't the foreman," said paw at last.

They continued to draw their careful, meaningless symbols in the dirt.

"Hit's about dinnertime," said one man and dropped the twig with which he had been marking in the dirt and rose and wiped his hands on his overalled legs and turned and went into the house.

The rest of them dropped their sticks and rose one at a time and followed him inside.

Seventeen

Maw was standing over the stove stirring the contents of a pot when paw came in Friday just before dark. Her face was red and flushed from the heat and sweat beaded her forehead and stood in small globules on the back of her neck. Her dress was plastered to her back and her forearms were dripping. She turned as paw came into the kitchen.

"That boy of Mr. Browning's was by to see us this evening," she said.

"Well now," said paw, "I wisht I had of seen him. I ain't heared from Mr. Browning since we left the country."

"I was right glad to see him, myself," said maw. "Hit kind of made me homesick a-talking to him. He said they ain't no one in our place yit."

"I knowed that," said paw. "Someone, I fergit who, told some the boys down to the job one day."

"They's a good many of the houses vacant now," said maw.

"I 'lowed they would be after most of us left," said paw.

"He said the crop weren't much this year. Said hit looked like to him they weren't much land worked as usual. Seems like hit's kind of hard to git no one to farm no more. He done got him one them jobs driving a truck fer the contractor."

"Well now," said paw. "That might be a pretty good kind of job to have. I wisht I had thought of it sooner. But no, hit wouldn't do me no good to know about it. Somehow I never learnt to drive no truck. What kind of hauling is he a-doing?"

"He said he was a-hauling sand and gravel from a pit some'ers. 'Bout thutty mile he said. They pay right good too. He tried to git Mr. Browning to move to town but Mr. Browning said he was a-gitting too old to move anywhere now. Said he done already moved twict in his life. Onct to the house we had afore we moved into hit and onct back to where he lives now and he never intended to move no more. Said he aimed to die and be buried from the place where he is now."

"Well now, some folks is like that. Don't never like to stir around much."

"Mr. Browning said ifen they lived in town they wouldn't be no place to go Saddys."

"Some folks is kind of hard to please," said paw. "Where is that boy of hisn staying?"

"He never said," said maw.

"We might could take him in here," said paw. "With all the money he's making he ought to be willing to pay us a little board. Say about three dollars a week."

284

"They was two more fellers with him," said maw. "They're all three staying together some'ers."

"Well, we'd ought to be able to fix up fer the three of 'em. That would kind of help out until Mr. Will gits back from Hot Springs and we can git our cards back. I just believe I'll see 'em up to the Square tomorrow evening and talk to 'em some about it."

Saturday. On the Square. Cars parked fender to fender against the curb, lining it solid from corner to corner. Cars parked on the red-painted danger signs in front of the fire plugs. Cars parked on the Reserved No Parking signs in front of the drugstores and hotels. Cars parked against the rear fenders of the cars parked against the curbs. Cars parked double in the single parking section along the center of the pavement between the traffic lane in front of the stores and the traffic lane around the Courthouse. Cars and trucks and busses with home-built bodies parked against the curb around the Courthouse yard. New cars, old cars, clean cars, muddy cars. And the sidewalks crowded with standing groups, talking and laughing in the sunlight. Black groups, sunburned groups, tobacco-spitting groups with nothing to do on Saturdays but come to town and stand and talk and laugh and spit.

Hurrying clerks. Going home to dinner. Going into the café for a quick sandwich. Going into the next door to replace a suddenly discovered shortage in stock. Slow-moving, country people. Going nowhere. Elbowing their way through the standing, laughing, spitting groups. Young girls in fresh dresses with faces painted and powdered and lips smeared with too bright red, with questing eyes beneath the metallic unnatural sheen of permanents. Cheap gaudy bracelets and red fingernails. Fresh dresses and starched and iron-slicked slacks, too short, too tight, pale blue with half-dollar size white buttons making gaps over pink silk hips. Unaccustomed spike heels and red-painted toes in open-end patent leather.

Swaggering boys with slicked-back hair above sun-browned faces. Two-toned sport shoes, too short trousers, broad-shouldered, wasp-waisted coats tight buttoned across tieless shirts. Laughing and cursing and swaggering self-consciously in and out the beer joints.

Well, if there ain't old Ed. Ain't saw you in a coon's age, Ed. How you been making it? How's your folks? Hello there, Tom. How you been making it? Ain't saw you in a coon's age. How's your folks? Well, if there ain't old Joe. How are you, Joe?

Let's walk around the Square again. Maybe they'll see us this time. I ain't got a date for that ser'ul at the show this morning. Wisht I hadn't bought these old high-heel shoes. They're just killing my feet.

Come in here, you son-of-a-bitch, and have a beer with us. You all know this bastard, don't you? Three more beers right here. How'd you like some of that that just passed the door? Boy, howdy.

Paw found Stan Browning that evening and Stan's two partners were with him. They agreed to move in the next morning and just as paw completed his arrangements with them the rent man passed.

"Hello, there," said the rent man. "I just came from your place. Got that rent?"

"Well now, I ain't got it right with me," said paw, "but I just completed a deal with them three gentlemen to come board with us and they are going to move in fust thing in the morning."

"Move in? Where are you going to put them?"

"Well, maw kin likely find a place fer 'em. We might be a mite crowded right at fust but I 'low we'll git used to it in a few days."

"Look here, Mr. Taylor. I told you the other day that you would have to have that rent for me today."

"Well now, I kind of rec'lect you said something about it," said paw, "but I felt shorely with us just gitting started in the boarding business like we are, a day or two wouldn't make no difference."

"But with none of you working and seven families and these three new men having to eat out of what board just three men can pay, how are you going to have anything left to pay rent with?"

"Well now," said paw, "we'll likely git something studied out when the time comes."

"When the time comes? The time is here now."

"Why, you wouldn't make no feller move out this time of evening shorely. Hit'll take us a spell to find another place to go to."

"Listen," said the agent. "Listen. I can't just throw

you out. I wish I could. I wish I had that much sense. No, if I had that much sense I wouldn't be a rental agent. But even the fellow you beat out of the rent deserves a little bit of mercy. Will you do one thing for me? Just one thing. Will you get rid of that God-damned dog that bites me every time I go down there?"

"Well now," said paw. "I never knowed he was a biting dog. I will shore 'tend to him. We aim to make ever' body welcome to our place and we don't aim to have no biting dogs around. How-some-ever hit'll take some figgering on just how to go about it. Hit belongs to one of my little girls and I'm afeared she'll be right put out ifen I make her git rid of hit."

"Well, just don't bother about it," said the agent. "Just don't bother about it. I guess if I ever go back down there again expecting to collect any rent I deserve to get bit."

Paw stopped by the City Hall on his way home but the offices all closed at noon on Saturday and there were only two or three of the overalled men there and they were sitting on the front steps. Paw walked in and sat down by them and they sat quiet, listless, their hands hanging limp over their bony knees.

"Well, I've got to be gitting on home," said one of them at last and he rose and walked slowly down the street.

"We might's well be gitting on too," said another and two more of them departed.

Paw sat on for a while, then he too rose and left.

✦

Paw was nearly home when the agent pulled his car in to the curb beside him.

"Mr. Taylor," he called. "Mr. Taylor."

"You mean me?" said paw, slowing to a stop.

"Of course," said the agent.

Paw walked over to the car and raised one foot to the running board.

"One thing I forgot this afternoon when I saw you uptown," said the agent. "The man downstairs and some of the neighbors have been to me about some awful smell down at your place. Do you know what it is?"

"Why, yes sir," said paw. "I expect that's Rinno. He's been smelling right strong fer the last few days."

"Rinno? What is rinno?"

"My oldest boy."

"What makes him smell so? Does he need a bath?"

"Well, no sir," said paw. "I don't hardly reckon so."

"Is he sick?"

"Well, he was."

"Was?"

"Yes sir. He taken and died about over a week ago."

"Died? Over a week ago? You mean you've—you haven't—you—"

"Well, yes sir. We got him in a box under the bed."

"Under the bed?"

"Well, yes sir. The box is nailed up good."

"Great God-o-Mighty."

"We was aiming to take him out to London Hill to bury him but I ain't never got a-holt of Frank yit."

"Frank?"

"Yes sir. He drives the bus from out there."

"Get in here," said the agent.

"I don't want to put you to no trouble," said paw.

"Get in!" said the agent again. "Trouble? God-o-Mighty."

Paw came around to the side of the car and climbed into the seat by the agent and he whirled the car around in the middle of the block and ran both red lights on his way back to town.

So they loaded Reno into the funeral hearse that the agent paid for and the agent used his car to take paw's family out to London Hill. They drove into the weed-grown cemetery before sundown and the undertaker and the agent lifted the flimsy box out of the hearse and set it on the ground.

"Where's a shovel?" said the agent.

"Hell, I don't carry shovels with me," said the undertaker. "They always have these country graves dug for me when I get there."

"We could most likely git one over to old man Harvey's," said paw.

"Where is old man Harvey's?" said the agent.

"Hit's about two mile through the woods," said paw.

"Can we get there in a car?" said the agent.

"Well now," said paw. "I just don't know. They ain't no road there."

"Here, son," said the agent to Jutland. "Here's a five-dollar bill if you will have two shovels back here in an hour."

Jutland started off through the woods at a run and

the agent sat on the running board of the hearse and smoked one cigarette after another. They heard Jutland's feet pounding through the woods in fifty-five minutes and soon they could hear his gasping breath.

The agent had his coat off when Jutland panted up to the hearse with the two shovels and he took one of the shovels and said, "Where do you want to bury him?"

"Some'ers along about here," said paw with a wide sweep of his hand.

"Is this all right?" said the agent with his foot poised on the shovel a few feet from the rear of the hearse.

"Well, I guess so," said paw.

"We'll take turns with the shovels," said the agent and pressed the shovel into the ground.

Maw and the children stood to one side and watched the deepening grave and when night came the undertaker and the agent backed their cars around so the lights would shine on their labors and into the yawning hole.

They threw the last shovelful of dirt out and the agent said, "All right. Let's lower him."

The undertaker fitted the slings under the flimsy box and they swung it over the hole and lowered it into the ground. The children stared at the agent and maw watched the box disappear with lackluster eyes and the snuff stick drooping from her lip.

When the first clods thudded on the box, paw said, "We done fergot the preacher."

"Preacher?" said the agent, transfixed with his foot raised to the shovel in the pile of loose dirt.

"Yes sir," said paw. "Our folks is allus been buried with a preacher."

"Can't you say a prayer?" said the agent to the undertaker.

"Hell, no," said the undertaker. "I never said one in my life."

"Can't one of you say a prayer?" said the agent to paw.

"Well, hit wouldn't be like no regular preacher," said paw.

The agent dropped his shovel.

"Where is a preacher?" he said.

"Brother Smith lives about three mile back down the road we come," said paw.

"Well, let's go get him, then," said the agent.

The agent and paw got in the agent's car and returned down the road to Brother Smith's house and paw called "Hello" into the dimness of the porch.

They heard steps inside the house and then the door swung open revealing a tall thin woman in the lamplight and she called back, "What is it?"

"Is your man to home, Miz Smith?"

"No, he ain't. Who wants him?"

"This is Mr. Taylor. We are burying Rinno over to London Hill and we sort of wanted Brother Smith to say a few words fer us."

"Well, he ain't to home."

"Where is he?" said the agent.

"He went over to Spring Hill to the meeting this morning and won't be back till Monday."

"Where is Spring Hill?" said the agent to paw.

"Hit's about ten mile the other side of town," said paw.

The agent opened his mouth and he and paw stared at each other in the glow of the dashlight, paw in mild astonishment and the agent in outraged fury. He snapped his mouth shut and slammed the car into first and swung it viciously out into The Rock.

They returned to the cemetery with one of the town preachers and he stood in the light of the car lamps above the grave with his Bible folded in his hands and briefly sketched Reno's life and the futility of human endeavor and the promise of eternal manna and consigned Reno to the dust from whence he came and the children sobbed openly and the tears of sympathetic vacillation flowed over maw's flabby cheeks. Paw blew his nose loudly and wiped the sleeve of his jumper across it and the agent and the undertaker dropped dirt on the flimsy box and the shrill sounds of the night insects overtoned the spent sobs of the children and the hollow thuds of the clods on the flimsy coffin.

"I never knowed how pitiful Rinno was until that preacher talked about him tonight," said maw when they were home again.

"He was pitiful, kind of," said paw. "He was a monst'ous cur'osity."

✦

The three new boarders came the next morning. Came in their individual trucks with their second lows and their straight exhausts. They heard them when they left the Square—heard the long snoring sound of their acceleration and the entire upstairs with the exception of Virginia emptied into the yard to greet them.

Paw as head of the household stood in the forefront of the crowd with a smile of welcome on his face and raised his hand in ostentatious salute as they slipped the gear levers into second for the abrupt climb into the gravel driveway at the side of the house. The neighbors covered their ears at the window-rattling din and looked at each other in consternation as the newcomers reached their shabby suitcases from the metal dump beds of the trucks and moved in the midst of an admiring group into the house.

"Boy, did you hear old Stan throw it into hisn when he took that rise?"

"Stan told me he was aiming to git him a cut-out soon's payday come."

"They had their mufflers off but the Marshal made 'em put 'em back on."

"Boy, with ever thing still I bet you could hear 'em come over that two-mile hill."

"God in heaven," said a neighbor from across the street. "We can't put up with that. Why, it's awful. It oughtn't to be allowed in a civilized country. It ought to be against the law."

"Why don't you go down and see the Mayor about it in the morning?" said his wife.

"By God, I will. I'll go see the Mayor."

Have you heard the latest one? That bunch of WPA folks took a crowd of these gravel truck drivers to board and the truck drivers kept their trucks down there, not in the house but in that gravel driveway by the side of the house—but they might as well have took 'em on inside because the only difference in the men and the trucks was the trucks had straight exhausts on 'em and the men didn't have no exhausts at all. Them folks that already lived there didn't have no jobs and didn't have to be nowhere at no certain time except up to the pitchure show to see who come out after each show and at them beer joints to see if the folks in them was getting along all right and it took from about nine-thirty till about twelve to get all the pitchure shows and all the beer joints attended to and they must have attended to them in some sort of shifts because didn't none of 'em get home at the same time. About the time the folks downstairs quit laying awake listening and decided they was all in, them gravel drivers would have to get up and start cranking them trucks that sound like airplanes and then everybody on that street would just give up trying to sleep and go ahead and get up. Them trucks kept on waking some feller's little baby up until the baby got sick and the baby's papa got a gun and went out in the street and shot at a couple of them truck drivers one evening and they went and got the mayor and the marshal. The feller that had the sick baby took some shots at them too and then them truck drivers had to start coming in from the back and leaving their trucks in that alley right under the windows where the folks that lived downstairs had been trying to sleep and the downstairs folks just give up and moved. Said they just be damned if they could stay any longer. Said it was bad enough to live under a mule barn or by a airport but to live between the two of them was just asking too much of any man. And the feller that collects the rent from the place never had been able to get the folks upstairs to pay him nothing and now the folks downstairs have done moved and when he took some folks down there the other day to try to rent them the downstairs them WPA folks upstairs had done took over the whole house and they have done got them a dog that they sick on the rent man every time he goes down there.

Eighteen

Paw was standing in front of the City Hall when a young sun-burned fellow walked up to him.

"Hello, Mr. Taylor," he said.

Paw stared blankly at him.

"I'm Alex Duncan's boy, Mr. Taylor. Don't you remember me?"

"Why, shore. Shore," said paw. "How's your paw gitting along?"

"Haven't saw him in quite a while, I been over in Arkansaw with Hub."

"Well, I declare," said paw. "What do you know about that? I never knowed Hub was in Arkansaw."

"Yes sir. We been working out in a lumber camp."

"Well, well," said paw. "We ain't hearn from Hub since he left."

"Hub's been sick. Fell and tore that old sore open in his side again."

"Well, that's too bad. How did he hurt hit the fust time?"

"I don't know. Hit was already hurt when he come over there. He's back at work now though."

297

"I know his maw will be glad to hear that."

"He said to tell you all how come he ain't sent no more money. Said to tell you all and Buddy special he'd send some more soon."

"Well, I declare," said paw. "He must not know about Buddy."

"Is something wrong with Buddy?"

"Well, yes," said paw. "Buddy ain't with us no more. He has passed on."

"I know Hub will hate that. He's allus a-talking about Buddy. He worried a lot about Rinno too."

"Well, I do know," said paw. "And Rinno has done passed on to his reward too."

"Well, that's too bad," said the young man. "Hub never knowed hit."

"Did he 'low when he would be home?"

"Not fer quite a spell anyhow. Said he reckoned he better not try to come back any time soon."

"Well," said paw. "His maw will be disappointed about that."

"Well, I got to be going. Don't fergit what he said about that money."

"I won't," said paw. "And I'll be right glad to git it too. What with me not working now. That feller is gitting right persistent about them payments on that raddio too. Yes sir, I'll be right glad to see Hub sending in a little money."

The men from force of habit and from lack of something to pass the time or perhaps from the final urgings

298

of forlorn hope still stood in front of the post-office window while the mail was put up, then moved up in line and one by one called their names across the counter. Occasionally one of them would receive a communication of some kind—a notice from a finance company, an advertisement from a patent medicine company, a rare personal letter addressed in pencil with its scrawling chirography in the rounded penmanship of a third-grade student but the unmistakable waverings of the aged hand that held the stubby not sharpened pencil in the letters themselves.

Paw was in line this morning and he received a letter. It was unstamped and the small lettered penalty clause showed through the cancellation. The heading of the Works Projects Administration was stamped in bold type in the upper left corner. Paw tore the flap open with trembling hands. A work card. A Four Oh Two. Report to the Road Project at seven o'clock on the fifth. Next pay period.

"Look here," said the Road Supervisor. "I've got a work card for that old Taylor fellow. To go to work on the fifth. That's bound to be a mistake. What must I do?"

"Did you get all four copies or did they send him his?"

"Must have sent his to him. I only have three."

"Well," said the Area Engineer, "we'll just have to fix up a Four Eighteen on him and have it waiting on the job for him when he reports on the fifth."

✦   *299*

And paw. On the morning of the fifth. In clean, blue home-made shirt, clean faded overalls, cracked shoes, and felt hat pulled low against the rising sun, a paper of lunch in his gnarled, hooked hand, complaining to himself already at having to walk the short blocks to town in order to catch the truck, seeing the first blue check and new radio tubes, bewildered no longer but vaguely concerned at being once more engulfed into a time-ordered existence and shackled to the security of two moving clock hands by the magic of his name on a slip of paper in impersonal print, drawn to a fate that he did not recognize as unkind; for kindness and unkindness are only intangible comparisons and the only unkindness that he knew without even recognizing was the fact that he had been born. Not compelled by seasonal or even yearly mutations, the limits of his development or even changes were as stagnant as the land from which he sprung, and only the erosion of complacent unendeavor etched small crow's-feet at the corners of his mild unfaded eyes. Paw, headed for work, a vaguely remembered symbol against a rising sun.

THE END